CATCH ME IF YOU CAN
CHRISTINA C JONES

WARM HUES CREATIVE

CONTENTS

1.
2.
3.
4.
5.
6.
7.

8.

9.

10.

11.

12.

13.

14.

15.

 Created with Vellum

AUTHOR'S NOTE

So this was a tough ride. This project is a romantic suspense, which is a completely different kind of thing for me. So many different elements, dropping clues, keeping everything straight... it's been a challenge. But, the end result is a project that I'm happy with, and I hope that you as the reader leave this project with the same feeling. I wish I could just copy/paste the acknowledgements from the last book, because those same people came through for me in this project. Betas, family, friends, and last but not ever *least, the readers, I appreciate you all.*

Please enjoy!

ONE
NAOMI

NAOMI OFFERED a warm smile to the cashier, tossing a casual *"Au revoir!"* over her shoulder as she exited the patisserie with a small paper bag of sweets. She didn't want them, but they were an important part of appearing to belong.

The stop at the chic little bakery had given her the opportunity to duck into the cramped bathroom, toss her wide-brimmed sun hat and glasses into her oversized tote, and change into the summer dress tucked neatly into the bottom.

In the mirror, she removed the pins from her sleek bun, using wet hands to coax curls out of her pressed hair. Then, she used moistened wipes to remove the thick layer of contouring makeup, applied with the specific purpose of changing her features and skin tone. Satisfied with the change in appearance, Naomi ducked out of the bathroom to join the service line, bought her pastries and left, carefully avoiding the gaze of a uniformed police officer on horseback a few feet outside the door.

She was confident they hadn't seen her face, but she was *sure* the police had spread word they were looking for a brown woman in black jeans, walking with a serious limp. Several of them witnessed the disgraceful tumble she'd taken after slipping in a puddle left behind by a short summer rain. But, even with what she suspected to be a slightly twisted ankle, she was quick on her feet, and managed to elude the officers in the private, greenery-clad alleys of the 16th arrondissement, then made her way to the bakery.

Now, Naomi tread cautiously as she turned onto a quiet, tree-lined avenue. If she kept her pace slow, her faltering steps were barely noticeable. But she wouldn't be able to stay on her quickly-swelling ankle very long. She needed an out, and she needed it *fast.*

There was no way she was calling Quentin. It was *his* fault she was in this mess anyway. If he'd been as focused as he should have, and planned properly, they would have known about something like an extra security guard, and she wouldn't have nearly gotten caught.

Relax.

Relax.

Relax.

Naomi silently repeated those words like a mantra until her head, heart, and lungs caught up with each other and obliged that command. This wasn't the time to freak out. Her freedom depended on *not* freaking out, so she ignored the throbbing pain in her ankle and went back to work.

As Naomi stepped onto a busier street, lined with the seated patrons of numerous cafes, she mentally thumbed through her list of suitable contingency plans. She needed to get back to her hotel, where she wouldn't have to worry about standing out, but it wasn't as simple as just hailing a car. She would have to either make it to a taxi stand, or call for a cab, both of which required waiting, neither of which sounded like desirable options. And that wasn't even considering that *of course* the police would be checking cabs leaving the area. She would have to do something else.

Crap.

Flutters of anxiety rose in Naomi's belly as a group of uniformed cops appeared in her path, seemingly out of thin air. She shook her head, frustrated that the sudden turn of events was putting a heavy strain on the skills she prided herself on.

Diligence. Focus. Agility.

That became her new mantra. Despite the overwhelming urge to duck her head, she kept it held high as she passed them, even tossing a smile and a wave to a nice-looking officer in the crowd. She was surprised when he sent back a flirtatious smirk of his own, even turning backwards to hold her gaze. Not wanting to draw suspicion, Naomi winked at him before turning her attention back to the problem at hand.

She'd barely taken two steps when she collided with a pedestrian. Her body went one way, and her foot went the other as she dropped to the ground in a heap. White-hot pain shot through her ankle, sending a wave of nausea to settle in her stomach.

Barely, she registered someone speaking American-accented French to her, in a deep tenor.

"Je suis désolé."

When Naomi looked up, she was immediately struck by dark grey eyes, brimming first with apology, then compassion when he noticed the distress on her face. For a moment, she froze, taking in smooth, copper-brown skin and a handsome face surrounded by neatly trimmed facial hair.

"Non, Excusez-moi," she stammered, fighting a swell of dizziness as he helped her to her feet, supporting her in his arms.

"Besoin d'aide?"

Naomi shook her head, even though she was still using him as a crutch. She didn't want his help, she wanted to get the hell off the street before whatever minimal cover she still had was blown.

"Je vais bien." To prove that she *was* fine, as she'd so boldly declared, she pushed away from him. *"Voir?"*

Forcing a smile on her face, Naomi put her full weight on her ankle. *"Je suis— goddamn it!"*

Almost immediately, she buckled to the ground in agony. *I wonder how long I'll be in a French prison* was Naomi's last thought as her head hit the ground and she descended into blackness.

MARCUS

HOW LONG IS this gonna take?

Special Agent Marcus Calloway paced the hospital room, anxiously awaiting the nurse's return. He didn't have time to spend hours in this God-awful place, playing babysitter to a woman he didn't even know. Still, a sense of remorse had spurred him to bring the woman to the hospital himself when she blacked out, nearly giving herself a concussion. It was, after all, his fault that she'd been injured. Marcus cringed as he thought about how bad her ankle looked when he brought her in. It was elevated and wrapped in elastic compression bandages now, but not ten minutes ago the bruised, swollen mess was in full view.

Marcus sighed in relief when the nurse re-entered the room, wielding the plastic ID card that identified the woman as Collette Douet. The picture on the front of the card was *terrible*. In it, her features looked pinched and sharp. Her cheeks seemed hollow, and her eyebrows were shapeless masses on her face. Her skin held a peculiar cast that almost made her look sick. In fact, it barely looked like her at all, if it weren't for those heavily lashed, almond shaped brown eyes. They were the only thing in the picture that held any resemblance at all to the strikingly beautiful woman who lay asleep in front of him. In person, her flawless mahogany skin had a healthy glow, and impeccably shaped eyebrows complimented the full, gently rounded features of her face.

Shaking his head at the picture, he shoved it into her tote bag where he'd found it and headed out. The nurses could handle making sure she got proper care. Right now, Marcus needed to get back to his team at the police station and get caught up.

For the past three years, Marcus Calloway had been working his ass off for the Major Thefts division of the FBI. He was on a special task force that focused on Jewelry and Gems, or J&G as they referred to it. They tracked jewel thieves both home and abroad, but Marcus had a fixation on one in particular.

Jolie Voleuse — the pretty thief.

It was a pseudonym she picked up in France after getting away with nearly five million dollars in jewelry at the rumored age of 19. That was nearly 10 years ago — back when Marcus was still a cop, and the FBI was a distant dream. Still, no one knew her true identity, and somehow, even in this age of a camera on every corner and in every hand, the only pictures of her were grainy stills from security cameras, none of them featuring an unobscured view of her face. Supposedly, she was *that* good, but Marcus refused to believe that. She was just *lucky*.

Today, for example. Marcus had zero hard evidence to back it up, but he felt in his gut that the suspect the police had allowed to escape was the legendary thief. *I hope she's enjoying her freedom*, Marcus thought, smirking as he headed for the door. The apartment building the "pretty thief" had chosen for her latest illegal activities wasn't as archaic as it looked, at least not when it came to security. They'd already handed over their security footage to the police, and Marcus was actually tingling with excitement at the thought that he was *finally* going to see *Jolie Voleuse*'s face.

This was *big*. A bust like this was precisely what he needed to get back into his superior's good graces.

Across the room, Collette stirred, a deep scowl crossing her face as consciousness returned, presumably bringing pain with it. Marcus quickly ducked out of the room, not wanting to get wrapped up in a conversation when he had somewhere else to be. He informed the nurse that her patient was waking up, then got the hell out of there, relieved to finally be on his way.

Under other circumstances, Marcus would have stuck around to make sure his face was the first thing the gorgeous Collette saw when she awoke. A sincere apology, flowers, and if things went well enough — meaning that she didn't throw him out of the room, since he was the reason she was there in the first place — an invitation to dinner, maybe a bicycle pizza delivery from Rue Bichat at the Canal Saint-Martin. Afterwards, perhaps a walk along the Seine, or jazz in Montmartre. Marcus didn't *live* in Paris, but he'd been there often enough to know exactly how to charm the panties off a beautiful woman.

But not today.

Today, adrenaline coursed through Marcus's veins as he pulled open the door to the police station and allowed his memory to lead him to the stuffy, cramped room his team used when they were in Paris. He could — and usually did — complain about the lack of respect he and his counterparts received, being stuffed in here when there was a conference room with plenty of space next door, but *not today*. He was beaming as he entered the room where agents Renata Parker and Kendall Williams were preparing to watch the security video a third time.

Kendall glanced back as Marcus pulled a chair, positioning himself between the other two members of his team. "'Bout time you got here, sleeping beauty. What took you so long?"

"Ran into somebody on the street. Messed her ankle up, had to take her to the hospital." Marcus kept his eyes on the screen as he spoke, trying to decipher what was happening in front of him. "What am I looking at here? Fill me in."

Renata spoke next, pushing her long braids over her shoulder before she started. "*This*," she said, pointing to a slim figure carrying a large tote as she stepped off an elevator into the hallway, "Is our suspect." Marcus watched, transfixed, as the unidentified subject made her way down the hall in no apparent hurry, approached an apartment, and broke in as quickly and easily as if she had a key. Not even five minutes later, she was back, leaving no outward sign that she'd been there.

She kept her face angled away from the security camera as she distanced herself from the door, but off-camera, something got her attention. Marcus and his team knew from the reports that an added armed security guard, picking up spare hours to supplement his income, had seen the suspect exiting the apartment. When he called out, he was simply saying hello, but when she turned around — giving the camera a full view of her face — he didn't recognize her as a resident. She'd almost talked her way out of suspicion when the guard remembered the note the residents had left at the front desk, with instructions that *no one* should be in the apartment until they returned from their visit to Barcelona.

The guard made the mistake of saying this out loud, and as they saw clearly on the tape, she took off down the hall before he thought about drawing his weapon. The agents watched, almost impressed as the suspect easily evaded the security guard and his counterparts who'd joined the chase. She would have been in the clear when she climbed out of the second-floor window if the security guards hadn't alerted the police, who were nearby after responding to a minor car accident.

Video footage from the bank across the street showed the suspect glance to either side as she hung out of the window. The police spotted her, and she quickly dropped to the street, hesitated as if in pain, then sped down away with a limp that became less pronounced as she maneuvered down the busy street. An electronics store provided the next segment, showing the suspect ducking into an alley, emerging clad in a wide-brimmed hat and sunglasses she'd probably pulled from the oversized tote. A traffic camera showed her walking calmly into a bakery, which she never exited, at least not that any of them could see.

"I guess you can relax, Marcus," Kendall said, clapping the other man on the shoulder as he rewound the compiled video to the clear shot of the woman's face. "This chick is a criminal, without a doubt, but nobody can tell the lie that she's pretty. She's not your *Jolie Voleuse* after all."

Marcus pulled his face into a pinched expression, shaking his head at Kendall. "*Or*, it means that *Jolie Voleuse* is actually—"

"*Voleuse* Moche," Renata finished, chuckling as she hopped down from her perch on the end of the table. "We called you away from your fancy Parisian vacation to catch an *ugly* thief. Aren't you excited?"

"*Thrilled.*"

Truth was, it didn't feel like much of a vacation anyway. A vacation would have been sipping tequila while beautiful bikini-clad women served him *more* tequila and rubbed sunscreen on him on a remote Caribbean island. Marcus had been *forced* to take time off after leaving a trail of destruction nearly a block long in an effort to take down a minor jewel peddler who turned out to be a *major* drug peddler. But nobody wanted to talk about *that*. They just wanted to go on and on about "destroyed national monuments" and "wildlife preserve set on fire" and "demolished historic bridge" as if those things were more important than "dangerous criminal in custody". It wasn't like anybody died — punk-assed crooks included.

Still, Marcus took his "highly recommended" vacation with minimal complaint, and headed to Paris. He didn't even *like* Paris, but a hunch — just a little inkling — told him that *Jolie Voleuse* was overdue for a little action in the city where she was minted. That gut feeling had *never* led him wrong. And he *needed* to get through this case.

The video was playing again, and something interesting caught Marcus's eye. Another bank, down the street, showed Collette stepping out of the bakery where the suspect had disappeared, looking flawlessly beautiful in the Parisian sun. Well, *almost*. She was trying very hard to hide it, but Marcus could see the stress lining her face with each step she took. Collette was *limping*.

Marcus glared at the screen, unblinking, as she continued down the street with a well-concealed falter in her steps. He saw her shoot the passing officer a flirtatious smile, just before the back of his head came on-screen, rushing down the street to get to the police station from his hotel. Renata and Kendall had abandoned the recording, and were talking about going back to the apartment building, but Marcus's gaze was focused. He cringed seeing the moment of impact between he and Collette, hard enough that she went tumbling to the ground.

As his on-screen self knelt to help her up, Marcus's eyes fell on the tote bag he'd picked up and placed back on Collette's shoulder. A prickly feeling crept over his skin as he snatched the remote from the table, rewinding the recording to the spot where the suspect walked out of the apartment door.

Right there.

There it was, the same tote bag he'd shoved the ID card into not even half an hour ago.

TWO
NAOMI

I HAVE to get out of here.

That was Naomi's first thought upon opening her eyes to the bright, clinical lights at the hospital. She recounted the events before she'd blacked out, and determined that *getting her ass out of there*, as quickly as possible, was indeed the best plan. The last thing she needed was another visit from Agent Calloway.

Naomi shuddered. She'd heard one of the nurses call him that as she drifted between conscious and not, high off whatever they'd given her for the pain. It was an unusually bad stroke of luck, to pass out in the arms of law enforcement, while you were on the run *from* law enforcement. What agency he belonged to was a mystery — one she didn't plan on sticking around long enough to solve.

She shifted positions as she sat up, cringing as pain shot through her elevated ankle.

Damn. Okay... focus, Mimi, focus.

With her bottom lip pulled between her teeth, Naomi carefully maneuvered her foot down from the pile of pillows. Limited mobility certainly didn't *improve* the likelihood of making it out any time soon, so Naomi leaned back into the pillows, massaging her forehead as she tried to come up with a plan. Somewhere, somebody was watching the surveillance tapes from the streets she'd used to get away. If that somebody was competent at all, her freedom was in jeopardy.

"*Jolie Voleuse*, you're under arrest! Hands in the air!"

Naomi's eyes darted toward the door as her heart slammed to the front of her chest. The woman in the doorway had her face pulled into an expression that was half scowl, half smirk as she stepped in.

Naomi looked heavenward, pressing her palm to her heart in relief at the sight of Inez. She welcomed the sight of her olive-skinned friend and occasional partner-in-crime, and had to fight back the lump in her throat.

"*Inez*, I don't think I've ever been so glad to see you. I'm not even gonna kick your ass for trying to scare me half to death!"

Inez smile. "Looks like you could use a rescue mission, amiga," she said, pushing her thick, wavy hair back from obscuring her face.

Naomi angled her head to the side. "Yeah... looks that way."

Both women grinned, but in the next moment, Inez was all business, pulling her sheet of jet-black hair over her shoulder before she produced a tennis shoe and a sophisticated, hinged ankle brace from her bag. She strapped the brace on Naomi's leg, assisted her in getting the shoe on the other foot, then handed her two pills, passing a cup of water from the bedside table to help her swallow them.

"Estas bien?" Inez asked, helped Naomi down from the bed.

Naomi gingerly placed her weight on her ankle, testing the strength of the brace. When it held easily, and the hinges allowed her to move her foot with relative ease, she smiled. "Si, gracias."

"You know… you're gonna owe me *big time* for this one. Quentin called me when he lost contact with you this morning. You're lucky that I was only an hour and a half away by rail, in Belgium."

Naomi cringed. "*You* used the rail system?"

With her face pulled into a scowl, Inez nodded. "Mmhmm. So you actually owe me *double*."

"I'll keep that in mind." Treading carefully on her injured leg, Naomi gathered her things, carefully checking the tote to make sure everything was still there. After all of this, it wouldn't do to misplace the entire reason for the trip to Paris. When she was done, she secured the bag on her shoulder and followed Inez to the door.

Inez peeked out first, making sure that her hair fell in a way that masked her face from the security cameras she scouted on her way in. "I know you'll check things out for yourself, but you should avoid these areas," Inez said, giving Naomi a brief rundown of areas to avoid, and a quick description of the route she should take.

"A car is already waiting for us. If you get down there and I'm not with you, *go.* Got it?"

Naomi smiled. "It wouldn't do for us to get caught together, now would it?"

"Not at all," Inez chuckled, taking one last glance down the hall before she ushered Naomi out of the room.

Before they entered the stairwell, Naomi grabbed Inez's hand. *"Thank you."*

Inez shrugged. "Thank Quentin, for having the common sense to put a working emergency contact number on your fake hospital records. I wouldn't have known where the hell you were or that you needed the brace, nothing."

Naomi rolled her eyes, sucking her teeth as they headed down the stairs to the waiting car. "Quentin will be lucky to not get his ass kicked for getting me in this mess in the first place."

MARCUS

SO DAMNED CLOSE.

He'd seen her face.

He'd *touched* her.

And yet… somehow, she'd still gotten away.

"This is bullshit," Marcus mumbled under his breath, adjusting his position in the uncomfortably hard chair. Where the hell were Kendall and Renata? After all, this was *their* case, technically. Marcus was off the clock.

That little fact was his only saving grace. Marcus and his team reported directly to only one person — Supervisory Special Agent Wilhelmina Black. For the most part, SSA Black didn't have much to say. She trained her agents to execute their responsibilities as quickly and quietly as possible, then stood back and let it happen. The ten agents under her enjoyed a level of clearance, autonomy, and access to resources not afforded to many in their agency, right up there with the agents in counter-terrorism, because too often, the two intertwined.

SSA Black didn't care about any of their quirks, as long as they brought value. She knew how to mold a person into a "team work!" frame of mind, so she was content to allow them to remain misfits, until they started messing up.

Today?

"*Major* screw up." Black's voice was agitated as it resonated from the crappy speaker of the phone. It was a lousy old landline, which had been set up in the dusty conference room for the specific purpose of facilitating the scolding of Marcus, Kendall, and Renata. She blew out a heavy sigh, and Marcus imagined her lighting a cigarette and taking a long drag — even though no smoking was allowed in their headquarters back in the US. "You're on *vacation*, Calloway. How do you get your hands on a woman we've been looking for, and just... let her go? *On vacation?*"

"I didn't —"

"You didn't know. Yeah, you said that already. But the problem now is that we're still no closer. The video of her leaving the bakery is too grainy to run facial recognition, and all of the video from you bringing her into the hospital is "mysteriously" corrupted."

Marcus sat up, scrubbing a hand over his face. He'd almost put his fist through a wall when he called the hospital to have guards placed at her door until he could get there, only to find out she was already gone.

"Marcus," Black said, softening her voice. "I need you to focus. I'm not sure that anything could have been done differently today, but we've got a jewel thief still on the loose, and unhappy tenants from the apartment she hit. Ten *million* dollars' worth of black diamonds, gone."

"Ten *million*?" Marcus lifted an eyebrow. "That's not what they told the police. And the security was shoddy at best. Why would they keep diamonds of that value in that apartment when they weren't there?"

"Your guess is as good as mine, but..."

"I can guess there's more not being said."

"Precisely. That's why I need your head in the game. Finish your vacation, then get back to work."

Before he could respond, the line clicked, and SSA Black was gone, leaving the dial tone blaring in his ears.

Marcus hit a button to close the line as he stood, then paced the room. Hands on his hips, mind racing, he replayed the day in his head, trying to pinpoint anything he'd missed. The address on the fake ID was a dead end, and the picture was even less helpful. Renata guessed that she'd used stage makeup to alter her look, and the stop at the bakery had been to wash it off, returning to her normal appearance.

Her normal, gorgeous appearance.

Marcus shook his head. He didn't really give a damn how she looked. He was more concerned with the fact that he'd gotten closer than ever, had her right under his nose, and she'd evaded him again.

"For the *last* time," Marcus declared, stalking to the door and flinging it open. She may have gotten away this time, but the very next chance he got... she was *his*.

THREE
NAOMI

JAB. Jab. Hook. Jab. Hook. Duck. Jab.

Naomi ignored the bite of pain in her ankle. She continued her assault on the heavy-bag, pretending to take no notice of a shirtless Quentin as he sauntered into their private area of the gym, hands shoved in the pockets of his sweatpants. He was a slim guy, but years of training and disciplined eating had given him solid layers of muscle, and his presence exuded obvious power.

"You probably shouldn't be on that ankle." He stopped beside her, close enough that she could smell his cologne, mixed with perspiration from the umpteen miles he'd just finished on the treadmill. Sweat clung to his golden skin, making her mouth water as her temperature rose. She swallowed hard, not giving him the courtesy of looking at him as she hit the bag again, with more force than she had a few moments before.

Warranted or not, she was still mad at Quentin. He'd messed up with the Paris job, and almost cost her freedom. Maybe even her *life,* if that security guard had been feeling trigger-happy. Sure, he'd helped by calling Inez, but what if she hadn't been available, or had been too far away? What then? She hit the bag again, imagining that it was Quentin's face.

When he grabbed her wrist, she jerked away, aiming a right hook for his jaw, followed by a quick left when he dodged it. "Simmer down, *cher*," he said, catching her wrist again before the punch landed. He evaded the blow from her left hand as well, then backed her against the wall, pinning her hands at her sides. "Gone hurt ya'self tryna be tough."

Naomi sucked her teeth, trying not to be affected by the sexy cadence of his Louisianan Creole accent, or the heat drifting from his body to hers. "If my ankle didn't still hurt, I'd kick your ass."

Quentin grinned, sparking a jolt of warmth between Naomi's thighs. "Used to be you could kick my ass injured or not. Getting soft on me, Mimi?" He spoke those words right against her ear, close enough that she could feel the minty-coolness of his breath on her neck.

Against her will, she moaned as he put his mouth there, trailing kisses over her sweat-dampened skin. "No. Not getting soft... getting *smart*," she said, biting her lip as Quentin released her wrists and dropped to his knees in front of her. "I have a class to teach in an hour. Can't risk hurting myself again. Not for you."

Chuckling as he shook his head, Quentin grabbed the waistband of Naomi's leggings and underwear, yanking them down over her thighs. "So I take it you're still upset? Been a week now."

He was gentler about getting her clothes over her injured ankle, taking care not to pull too hard as he removed them from her foot, then tossed them aside. He grinned up at her, his strong hands greedily gripping and caressing her exposed flesh, urging her to open her legs.

"Hell yes, I'm still upset. I don't care how long it's been. You're supposed to be on my team, my *hacker*, and you weren't on your job. *This* doesn't excuse the fact that you messed up."

Quentin nodded absently as he gently lifted her leg, hooking it over his shoulder. He kept his gaze centered on his destination as he planted scorching, wet kisses from her knee to the apex of her thighs, then stopped. Trembling with anticipation, Naomi pushed her fingers into his thick, curly hair, gripping a handful to pull his head back so they were looking at each other. With his eyes locked on hers, he covered her with his mouth, and went to work.

Hell yes.

Naomi tossed her head back against the wall, her arousal heightened by the throbbing music from the spin class happening on the other side. She claimed that this wouldn't fix anything, but the things he was doing with his tongue were making it quite easy for Naomi to forget his error. Shamelessly, she thrust herself against his face as pressure built at her core. He devoured her with a level of skill only obtained by experience — something he had plenty of with Naomi.

They'd known each other since they were kids, had grown up together in New Orleans. Between them, they'd played many different roles for the other — friend, protector, lover, partner-in crime. Presently, they were all four.

Naomi moaned her pleasure, thighs quivering as Quentin pushed a first, then second finger into her, burrowing deep with one hand, squeezing a handful of ass with the other. She gripped his hair tighter, squeezing her eyes shut as the pressure coiled, tighter, and tighter, and *tighter*, until it exploded, taking her over the edge.

Quentin rose to his feet, smirking as he freed himself from his sweats, then stepped closer.

"What are you doing?" Naomi asked, pressing her hands to his chest to stop him as he gripped her by the thighs to pick her up.

He lifted an eyebrow. "Finishin' what we started."

It was Naomi's turn to smirk as she pushed him further back, shaking her head. "Uh-uh. I told you I have a class to teach. I'm hitting the shower."

"So whaddya expect me to do with this?"

Despite herself, Naomi's heart rate sped up as he pointed to the erection bobbing in front of him. Quentin was beautiful all over, but *especially* there, and if she weren't supposed to be mad, she would — no. *No.*

24

Quentin was distracted lately, and Naomi had nearly been a victim of that lack of focus. She was supposed to be able to depend on Quentin. Second-guessing him meant second-guessing herself, and that took valuable time she usually didn't have when they were on a job. She wasn't about to reward him for that.

"I guess you better hit the shower too, *cher*."

Naomi winked at him, then turned to walk away, not caring that her obvious limp stunted her triumphant exit.

He got the point.

IN THE SHOWER, Naomi closed her eyes, letting the hot water soak her skin and hair. She cringed as it hit her still-tender ankle, but relaxed as the heat began to work through the soreness. At the very least, enough luck had been on her side that it wasn't broken, merely sprained. She hadn't seen her five and six-year-old little ballerinas in a week, and missing another class would have been the last blow to her already fragile mood.

Naomi didn't particularly enjoy kids, but she loved the ten little dancers who rushed up to her for hugs when she entered the room. They reminded her of herself at that age, dressed in a simple leotard and soft ballet slippers while she watched her mother in the mirror, mimicking her as she practiced her positions in front of the barre.

With a heavy sigh, Naomi pushed the memory from her mind as she soaped her skin. She washed quickly, removing all traces of sex and sweat before she stepped out, toweled off, lotioned, then surveyed herself in the mirror.

Her hair was back to its normal state, a thick mass of kinky, unruly curls that reached past her shoulders. Noting the time, she picked up her brush, and ten minutes later, she'd managed to wrangle her mane into a tight bun against the back of her neck. She donned her leotard and tights — the same the class would wear — then pulled a simple ballet skirt on, to cover the swell of her hips and butt. More than once, she'd had to give a stern warning to a student's father — and a couple of mothers too — that ogling the instructor wasn't conducive to a healthy learning environment.

When she was dressed, Naomi strapped her ankle back into the brace and stepped out of the private bathroom, which was located just beyond the office she shared with Quentin. It was empty, but she didn't have to wonder for long where he was, because as soon as she stepped onto the main floor, she spotted him at the door that led to the spin class, flirting with the attendees as they filed in for the next session.

Quentin— dressed in sweats and a tee shirt, looking freshly showered himself — winked at her from across the room. Naomi's only response was a raised eyebrow as she pulled open the door to her classroom and stepped in.

The gym, Five Star Fitness, had been Quentin's idea, nearly four years ago. He thought they needed a "legitimate venture" to cover for their... illegitimate ventures, and concluded that merging their mutual love of fitness with the necessity of a business was an ideal plan. Naomi hadn't been exactly *enthusiastic* about the huge, dusty space he showed her, on a sketchy-looking street in the heart of downtown, but she had to admit that Quentin had turned it into a success.

And, he'd been correct about the rebirth of the neighborhood. Urban Grind, the coffee shop just around the corner, had been the only other black-owned business on the block when they purchased the space. Now, there was a barbershop, a tattoo and piercing parlor, a flower shop, a chocolate sop, and several restaurants, boutiques, and other businesses, all black owned. They'd banded together to clean up their neighborhood, and turned it into one of the most beautiful areas in the city, one they were all proud to call home.

But Naomi's pride and joy was this little 20x20 room. Two of the walls were mirrored, with glossy wooden barres bolted to the glass. On the other side of one of those mirrors was a place for parents to sit and watch their little ballerinas through the two-way glass. She looked up as her first student, followed quickly by a second, came running in, both hesitating at the sight of the robotic-looking contraption on her ankle. Soon, her classroom was full, and she gave her pupils a reassuring smile as she explained that she'd slipped after spilling a bit of water.

Naomi took a moment to teach the girls a lesson about cleaning up behind themselves so no one would get hurt, then, took her position at the front of the class. She glanced expectantly back at the girls, who scurried into place, their giggles replaced by faces that spoke of incredible focus, despite their young age. They knew their teacher expected discipline, focus, and agility, and they were eager to please.

When she was satisfied that they were ready, she gifted them with another smile. "Alright, my baby ballerinas, we start with our stretches, right? Let's touch our toes!"

MARCUS

MARCUS COULDN'T BELIEVE his luck.

He'd griped, groused, *and* grumbled about the last-minute phone call, begging him to retrieve his niece from her ballet class. It was all the way across town from his comfortable, air-conditioned desk at the FBI field office in the city. *All the way across town* in the stifling summer heat, but he loved his little sister, and he loved six-year-old Sophie, so if Meagan couldn't pick her up, *of course* Uncle Marcus would.

And he was so damned glad he'd agreed.

A grin spread over his face as he watched his niece's ballet instructor. The woman was honestly gorgeous, but that wasn't news to Marcus. He allowed himself a moment to rake his gaze over perky breasts, a flat stomach, and *have-mercy*, how had he not noticed the *ass* on this woman back in Paris?

"Good thing the other side is a mirror, huh? Looks like you're enjoying the view, bruh."

Marcus startled as a hand clapped his shoulder, followed shortly by a familiar face as the owner of the voice came to stand beside him.

"Roman, what's up dude?" Marcus extended his hand to the other man, but kept his eyes trained on the ballet instructor as she circled the room, helping her students adjust their posture. He knew Roman because they not only shared the same barber, but Marcus stopped by his coffee shop regularly.

"Not much. I didn't know one of the girls was yours. Didn't know you had kids at all, actually."

Marcus shook his head. "I don't. Picking up my niece — the one wearing the cat ears she won't take off!"

"Butterfly wings," Roman said, laughing as he pointed out the little girl beside Sophie. "Zahra was ready to fight me, her mom, *and* her stepmom all last week because she had to take them off for bath time."

"These damned kids man."

"Right."

Tilting his head to the side, Marcus stroked his chin. "Listen, man… about this ballet instructor… she's the same one that's always here?"

"Who, Naomi? Yeah. She and Quentin own the place."

For some reason, the mention of a male counterpart sent a flash of angry heat through Marcus's blood.

"Who is Quentin? Her husband or something?"

Roman grinned. "Why… you tryna holla?"

Marcus shrugged, shoving his hands in his pockets. "Maybe… maybe not."

"Yeah, right," Roman laughed. "But nah, I don't think they get down like that. At least not that I know of."

The class ended, and half of the girls — including Sophie and Zahra — came running into the waiting area to join their parents, while the other half lingered. A few of the parents went to speak to the instructor, distracting her from stepping out.

"You said Naomi, right?" He asked Roman, stopping him as he guided his daughter to the door to leave. "You know her last name?"

"Yeah. Naomi Prescott."

The two men exchanged goodbyes, and Marcus led Sophie to his car. When she was strapped securely into the spare booster seat he'd pulled out of his trunk, Marcus climbed into the driver side of his car and pulled out his phone. He remained parked as he navigated to a number and hit the dial button, putting the phone up to his ear. Marcus smiled as he glanced back at the gym reflected in his rear-view mirror.

"Gotcha."

Naomi

"How many showers you gonna take today, woman?"

Naomi rolled her eyes at the sound of Quentin's voice through the speakers as it bounced off the tiled walls of the shower. She was in her apartment now, taking advantage of her custom shower while she spoke to Quentin over the phone.

"As many as it takes to wash your stink off me." Naomi followed her statement with a laugh as she pulled one of the sprayers from the wall to rinse herself.

"Ha, ha," was Quentin's sardonic response.

Truthfully, Naomi was trying to rid herself of the gross feeling that she was being watched. It first crept up near the end of her first ballet class, raising the fine hairs on her arms and keeping them at attention. Although no one who seemed suspicious was around, the feeling persisted, and stretched into the end of the day.

"Anyway, I'm callin' because Barnes reached out to me. Damien Wolfe is askin' around about his diamonds."

Despite the high temperature of the water blasting at her from several directions, Naomi's blood ran cold at the sound of that name. Damien Wolfe—the damned devil as far as she was concerned.

"Asking who?"

"One of Luca's men was found with a pocket fulla ice... head fulla bullets... if you get my drift."

Naomi swallowed hard. "I do." She inhaled deep, testing her expensive luxury body wash's claim to be calming.

"Mimi... you sure this is—"

"I am," Naomi snapped. "Don't get cold feet on me, Quentin. You agreed to this... you said you had my back."

"You know I do, cher."

"Then... hang in there with me. We knew this was gonna be dangerous when we started. We're too close to the end to change our minds. I took those diamonds, Q.

We're too far in to back out. I *need* you on my side. I need you *focused*."

"I *am* focused."

"You're *not*." Naomi shut off the water, then pulled body oil from the shelf and dropped herself onto the built-in shower seat. "You're distracted, and I wish you would tell me why."

When Quentin didn't answer, she sighed. "Q, I really wish—"

"*Cho Laud*! Mimi, you seein' this?"

Recognizing his expression of shock, Naomi looked up from her task of moisturizing her skin. "Seeing what?"

"The cameras!"

Naomi's eyes flew to a set of video monitors connected to her security cameras on the bathroom wall. She watched, heart racing, as people with guns, wearing jackets with the letters FBI emblazoned across the back kicked in the front door and swarmed her townhouse.

"*Mimi*," Quentin said, in a tone that made it obvious he'd already tried to get her attention several times. "Why is the FBI at your place?"

She shook her head as she stepped out of the shower, patting herself dry with her towel before securing it around her body. "I have no idea, but I'm glad I decided to stay at the condo tonight instead." Her gaze traveled to the monitors that showed the feed from the surveillance cameras that lined the building she called home when she wanted to be in the city. *Those* screens were free from activity.

Naomi's shoulders sagged in relief. The townhouse was in her given name — the condo was *not*. It was in the name of her deceased mother, and Naomi had taken her father's name. But if the FBI was involved, it wouldn't take long to dig up her family and put them under scrutiny as well. She wasn't sure what they wanted with her, but she didn't intend to stick around and find out.

"Meet me at the safe house in twenty minutes," she told Quentin, before pressing a button on the remote to end the call. In the newly formed silence, Naomi sucked in a breath, then pushed it back out, trying to calm her racing heart.

Remember what you're made of. Diligence. Focus. Agility.

Squaring her shoulders, Naomi pushed her trepidation to the side and pulled open the bathroom door. Once she was with Quentin, she would call Barnes, if he hadn't already—

"Hi, Collette— I mean, *Naomi.*"

Cold fury washed over Naomi as she looked into the familiar grey eyes she'd tried to forget, ever since that day on the street in Paris. Her uninvited guest's lips perked up into a triumphant smile as he stood there in the doorway, blocking her exit and flashing his badge. Naomi's nostrils flared in anger, and her gaze shot around, looking for an escape. When she found none, she pulled her mouth into a derisive grin that matched his.

"Hello, Agent Calloway."

FOUR
NAOMI

JUST TAKE A DEEP BREATH, Naomi. Count to ten. Do it again. Now do it backwards.

Shit.

It wasn't working. Despite her best efforts to calm down, Naomi still wanted to choke the man in front of her so badly it was making her hands itch. She clenched her fists as tightly as she could, not wanting to give him the satisfaction of seeing her angry. Closing her eyes, she searched for something, *anything* to breathe positive energy over her.

"Answer the damned question, Prescott!" he demanded, smacking the tabletop with such force it shook violently. His outburst broke Naomi away from her thoughts, and the loud bass of his voice triggered a dull headache that began at the nape of her neck, then traveled forward, settling between her eyes.

"I've *already* answered you, several times." Naomi massaged her temples with her thumbs as she rested her head in her hands. "I don't know anything about any diamonds."

She sat back in the cold metal chair, wishing she'd worn something a little warmer than the tee shirt and jeans she'd donned under the watchful eyes of a female agents on the team Calloway had brought with him to storm her apartment. Naomi still wasn't exactly sure how they'd gotten past her security undetected, but she'd overheard something about rerouting cameras in a loop, and hacking into the system. So… Quentin had failed her again.

"You really expect me to buy that?" Agent Calloway asked, standing to pace around the table, with his hands shoved in his pockets. "You were there, on the street, carrying the same tote bag as our suspect. You came out of the same bakery the suspect went into. You were carrying a photo ID that *looked* like the suspect. Do you see where I'm going with this?"

Naomi laughed, which elicited a scowl from the agent. "No," she said, crossing her arms. "I don't. If you had *proof* that I'd done anything wrong, you'd be arresting me for something… but you're not. So… if you're holding me here with no evidence, I'd at least like to speak to my lawyer."

Agent Calloway's face was grim as he stared at Naomi, ignoring the loud chime of his cell phone. "Terrorists don't get lawyers."

"*Terrorist?*" Naomi's eyes went wide in disbelief. "You know goddamned well I'm not a terrorist."

He shook his head. "I don't know anything, except that if you don't start talking about the ten million dollars' worth of diamonds you stole, I'm gonna make sure you end up in the deepest, darkest hole I can find."

"I. Don't. Know. Anything. About. Any. Diamonds."
Naomi repeated. "I want to talk to a lawyer. Are you
denying me my right?"

Agent Calloway scoffed, then stopped to scrutinize
her face. "You know, you're a really beautiful woman."

Naomi's eyes narrowed as the agent switched gears.
Did he really think she was stupid enough for *flattery* to
make her talk?

"I'm serious," he said, taking a seat on the edge of the
table. His leg brushed hers, and Naomi snatched hers
away, wrinkling her nose in disgust. "You're obviously
well-taken care of. The nice apartment, expensive
furniture… perfect skin, the hair, the body… somebody is
funding all of that for you. So… what is this, next level
prostitution or something? Instead of fucking, you steal?"

Naomi's mouth dropped open, and she stuttered over
her words for a few moments before she got them out.
"What the hell is your problem?"

"My *problem* is that I don't believe you. My *problem*
is that you're a wanted criminal, and you're sitting here
playing innocent. My *problem* is that you're a liar, and I.
Don't. Like. Liars."

With each word, Agent Calloway had leaned closer
and closer. As Naomi's pulse shot up, she ground her
teeth together, trying in vain to rein in her temper. But by
the time he shot out the words "liars", he was right in
Naomi's face, their noses nearly touching, and before she

could check herself, her palm was connecting with the side of the agent's face.

Instead of recoiling, he smiled.

Naomi jumped from her seat, her hand stinging from the force of the impact as she backed away from the table. That was a bad decision. An impulsive, careless, angry decision completely opposite of the control she prided herself on. But this — this entire situation was as far out of control as it got. So many things had gone wrong at this point that it was almost funny.

Almost.

"You know I could arrest you for that shit, right?" Agent Calloway asked, his voice dangerously quiet as he ignored his phone again to stalk toward Naomi. She took as many steps backward as she could, until her back met the cool brick wall. "Assaulting a federal agent... *lying* to a federal agent. You're just breaking all kinds of laws tonight, Miss Prescott."

He stopped right in front of her, leaving barely an inch of space between them.

"You had no right to get in my face like that. Or *this*." She met his eyes. Naomi wasn't about to let him know his attempt at intimidating her was working. "I don't know anything about any diamonds, but I'll take a charge for defending myself."

"Oh really?" Agent Calloway smiled as he placed a hand against the wall on either side of her. "You think you could take me on, huh?"

"I'd love the opportunity to try," Naomi shot back, lifting her chin defiantly. She was bluffing like crazy. Agent Calloway was over six feet tall, and his athletic frame had to easily top two hundred pounds. She was confident that she could best him in speed and agility, but if they were measuring in strength, he could kick her ass with minimal effort. But he wouldn't do that in the middle of an FBI field office... would he?

Agent Calloway allowed his eyes to drift over her body in a way that *should* have disgusted her, but instead sparked an unholy mixture of rage and excitement. "It could be arranged... after hours." He winked, and that little gesture set off the appropriate anger as she shoved him away.

Crap.

Before she could get in trouble for *that*, the door to the interrogation room opened, and a pretty cinnamon-skinned woman with long braids walked in. "Calloway," she said, her voice edged in agitation as she gestured for him to come to the door.

"Kinda busy here, Parker."

"Not anymore."

At that, a frown marred Agent Calloway's handsome face, and he turned to the other agent, freeing Naomi from the trap of his arms.

Agent Parker shrugged. "SSA Black says to cut her loose."

"*What?*"

Agent Calloway's nostrils flared in anger, but she pumped her fist, muttering "hell yeah!" under her breath. His mouth was still hanging open when she shot past him, then squeezed past the other agent in the door. Naomi turned back, looking at him over her shoulder to blow a kiss in his direction.

"Nice meeting you again, Calloway!"

MARCUS

WHAT THE HELL JUST HAPPENED?

Marcus stood in the hallway outside the interrogation room, watching the swing of Naomi's hips in her tight jeans as she walked away, still maligned by a slight limp. As if she could feel his eyes on her, she paused, turned, and shot him a rude gesture with her hand before she disappeared around the corner. Bringing his hand to his face, Marcus ran his fingers over the place where she'd

slapped him. It was still stinging, and for some reason...
that kinda turned him on.

"Well I'll be damned," Renata said, grinning as she
came to stand beside Marcus. "A woman that can make
you speechless. I have to say— I'm impressed."

Marcus shook his head, turning to face his partner as
he crossed his arms over his chest. "I'm not about to
entertain *that* with you Renata. Why the hell are we
letting her go?"

"I've already told you what I know. Black said to cut
her loose, so I passed the message on. And... she wants
to see you."

With a heavy sigh, Marcus glanced down the hall,
toward the heavy glass door that led to SSA Black's
office. "Did she say what *that* was about?"

"Nope. Her exact words were: send Naomi Prescott
home, and tell Calloway to get his ass to my office."
Renata stopped, a slow grin spreading across her face
before she poked Marcus in the chest. "You're in
trouble," she sang.

Marcus shot her a glare before he turned away, but
said nothing else as he headed down the hall to his
superior's office. His mind raced, flooded with possible
reasons why he'd been ordered to let Naomi go. He knew
he'd made the right choice in only mentioning her latest
crime. The more he accused her of, the more he had to
prove, and *that* was exactly the issue. The only concrete

proof Marcus had was a gut feeling that Naomi Prescott and *Jolie Voleuse* were one in the same. Unfortunately, his unsubstantiated hunch wasn't enough to put her behind bars for *one* crime, let alone the other 32 thefts that had been attributed to her over the years. It wasn't even enough for an official warrant — and maybe *that's* why he was in trouble.

He shook his head.

Shit.

As Marcus approached SSA Black's door, a sudden weariness swept over him. Maybe this was a sign. A huge, bright green, flashing neon sign screaming "Hey, asshole, the "pretty thief" just isn't yours to catch."

This wasn't the first time he'd been close, but it was the first he'd been *this* close. Now he'd felt the softness of her skin, inhaled the seductive aroma of her perfume, sensed the raw sensuality oozing off her when he had her pressed against the wall in that interrogation room. He fought the urge to smile as he recalled her feisty attitude. Not many women would look an FBI agent in the eyes and threaten to kick his ass.

To Marcus, that only further proved her guilt.

In his experience, an innocent woman would have dissolved into tears as she proclaimed her innocence, maybe begged for mercy. Not Naomi. Her words, her tone, her body language... she was combative, yet centered. *Controlled* — until he called her a liar. He had the sore cheek to prove she didn't like that one bit.

A sinking feeling was beginning to grow in Marcus's stomach as he knocked on his supervisor's door. His suspicion was confirmed after he received permission to enter, and found that SSA Black was not in her office alone.

Seated across from her at her desk was a man Marcus knew well. On more than one occasion, Supervisory Special Agent Richard Barnes had tried to recruit the younger agent to his division — whichever one that was. Marcus didn't appreciate the intentionally vague nature of Agent Barnes's approach, and had taken to avoiding the man whenever he was around. He just gave off the vibe that he knew something he *should* be telling you, but wouldn't.

Now, Barnes was sitting in SSA Black's office — *on* her desk, to be precise — and Agent Black didn't seem to mind. His curiosity piqued, Marcus stepped in and closed the door behind him, looking between the two in an attempt to assess their body language. Agent Black was an attractive woman — a shining example of the saying "black don't crack" — so he wouldn't be surprised at all if Agent Barnes was —

"Have a seat, Calloway."

Marcus lifted an eyebrow. He'd never heard Agent Black sound so... *soft*. He did as he was told and took a seat in front of the desk, shifting uncomfortably in his chair under the dissecting gaze of the two higher-up agents.

"Naomi Prescott," SSA Barnes said, folding his arms over his chest. "She's off-limits, young man. Anything you have on her... make sure it never sees daylight again."

A vein throbbed at Marcus's temple. Was he *really* being told to bury a case?

"If you don't mind me asking, sir—"

"I do, but ask anyway."

"Why do I have to disregard Naomi Prescott? The woman is a major criminal, and if you just give me a little time, and the resources I need, I can prove it."

Barnes chuckled, half-turning to Black to share his laughter. "Son... with enough time and money you can prove *anybody* is a criminal."

Marcus scowled as his superiors shared a laugh at his expense.

Yeah, laugh it up. Everything is funny until she's sneaking in your house at Christmas, taking the ornaments off your tree.

"With all due respect, sir, I—"

"You're just trying to do your job, uphold the law, and get a criminal off the streets, yeah, yeah. You're a good kid, Calloway. I get it. But trust me... Naomi Prescott isn't a criminal you want off the streets."

"And why is that?" Marcus asked, cocking his head to the side.

"Because she's not a *criminal* at all."

Marcus narrowed his eyes. "Again… with all due respect Agent Barnes, I know different."

"You *think* you know different. Fact is, she is extremely valuable to our organization." Agent Barnes pushed his hands into his pockets as he stood. "Naomi Prescott possesses a unique skill set that she has agreed to put to use in service to the FBI. Technically, she's an agent, but you won't find that information available to anyone below *my* clearance level."

"So why are you telling *me*?"

"Because you marched one of our best covert operatives into an FBI field office. And the raid you conducted? Couldn't have been pushed through the proper channels, because if it was, you would have set off a shit ton of red flags."

Marcus smirked. "Yeah… I suspected she probably had somebody, somewhere pulling some strings for her, so I pulled a few of my own to get my information and plan my takedown. I would say it worked pretty well."

"Except now, a dozen or more people will recognize Naomi's name as connected to the FBI. A half dozen saw you bring her in. Two other members of your team saw you interrogate her… do you see where I'm going with this? It was good investigative work… but you got lucky.

Running into her on the street, happening upon her in her normal life, catching a flaw in her security... A mistake by someone on her team snowballed, and fortune was on your side. This is good for you, Calloway... but it's not something you get to add to your resume."

That deflated every little bit of pride he had left about finally catching up to his prey. Running his tongue over his teeth, Marcus carefully considered his words before he spoke again. "So... you're telling me that all of the time, energy, resources spent chasing *Jolie Voleuse*... that was all for nothing, since you've known who she was, and have been protecting her the entire time."

"Not the whole time," the other agent responded, shaking his head. "Prescott has been in partnership with the FBI for the last seven years, referred to by code name Black Swan — her choosing. Before that, she'd been building her reputation as a faceless, traceless, uncatchable thief. She was known as Arabesque for three years before the Frenchies renamed her *Jolie Voleuse*."

Marcus scratched his chin, glancing past Agent Barnes to Agent Black, who was enthralled as if she was hearing this for the first time. *Was* she hearing this for the first time?

"So what changed?" Marcus asked. "How did she end up working for the FBI?"

Barnes smiled. "I caught her. But... for the sake of transparency, she was double-crossed by a team member.

A similarly talented young woman who went by the name "Royale" set her up. Naomi had to choose between FBI custody and the *very* nasty Parisian criminals she'd just hit for five million dollars. Obviously, she chose to come over to the legit side of the law."

"So you're telling me that the only times this woman has ever gotten caught were because of her team?" Marcus lifted an eyebrow in disbelief.

Agent Barnes nodded. "That's *exactly* what I'm telling you. A jewelry box hasn't been safe around Naomi Prescott since she was sixteen years old — and *that's* just what she'll actually admit. Black Swan has had *plenty* of time to perfect her craft. On her own, she's impeccable, but some jobs just require a second set of hands, or eyes, or muscle. She has autonomy there, and sometimes… they drop the ball."

Sitting back in the comfortable leather chair, Marcus used the moment of quiet to process the load of information SSA Barnes had divulged. It certainly cast things in a different light. "But… if you knew it was her all this time, why not take her alias off the wanted list, scale back the investigations?"

"To preserve her cover. A very limited number of people know that "Black Swan" is Naomi Prescott. Even fewer know that Naomi Prescott is *Jolie Voleuse*. But, *Jolie Voleuse* is a well-known name in the crime world, and we need it to stay that way. The idea of this uncatchable thief has allowed us to manipulate crime families, gangs, terrorist rings, and all manner of other criminal enterprises. To pull the investigation into those crimes would mean pulling away our foothold into that world. They all think they're stealing from each other, but really…"

"The government is. Got it." Marcus leaned forward, propping his elbows on his legs. "So… enough history lesson. Why are you telling me this stuff if Naomi Prescott is supposed to be an enigma, no connection to the government?"

The other agent smiled. "I thought you'd never ask."

EVEN THOUGH IT was dark out, a persistent drizzle of rain added a sultry, stifling quality to the summer air. Humidity lay heavily on Marcus's skin as he climbed out of the passenger seat of Agent Barnes's car. The blackness of the alley where they'd parked stretched all around him, layering apprehension on top of the irritation he already felt.

Marcus wasn't really a fan of being *forced* into anything. He liked having at least the *illusion* of a choice, and SSAs Barnes and Black had stripped him of that. It was nearly 11pm, on a Tuesday night, and instead of lazing in front of his TV with a beer and the remote, he was walking into Five Star Fitness. This time, he was using the private entrance in the back.

Barnes held the door open for Marcus, then followed him in, directing him toward a black-tinted, tempered glass door engraved with the word "Private". When he opened the door, the first person he saw was who he assumed to be Quentin. A "pretty-boy" Marcus decided, giving the man a once-over as he looked up from his laptop. Light eyes, curly hair, a scruffy beard, and thick black-framed glasses — not at all the type he would think of for a woman like Naomi.

"What the fuck is *he* doing here?"

Speak of the devil.

On the other side of the room, a sweaty, panting Naomi was poised in front of the heavy-bag. Her question was aimed at Agent Barnes, but her eyes were on Marcus, glaring at him with enough venom to make his cheek start tingling again where she'd slapped him, not even two hours ago. She'd changed clothes, and what a *glorious* change it was, into purple leggings and a sports bra that fit her like a second skin, accentuating toned thighs and other assets that Marcus shouldn't have been studying so closely. When his eyes made it back to her face, she wore an expression of disgust that burned through him until he finally looked away, glancing at Agent Barnes.

"Quentin, Naomi, meet the new addition to your team — Special Agent Marcus Calloway."

Naomi's lips parted, and she looked between the three men without saying anything, as if she were waiting on one of them to start laughing. When no such thing occurred, she shook her head, rolled her eyes, then started hitting the bag with renewed vigor. Quentin hadn't looked up from his laptop.

"Tough crowd," SSA Barnes snickered as he took a seat at the small conference table. "But they'll come around. Have a seat, Calloway." He gestured to the chair beside him, looking expectantly at Naomi as Marcus sat down. "Miss Prescott." Barnes's voice took on a little more authority in the wake of Naomi's obvious lack of acknowledgement. She let out a growl of frustration as she hit the bag one more time, then snatched a towel from a nearby hook to wipe the sweat from her face.

Moments later, Naomi was seated across the table from Marcus. As far as he could tell, she was making it a point not to look at him, and despite his annoyance with the whole situation, an amused grin turned up the corners of his mouth.

"The tide has changed, people," Agent Black said, commanding attention from the other agents. "Damien Wolfe showed his hand, outed himself as owner of those diamonds — not that we didn't already know that. But, now the rest of the crime world does, and our little plan to put him on Rochas's trail worked... only now, Rochas is running scared because one of his main guys is dead, and he's screaming to anybody who'll listen that he doesn't know anything about the diamonds. Which is a problem for us, because he *doesn't*. We weren't expecting Wolfe to act that fast, but he did, and now here we are."

Marcus shook his head. "Wait a minute... *Damien Wolfe?* The tobacco tycoon? You're talking about the head of one of the biggest, richest crime families in the country. Drugs, guns, prostitution... like... *real* shit. What the hell are *four* people gonna do against an operation of that size?"

"Anything we want." Naomi turned her heavily lashed eyes on Marcus as she finally acknowledged him. "All it takes is the right manipulation... but you'll learn."

"*I'll learn?*" Marcus propped his elbows on the table and leaned forward. "Listen, little miss—"

"Alright, *children*, settle down." The weight in SSA Black's tone made the three younger agents sit back, all wearing variations of a scowl. "The ego contest can wait until later... right now, we need to figure out what we're going to do about Rochas. He's in Brazil, so it looks like you'll be taking another trip."

"How soon?" Naomi asked, crossing her arms. "I'm still not at 100%."

Barnes groaned. "I was hoping for within the week. We've gotta move fast on this."

"Maybe not."

The other three agents turned to Quentin, who adjusted his glasses before he spoke. "Been trackin' the messages between Wolfe's people. Turns out, he's not happy 'bout the killing. He put everybody on ice until after his little girl's sweet sixteen next month. He don't want nothing messing that up, that's his pride and joy."

Naomi rolled her eyes. "*How sweet.*"

"Hey, don't be so sarcastic, Prescott." Barnes drummed an upbeat tune on the tabletop with his fingers. "His paternal dedication is buying us a month to prepare for what we need to do. I wanna hear ideas. Go."

"I say we go old school," Naomi spoke up first. "Since we uh... seem to be having some technical difficulties." It was impossible to miss the dirty look she shot at Quentin, who was seemingly engrossed in something on his computer. "As a matter of fact, I think I should go alone. If I need backup, I'll call Inez."

Marcus lifted an eyebrow. "Inez?"

"Inez Araullo. CIA. Personal friend of Naomi's," Barnes said, then turned his attention to Naomi. "And as for your idea, absolutely not. No way am I sending you after Rochas alone. Paris was one thing — Barbados is another. You're taking Marcus."

Naomi's eyes widened, then flashed as she turned to glare at Marcus. He shrugged. It wasn't *his* idea to travel with her, or anybody else for that matter.

"Why?" she asked, her voice dangerously close to a whine. "I don't know this man, don't trust him. And I'd rather go by myself than with someone I don't trust."

Quentin's deep New Orleans rasp broke in next. "I could—"

"*No*," Naomi and Barnes said in unison, causing an embarrassed flush to creep over Quentin's face. Marcus sat up in his chair, looking between the other three agents. His curiosity was piqued, but none of his table companions seemed keen on satisfying it.

"It's not up for debate, Prescott. We know Rochas likes to party, and we know *how* he likes to party. That's the weakness. So... okay. The story is that you're on a romantic vacation with your new lover, go to the private party at the house, do what you need to do, and get the hell out of there."

For a moment, no one spoke, then Naomi leaned across the table toward agent Barnes. "I'm sorry... I don't think I heard you right... I'm going on a *what* with *who*?"

Took the words right out of my mouth.

Smirking, Agent Barnes met Naomi's gaze. "You heard me, and you understood. And I want you to *sell* this cover. You travel with your own name, so it's airtight. It's well established that Naomi Prescott has a lot of stamps on her passport, makes sense for you to take a spontaneous vacation. Marcus, you said your niece is in

Naomi's class, right? You came to pick her up, couldn't get Naomi out of your mind."

"*Richard,* this is—"

"Exactly what we've always done, code name Black Swan, remember? Everything we do, every step we take… we're building on three identities at once. Marcus walked you into the FBI field office — that has to be explained in a way that *doesn't* implicate you as a criminal. We can sell it as some gesture to impress you or something. I'll figure it out. Star-crossed lovers have done crazier shit."

Naomi inhaled a deep breath, then pushed it out through her nose. "*Fine,*" she muttered under her breath.

Agent Barnes smiled. "Good. Marcus, I want you in this gym, *visible* at least three times a week until Barbados. Flirting, touching, *sell* it. You can hate each other all you want privately, but publicly, I wanna see that romance novel stuff. Losing your breath when they step in the room, can't keep your pinky fingers still, all that jazz. Got it?"

With that, SSA Barnes stood, and Marcus followed suit, still confused about what in the hell he'd just been ordered to do.

"Wait a minute," he said, holding up his hand. "Can somebody tell me what we're going to be doing in Barbados? What's the target, what are we taking?"

Naomi rolled her eyes, then fixed Marcus with a glare. "Who said we were *taking* anything?"

FIVE
NAOMI

"EXCUSE ME…"

Naomi checked herself from rolling her eyes in response to the deep rumble of Marcus's voice. Part of her annoyance was with herself — specifically, her *body* — for reacting so conversely to what was happening in her head. Marcus irritated her, big time.

His cocky arrogance aggravated the hell out of her, but in conjunction with that face, and those lips, and that *body*… she had to bite the inside of her cheek to remind herself that this was the guy who'd made her ankle injury worse back in Paris. This was guy who'd dragged her into an interrogation room. *This* was the guy who was now being forced on her as part of a team she needed to be able to rely on, yet she barely trusted him not to blow her cover.

Still, Naomi crossed her arms over her chest to hide the evidence of what his presence did to her. She was speaking to a student's mother, and the other woman's mouth dropped open slightly as Marcus approached.

"I don't mean to interrupt," he said, giving the mom a smile that would have made most women weak-kneed. "I just… I need to have a word with Ms. Prescott." Marcus winked, and the woman broke into a fit of giggles, shooting a sly smile at Naomi. She turned so Marcus couldn't see her, mouthed *"oh my GOD!"* then bustled away, leaving the two agents alone.

"Hello, Ms. Prescott,' he said, burying his hands in his pockets as he moved into the now-empty space in front of Naomi. He stepped close, much closer than necessary, and to keep from moving away Naomi had to remind herself that they were putting on a show.

She relaxed her posture, dropping her arms to her sides and tipping her head back so she could look him in the eyes. "Agent Calloway." He took another step, just barely leaving space between them, and Naomi swallowed hard. This proximity reminded her of the interrogation room the week before, and the confusingly raw lust she'd felt once anger was stripped away.

"What are you doing?" she asked, careful to maintain the low pitch of her voice.

A slow smile spread over Marcus's face as he leaned down, angling his head to the side to speak into her ear. "I'm making it look like I'm flirting with you... pretty convincing, huh?" Marcus dropped his gaze, and Naomi followed it to her chest, where the hard peaks of her nipples were straining, even through the thick fabric of her leotard.

"You egotistical son-of-a—"

"Uh-uh-uh," Marcus said, smirking as he grabbed her wrists and drew her hands up to his mouth. "Play nice in public, remember? We've got an audience."

Her back was to the other people in the room — parents picking up their kids from ballet practice, but she could imagine that several sets of curious eyes were on them. She straightened her face into an impassive mask as Marcus kissed her fingers, then released her hands.

"Good girl."

Naomi narrowed her eyes. "Get the fuck away from me," she hissed, then pulled her mouth into a smile that contradicted the roiling anger in her chest.

"Gladly."

He walked away, giving her what would have been a friendly salute if she didn't know better. Naomi took a moment to inhale a deep, cleansing breath before she turned around, and was met almost immediately by the curious eyes of two of the student's parents, including the one she'd been talking to before Marcus's interruption.

"So…?" one woman asked, with an encouraging nod.

Naomi bit back the urge to tell the woman to mind her damned business. "So… what?" she replied.

"You and Sophie's uncle!"

Shaking her head, Naomi turned to leave the room. At the last moment, she glanced back, giving the women a sly smile. "I have no idea what you're talking about."

She winked, then exited the class, leaving them to their speculation.

"WHAT'S ON 'YA MIND, CHER?"

Naomi flinched, startled by Quentin's melodic twang. She'd been deep in thought until he spoke, and she sighed when she glanced up, watching the flickers of light from the TV as they reflected in Quentin's eyes. They were at her townhouse, seated together on the couch. The movie they'd watched earlier was playing again, and Naomi had her legs draped across Quentin's lap.

She didn't even know where to *begin* answering his question. There was so much on her mind that she could barely filter through it in her head, let alone verbalize it.

The last two weeks of her life had brought about serious complications that Naomi was having a hard time processing. Before then, her extremely organized, extremely categorized lifestyle didn't require too much thought. Teach the ballet classes and fulfill her assignments for SSA Barnes. That was it. Both were second nature to her, though the class didn't require quite as much finesse or thought.

Quentin's screw up with the Paris job though — that was something that defied logic to Naomi. And he *still* hadn't given her a good explanation beyond the generic — and she suspected fabricated — "my system messed up". That was twice now, and that made only *three* known mess-ups in the twenty-something years she'd known Quentin. There was nothing wrong with his system. It was user-error, and Naomi didn't know if he was distracted, or scared, or *trying* to sabotage her — though she didn't, not even for a moment, actually believe the latter to be true.

What she *did* know was that she wanted her friend back — reliable perfectionist, unshakably confident, relentlessly flirtatious. She hadn't seen him in the last two weeks. He was unfocused, making mistakes, questioning everything… just not the Quentin she thought she knew.

She tried to pull her legs out of his lap, but he caught her at the thigh, running his hand up her bare flesh until he reached the hem of her cotton lounge shorts. "Hey," he said. "I asked you a question."

"It's nothing, Q. I just… I'm thinking about this job in Barbados. Hoping my ankle is completely better by the time we leave in two weeks.'

Quentin nodded, then eased his hand up a little further to dip it into the waistband of her shorts. He cupped her behind, squeezing the soft flesh before he lowered his head to place a kiss against her neck. "You worried about being alone in Barbados with this Marcus guy?"

Naomi rolled her eyes.

Leave it to Quentin to ask me about another man while he's gripping my ass.

"No. I can handle myself, and I don't think he's going to do anything to me, if that's what you're asking."

"Nah, cher. I don't think the man is crazy… just wanna make sure you're good." Quentin mumbled those words against her lips, immediately followed by a kiss that stirred up heated arousal at Naomi's core. She moaned as he repositioned his hand, bringing it underneath her tee shirt to cup her bare breast, flicking his thumb over her nipple.

Naomi closed her eyes, and she was back at her studio. Marcus was in front of her, staring at the hard peaks of her nipples as they strained against her leotard. This time, they were alone. She gasped as the heat of his mouth found hers, kissing her into dizzy excitement. She bit her lip as he tugged the top of her bodysuit down, leaving her breasts exposed to the chill of the air-conditioned room. There was a chair behind him for some reason, and he sat down, pulling her into his lap. Naomi was barely seated before his mouth was on her, nibbling and kissing and blowing and sucking her already rigid nipple until it was painfully hard.

He pulled away, caressing her breasts as their gaze met. "Mimi… can we…?"

"What?"

Naomi opened her eyes as Quentin pulled her into another kiss. She was straddling his lap, and her tee-shirt was pushed up, giving him full access to her breasts.

"I'm sayin'… we haven't in almost a month, unless you count the little taste you gave me that day at the gym."

Shaking her head, Naomi tried desperately to clear thoughts of Marcus's mouth on her out of her mind, but that was hard with Quentin doing the same thing. She pushed him away, removing herself from his lap as she tugged her shirt down.

"*We* may not have had sex in a month, Q, but I know *you* have," Naomi shot over her shoulder as she walked away. She didn't care who Quentin screwed, but she needed a reason to get away from him. *Why* was she thinking about Marcus like that?

Quentin caught up to her in the kitchen, grabbing her around the waist to pull her back against his chest. Naomi sighed as he pressed himself against her, pushing her hair out of the way to plant kisses along the back of her neck. She was aroused, and wet, and she *wanted* to do it, but as she closed her eyes again, her mind turned Quentin's fingers into Marcus's as they slipped into the front of her shorts, teasing her until she opened her legs wider for him, and he sank one inside.

"Mmm... Mar— maybe we shouldn't do this," she said, yanking away. "You know, Quentin... I've been thinking for a while that maybe we should put the brakes on anything that goes past friendship only."

Her words were true, but not as well-timed as she would have liked. Right now, she just needed to distract him from the fact that she'd very nearly *called him Marcus*. What the hell was her hang-up with *Marcus*?

Quentin lifted his eyebrows. "Oh... Uh... any particular reason, cher?"

"I just think it's for the best. I know you said you haven't been distracted lately, but you *have*, and I'm wondering if our sexual relationship has anything to do with it. Besides... I mean, Q, we do enough together as it is, right? We don't need an additional complication, especially since you and I aren't even... you know... *like that.* We're not secretly in love with each other or anything.... Right?"

"Right," Quentin chuckled. "Obviously I'm gonna respect what you wanna do, Mimi. I'd be lyin' if I said I wasn't gonna miss it, but you're still my patna', yeah?"

"*Always.*" Naomi stretched out her arms for a hug, sighing in relief when he returned the gesture. The fact that it *had* been on her mind to do this for quite some time eased her guilt over the *real* reason she'd just turned off the 'open now" sign for Quentin.

When he pulled away, Quentin gave Naomi a gentle pat to the face. "Now, don't be offended, cher, but... you started something that I need to talk to somebody bout finishing... if you get my drift."

Naomi lifted an eyebrow, then laughed as she rolled her eyes. "Get your ass out of my house, Quentin. You have my blessing to go and get yourself some booty."

Quentin joined in her laughter, then leaned to place a kiss against her forehead. "I want you to tell me something," he said, putting his hands on her shoulders. "This don't have nothing to do with the new guy does it?"

"*No.*" Was Naomi's quick reply. Maybe *too* quick, because Quentin shook his head, sighing as he dropped his hands to his sides. Naomi slipped his hands into hers, squeezing them between her palms. She let out a little sigh. "Maybe. Yes."

"Yeah... I saw you with him this evenin' in your classroom...looked pretty cozy."

Naomi groaned. "We're *supposed* to look like we're into each other, remember? It's part of repairing the damage his stupid ass may have done to my cover, and creating a *new* cover for us to be in Barbados together."

Quentin laughed. "I'm not saying nothin' Mimi. You're a groan woman... I'm just not sure we can trust him just yet. Watch your back 'round him, okay?"

"Okay."

"*Promise* me, cher."

"Okay, Quentin. I promise."

BUT AS SOON AS he was gone, Naomi brushed those thoughts from her head. Marcus wasn't necessarily by the book, as was the nature of his division— and hers — but he was no renegade. Beyond the self-importance and over-inflated superiority, Naomi sensed that Marcus was deeply loyal, and dedicated to his job. She'd been betrayed before, and every time, there had been an uneasy feeling about the person that went ignored. The feelings that Marcus ignited were vastly different.

As if on cue, his face drifted into her mind, followed shortly by his body. The day after appointing him to the team, Barnes had made Marcus come into the private room of their gym for a fitness test, without bothering to make Naomi aware.

She was speechless for a long moment when she walked into the room, her ability to move, speak, and apparently breathe snatched away by the sight of a sweaty Marcus— in nothing but shorts and protective gear on his hands— doing pull-ups, muscles rippling as he went. Up, down, up, down, over and over... *effortlessly*, like lifting his beautifully muscled body over that bar was nothing.

And that pissed her off.

He pissed her off.

In her brief experience, he was an asshole. A sexy one, and arguably good at his job, but an asshole nonetheless. What Naomi couldn't seem to figure out was why, exactly, that turned her on.

MARCUS

BEAUTIFUL.

Marcus sat transfixed, watching Naomi from the other side of the two-way glass. It was late — well after midnight, but instead of being at home in his bed, he'd been summoned to Five Star Fitness for another briefing. This time next week, he and Naomi would be boarding their ten hour flight to Barbados, but tonight, they'd run through their plan of action over and over, to the point of exhaustion. But, every detail was committed to memory.

Now, Quentin and Barnes were still holed up in the office, going over some type of tech stuff. Naomi had left nearly half an hour before, after being mostly silent through their long meeting. Marcus couldn't leave yet, because he'd ridden with Barnes, but the computer talk was making his head spin, so he set out to explore the gym.

It was the sound of music, pumping from the classroom where Naomi hosted her classes that brought Marcus to the front of the gym. Curious, he stepped into the area meant for parents to watch their kids during performances, and what he saw in front of him froze him to the spot.

Naomi was obviously mid-routine, and soaked in enough sweat that Marcus suspected she'd been repeating it since she left the office. In black leggings, a black sports bra, and black ballet shoes, Naomi was performing an impressively choreographed mix of classical ballet and modern dance, evenly sprinkled with overtly sexy moves that made Marcus's mouth go dry as he pulled a chair right up to the glass to watch. She was dancing to Ginuwine's *So Anxious*, a song that came out when Marcus was seventeen. It brought back fond memories of his seventeen-year-old self playing it for whichever girl he'd charmed into his room, in hopes that he could charm his way into her panties.

But, he didn't dwell on the memories long.

Naomi had dropped to the floor, crawling toward—from her vantage point — her reflection, but the way Marcus saw it, she was coming for *him*. She was winding her hips, tossing her hair, biting her lip as she got closer and closer to the mirror. It was sexy, no doubt, but it was somehow… deeper than that. Nothing about her movement spoke of vulgarity, just unrestrained sensuality, and Marcus couldn't decide if it was the woman or her moves that had blood rushing to his groin.

"Holy shit," Marcus whispered, leaning closer when she reached the mirror, did a series of moves on the floor that were downright erotic, then grabbed onto the barre to pull herself up in one fluid motion. With her hands clasped on the wooden rail, she dipped, knees together, back arched, rolling her hips with the music as the song led into the bridge. Her timing was impeccable, because the moment before the beat dropped, she was upright again. The moment after, she was… *off,* jumping and

twirling and leaping with a level of speed, agility, and grace that made Marcus's heart race. He was turned on, but more than that, he was *impressed.*

Both feelings annoyed the shit out of him.

Marcus had spent a good portion of his career with Naomi on his "hit list'. Hers was one of *very* few names that had never rotated out over the years. He was always searching, always moving, and always *just* missing his chance to finally catch *Jolie Voleuse*. The minute his luck *finally* caught up to his hard work, Naomi Prescott had shot his hopes and dreams of a career-making takedown in the chest with a heat-seeking missile.

That's why so much of Marcus's time over the last two weeks of forced teamwork with Naomi and Quentin had been spent doing everything he could to get under her skin. He *wanted* to get under her clothes, but after the way things had started, those chances were slim. So he would settle for watching her dance in the fearless, sexy way she probably only felt comfortable with because she assumed no one was watching.

Guilt pricked Marcus's chest at the thought of that. This was *her* time. According to Barnes, Naomi always withdrew into this room when she was preparing for a job. It wasn't okay for him to intrude on that.

Just as he was standing to leave, Naomi took one last leap across the room, landing on her previously injured leg. She pulled herself into what Marcus knew to be a perfect arabesque pose — he'd looked it up after Barnes's little history lesson that first night. She held it at first, but then a flash of pain crossed her face, and she collapsed, falling to the floor on her hands and knees.

Hesitation didn't cross Marcus's mind. He bolted to the door, and flung it open, rushing over to Naomi's side.

"Hey... are you okay?" he asked, helping her into a seated position.

She looked dazed for a few moments before she scowled. "I'm fine. Were you... *watching* me?"

Marcus scratched his eyebrow. "I... umm..."

Naomi let out a frustrated growl as she pulled away from him and stood, practically knocking her portable speakers to the floor as she turned off her music. "Unbelievable," she muttered under her breath as she gathered her things.

"I'm sorry." Marcus followed her to the coat rack, where she snatched a lightweight jacket from the hook and slipped it on, shielding her body from view. "I mean... you looked really good though."

Marcus recoiled at the look Naomi gave him then, and decided to switch gears. "Hey, you didn't look like you were okay when you landed on that ankle... are you sure you're ready to—"

"I said I was fine," Naomi snapped. "If you don't mind, I'd like to finish what I was doing."

For a long moment, they simply scowled at each other in a battle of wills. Then, Marcus shook his head. "Fine," he scoffed. "I'll leave you to it."

He stalked to the door and snatched it open, pausing in the doorway when Naomi called out.

"Marcus!"

He turned, his face set into an impassive mask. "Yeah?"

"Good boy," Naomi said with a smirk, then cranked her music back on full blast and turned toward the mirror.

SIX
MARCUS

"ARE you gonna marry Madame Mimi, Uncle Marcus?"

Marcus's eyes grew wide, then he shot a scowl at his sister, Meagan, who was pretending not to hear the questions Sophie had been peppering him with since he left his room. It was mornings like this that he *almost* regretted opening his home to them while Meagan's husband was deployed.

"Why would you ask such a question, lil bit?" he asked Sophie as she climbed onto the barstool beside him at the counter. Until she and Meagan moved in, Marcus's place was nothing but black and chrome, minimal and modern, but now, no matter how hard his sister tried to be unobtrusive, there were sprinkles of *girl* everywhere. A backpack in the shape of a cartoon cat — which Marcus had brought back for Sophie from Japan — , a makeup bag on the counter in his guest bath, four-inch heels parked beside his boots at the front door — all reminders that his space was no longer his own, but his sister and niece were the only family he had left. On the vast list of things he would do for them, giving up his home ranked low in level of sacrifice.

"Cause you're always staring at her, and talking to her, and you kissed her on the face, but not like you kiss me and mommy." All of that took her about two seconds to say as her mother put a plate of breakfast in front of her. Marcus watched in awe as she methodically ripped her bacon into pieces, a process that she'd previously explained as "making it last longer."

The kiss that six-year-old Sophie was referring to had happened just the day before. It wasn't something Marcus even planned to do, but when he arrived at the gym that day, Naomi's whole demeanor was off. Instead of the cold, haughty vibe she usually gave him — carefully concealed under the warmth and flirtatiousness the public saw, but *he* felt it — Naomi seemed stressed and distracted.

When he touched her — something he'd gotten strangely comfortable doing, at least when they had an audience — her skin was clammy, shoulders tense, and before Marcus could check himself, he'd leaned down and kissed her forehead. Naomi stiffened in surprise, but had the presence of mind not to pull away as Marcus caressed her cheek, giving her an encouraging smile. And... surprisingly, she'd actually smiled back. It wasn't even a big one, just a slight tip up at the corners of her mouth, but it moved Marcus to the point that he almost wanted to kiss her again, right on that bare hint of smile.

And then, he remembered that she barely tolerated him, and the feeling was mutual. This an act, orchestrated by someone else, to make the fact that they were boarding a plane to Barbados the next day as a couple believable. Rushed, and a bit ridiculous, but believable.

"Well," Marcus said to Sophie as she downed the rest of her waffle and eggs, then her bacon, "It's a little soon to talk about marriage, okay? We'll see how our trip goes first."

Sophie nodded, then left bacon crumbs on Marcus's face as she kissed his cheek, then jumped down from the barstool to finish getting ready for school. Marcus shook his head as he wiped his face, then looked up to find his sister studying him from the other side of the counter.

"So... Naomi Prescott." Meagan cleaned Sophie's place at the counter, then turned her attention to her brother again. "I... can't say I'm surprised you're attracted to her, because she's beautiful, but... I've *never* seen Naomi give anybody any steam. And trust me, I've seen *many* try... until you took over ballet pickup duties."

Marcus smiled. "Guess it's just that good old Calloway charm."

"Oh *please*," Megan said, rolling her eyes even though she smiled. "You ain't *that* charming, Marcus. You get a woman to go to friggin' Barbados with you after knowing her for three weeks, you must have put some kind of bedroom voodoo on her."

With a smirk on his face, Marcus leaned against the back of the barstool, propping his hands behind his head. "I confirm nor deny."

"Whatever, little brother. I know how you do. As a matter of fact… I actually *am* shocked that you went for Naomi. She seems much more… cultured, more sophisticated than your usual flings. Not the kind of woman for your whole drive-thru relationship thing you like to do."

Marcus shrugged. "Don't know what to tell you sis, other than that she's had my interest since I first saw her face."

This was one of the hardest parts of the job. When he was a cop, he talked to Meagan about his cases often, but once he joined the FBI, and *especially* on his current task force, that stopped. The information he dealt with now was much more serious, and usually, more dangerous. Even so, Marcus hated lying to his sister's face.

"Uh-huh. I'm just glad to see you going on another vacation. You've been kind of grumpy since you got back from Paris. Hopefully, work won't interfere this time, and you can actually *relax*… maybe even settle down. You know daddy warned you about that, remember?"

Marcus gave Meagan a weak smile as he thought back to the warning their deceased father had given him often, about getting so caught up in the job that you didn't get a chance to enjoy your life. Kenneth Calloway was a single father, following his Michelle Calloway's death in a car accident. He was a man who loved his family, but spent much of his time — perhaps *too* much

— holed up in his office poring over evidence, tracking down evidence, or chasing leads while his mother and sisters cared for Meagan and Marcus.

Marcus's career path mirrored his father's. Bachelor's in criminal justice, then police academy. Two impeccable years on the force earned him a detail with a special investigative unit, and two years after that, he became *Detective* Marcus Calloway. Now, he was Special Agent Calloway, just like his father, but Kenneth hadn't gotten to see any of that. He was, along with two other men — one of whom was a known criminal — gunned down in the second semester of Marcus and Meagan's first year of college.

Their father's passing was hard on both of them, but the worst part was not really knowing what happened. What little information he had was gathered by a private investigator hired by the twins. The PI quit not long after being hired, following a detaining by men in black suits. Meagan wanted to let it rest, but Marcus couldn't. Eventually, he *would* find out what happened.

In any case, it would have been ideal for Kenneth Calloway to follow his *own* advice, but instead he passed it down to his son. Marcus understood — and shared — his father's hunger for justice, the intrepid desire to see the bad guy fall. And despite his father's counsel, his job at the FBI — with the exception of the time he spent with Meagan and Sophie — was his life.

Marcus may have considered himself a magnet for beautiful women, but the long hours, nearly-constant danger, and unimpressive pay were strong repellants. His lifestyle wasn't exactly the type that women were lining up to share, and Marcus was okay with that. He enjoyed the freedom to come and go as he pleased, do what he wanted with his spare time, and not have to deal with the burden of a commitment. The only woman who questioned his movements now was Sophie, and *that* he could handle.

"I don't know anything about this "settling down" that you speak of, but I plan to relax in Barbados as much as possible," Marcus said, pushing his plate and cup into the steamy dishwater Meagan had prepared as he stood to leave. He actually smiled as he thought about it. They left for Barbados today, but the party at Rochas's house wasn't for another three days. They had a bit of reconnaissance to do on the island, but other than that, he and Naomi were supposed to appear as a couple on vacation. He planned to soak up plenty of sun — and Bajan rum —during their off time.

Meagan smiled. "Make sure you bring me back a tee shirt." She offered her cheek for Marcus to kiss, then extended her arms for a hug, which he returned.

"I'll be back in five days… try not to let lil bit wreck the place, will you?"

"I'm not making *any* promises."

"I'M SO JEALOUS," Renata said, peeking over Marcus's shoulder at the open envelope in his hands. It contained his and Naomi's tickets to Barbados, on a flight that left in less than three hours.

Marcus had stopped at his desk to make sure everything was locked up, and that he had everything he needed before he went to pick Naomi up from her condo. If anything went wrong on this trip, he did *not* want it to be his fault. He could imagine the look on Naomi's face now.

From his desk across from Marcus, Kendall chimed in. "Don't be. Marcus is the only agent I know who stays in so much trouble he's always "on vacation". What the hell did you do this time?"

Marcus shrugged. *This* was even worse than lying to Meagan. SSA Black had fed Kendall and Renata some bogus story about Naomi having an ironclad alibi, and they seemed to accept it and move on. All Marcus had to do was go along with it. They'd teased him mercilessly about "dating" Naomi after all of the hassle, but they both approved. Especially Renata, who admired Naomi's spitfire personality.

"I'm just making up for the Paris fiasco," Marcus said truthfully as he stuffed the envelope into his utility backpack, then pulled it over one shoulder.

Renata spoke up again as she followed Marcus to the elevator bay. "Well, I hope you have a blast. I wish *I* was on vacation."

"Didn't you tell me Taylor was staying with her grandmother for the summer?" Marcus asked, referring to Renata's fourteen year old daughter.

"That's *so* not the same thing. A vacation is not having to report to work, not just being away from your kids." Renata smiled, but Marcus noticed that it seemed strained, and didn't quite reach her eyes.

He smirked. "Uh-huh. Sending her away isn't as relaxing as you thought it was gonna be, is it? What's wrong, are you worried about her?"

Renata's throat bobbed as she swallowed hard, then opened her mouth to speak. "I... I... um..." Tears began welling in her eyes, and before Marcus could say anything else, she took off at a near-jog toward the women's restroom.

Damn. Guess she is worried about her.

Before he could go back to their team area to question Kendall about Renata's behavior, SSA Black poked her head out of her office.

"Calloway! I need to see you before you leave."

Shaking his head, Marcus decided he would figure Renata out later. He went to SSA Black's office and closed the door behind him, but she waved him off when he started to sit down.

"I don't plan to hold you long, because I know you need to leave so you can make your flight. But... I want to remind you that you don't only work for Agent Barnes... do you understand?"

"Yes ma'am."

SSA Black nodded. "Good. Marcus, you are one of my best agents, so I know you can see the... delicacies of this situation. It's important that you do your best to assist agents Prescott and LaForte, but remember that we have our own operation going. I need you to be careful that you don't compromise it. If it comes to a choice between Agent Prescott and you maintaining the hold we have on *our* target... I don't need to tell you what your decision needs to be, do I?"

No, she didn't.

Marcus didn't need *any* reminders that he still needed to make up for the mess that had gotten him put on the vacation that led him to Paris in the first place. SSA Black wasn't holding on to any grudges, but the supervisors over *her* head weren't quite so forgiving. He would help Agent Barnes, sure, but he had other things in the works as well. Things that could make up for the loss of *Jolie Voleuse.*

Marcus shook his head. "No ma'am."

"*Good*," Agent Black said with a smile that brightened her entire face. "Now, you go. Have as good of a time as you can while still giving us top notch work."

Marcus gave her a salute before he turned to leave. "Aye, aye, captain."

"Oh, and Calloway," Black called out, just before Marcus closed the door. "Try not to get slapped again."

"I KNOW THIS WOMAN SEES ME."

Marcus lifted an eyebrow, biting the inside of his jaw to hide his smirk over Naomi's frustrated attempts to get the flight attendant's attention. She unbuckled her seatbelt, and sensing impending trouble, Marcus put a hand on her knee to keep her in her seat. He flagged the attendant down himself. Naomi *did* have reason to be annoyed — the attendant was blatantly ignoring her.

When they were boarding, the attractive woman made an inappropriate comment to Marcus about the "mile-high" club, and Naomi cocked an eyebrow and said, "Oh, I guess you don't see me standing *right* here, holding his hand while you flip on the hot and ready sign? Okay, you are *bold*." She wasn't loud about it, and her voice actually held less disdain than she used when she spoke to Marcus, but the attendant blushed, her light skin flushing crimson as she turned away to speak to the next passenger.

Now, the woman was acting as if Naomi's comment had been unwarranted or abusive, and was purposefully avoiding their seats. Their *first class* seats.

The attendant — Stacy, according to her name badge — sauntered up to Marcus with a grin, barely acknowledging Naomi. "Stacy," Marcus said, flashing his dimples as he smiled, "I know you're busy taking wonderful care of the other passengers, but my lady needs something, if you don't mind."

"Not at all," Stacy replied, in a falsely cheerful voice through gritted teeth. "What can I do for you?"

"Dewar's white label, please. A double."

Stacy smirked. "Will that be all?"

"Yes please…. Actually, bring me the mini bottles — *unopened*. Two of them, please."

"Of course. Anything for you, sir?" Stacy asked, turning the charm back on as she addressed Marcus with a smile.

"No, thank you."

A few moments later, Naomi was swigging from a tiny bottle of scotch. "Thanks," she said, glancing over at Marcus. He studied her, interested, as she finished the first bottle, then didn't hesitate to open another, downing it just as quickly.

"Stressed?"

Naomi paused, with the third bottle pressed to her lips. She pulled it away, shaking her head. "Nope. Just don't like airplanes."

"Really? I'm surprised, as full as your passport is."

Naomi gave him a rare genuine smile as she held up the last bottle, right before she drained it down her throat. "Liquid courage has gotten me through many long flights… usually puts me to sleep."

"So… it's not that you don't like airplanes… you're afraid of flying."

"I didn't say that."

"Context clues."

Naomi stared at him for a second, then looked away. "Fine. I'm afraid of flying," she said, her gaze focused on the view out of the window. "Why does it matter?"

"It doesn't. Just… nice to know something about you."

She sucked her teeth, but kept her voice low when she answered. "Like Barnes hasn't already told you everything there is to know."

"What, all those random facts buried somewhere in a classified file?" Marcus asked, wishing she would look at him while they had this — their *first,* actually, that wasn't about going over the job — conversation. "That's not *you.* It's an on-paper approximation, but that doesn't tell me anything about you as a person."

At that, Naomi did turn around, eyebrow lifted as she met Marcus's gaze. "What makes you think there's more to me than that?"

For a moment, Marcus was hypnotized by Naomi's deep, expressive eyes. He had to pull his hand into a fist in his lap to keep from reaching over to brush her hair away from hiding her face. There was *something* there, behind that kick-ass exterior of hers that made Marcus wonder if there was anyone, other than Quentin and Inez who knew Naomi beyond what was in her file. Instead of asking that though, he smiled, then leaned closer to speak into her ear.

"Naomi… you're a thief turned FBI secret weapon turned ballet instructor in your spare time. I'm quite sure there's *plenty* of depth to the woman behind all of that."

Her eyes widened for a moment, then she bit her lip as she looked away. "I'm going to sleep. Wake me up when we're almost there… please."

Marcus nodded, shaking his head as she turned to her side, snuggled down into her seat, and closed her eyes. Several minutes later, the subtle rise and fall of her shoulders indicated that she had indeed fallen asleep, so Marcus sat back in his seat and closed his eyes too.

[COMMAND: open private chat]

painted_pixel: ..... are you there?

.....

CrawDaddy: yeah. any news?

... ...

...

CrawDaddy: p...you there?

...

painted_pixel: yeah. no news. is anybody asking questions?

CrawDaddy: of course. but i'm handling it. i said i would do whatever it took. meant that.

painted_pixel: she could die.

CrawDaddy: whatever it takes.

painted_pixel: you say that, but...

CrawDaddy: i'm a man of my word. i said i would do whatever it took, and I meant that.

painted_pixel: i hope so. because the alternative...

CrawDaddy: you don't have to remind me.

...

....

CrawDaddy: p?

[user "painted_pixel" no longer exists. aborting chat.]

"YOU SHOULD COME HAVE a drink with me."

Marcus watched the emotions play over her face before Naomi shook her head. She tossed her carryon on the bed, then took her suitcase from Marcus. He'd actually insisted on carrying both, plus his own, but Naomi had refused, citing the fact that she'd always taken care of her bags before, so she could certainly take care of them now.

"No thanks," she said, unzipping the suitcase to pull out her toiletry bag. "*I* am going to put the jetted tub to use for a long bath, and then hit the mini bar. You have fun though."

Marcus dropped his head, closing his eyes as he massaged his forehead. "Naomi... I can't go by myself. We're supposed to be a couple, remember?"

"Then I guess we're having a night in."

"We're on vacation."

"We're on a *job*."

"Where pretending to be on vacation is one of the requirements," Marcus said, taking a few steps closer. He stopped about a foot in front of her before he continued. "And the best way *I* can think of to do that... is to act like we're on vacation, which doesn't mean "a night in" on the first night."

"Marcus, I'm tired."

"Okay, so *one* drink, at the resort bar. We can look around a little, get our bearings, then you can have your bath and I won't bother you again for the rest of the night."

Naomi pushed out a deep breath as she propped her hands on her hips. "I don't even look presentable right now, Marcus, we just got off the plane."

"You look fine."

It was true. She was dressed simply, in sandals, dark-wash boot-cut jeans and a fitted black tee shirt, but somehow, the basic ensemble looked polished and sexy on Naomi.

"Can I at least take a shower?"

Marcus groaned. "Naomi... you know if you take a shower right now, the only thing you're gonna want to do is get in the bed. Stop stalling, and come have a drink with me."

If asked, he wouldn't have been able to give a good answer as to why he was working so hard at this, other than that the little glimpse of *something* he'd seen in her eyes on the plane made her exponentially more interesting than she already was. He wanted to see more.

"Fine, Marcus. Can I have... two minutes?"

Grudgingly, Marcus agreed. He fully expected those two minutes to turn into ten, then twenty, but Naomi stuck to what she said. She fluffed her hair, put on earrings, changed into a pair of strappy heeled sandals, and swiped deep red gloss across her lips. Naomi looked good before, but those subtle changes turned her up a notch or twenty.

"Are you ready?" she asked, lifting an eyebrow at Marcus.

Marcus rubbed his chin, then reluctantly pulled his gaze away to head for the door. He opened it for her, then closed it behind them, and grabbed her hand as they started away from their villa. Naomi tried to tug away, but Marcus held on, pulling her closer.

"What are you doing, *sweetheart*? An hour into vacation, and you're already being cold to me," Marcus teased, releasing her hand to instead loop his arm around her waist.

"Don't push your luck, Calloway." Naomi stepped away from his embrace, but allowed him to take her hand again as they continued toward the resort's restaurant and bar.

There weren't many people hanging around on the grounds, but somewhere in the distance, the rhythmic beat of steel drums hung on the air. The paths that led to the villas and main areas of the resort were paved, but lined with lit torches in the pristine white sand. It was warm— not overly so, but enough that the promise of a fan or an air conditioner to cool off made Marcus put a little pep in his step as he pulled Naomi along. As they got closer, the smell of *something* cooking over a wood-fire grill made his mouth water, and must have had the same effect on Naomi, because when they sat down at their table, they both went for the food menus instead of looking at the drinks.

Once the food was ordered, they requested their drinks, and once the drinks were served, *just one* quickly turned into *just one more*, which turned into *okay, this is the last one*, which resulted in a giggly, relaxed Naomi, and Marcus was *very* amused. The server came to ask if they wanted anything more, and Marcus waved her away. For some reason, even that was humorous to Naomi, and Marcus turned to her with a grin.

"What exactly is so funny?" he asked, pulling enough bills from his wallet to cover the meal plus a nice tip.

Naomi accepted the hand Marcus offered her to rise from her seat, slurping the last bit of her Bajan rum punch before she left the glass on the table. "*You* think I'm tipsy."

"*I* think your ass is *drunk*."

Marcus looped an arm around Naomi's waist. Giggling, she pressed her body against his as she spoke into his ear. "I'm *so* not."

"You so are," Marcus replied, chuckling as she rested her head on his shoulder. "I've never seen you like this."

"Like what?" As soon as they stepped outside of the bar, Naomi pulled away, lifting her hair off her face and neck. She lifted her chin, closed her eyes, and smiled as she moved her head back and forth.

Marcus lifted an eyebrow. "What the hell are you doing?"

"Feeling the island breeze on my skin. We're in *Barbados*." Naomi opened one eye to glance at him, then closed them again as she released her hair and took a deep inhale. "You didn't answer my question."

"What question?"

"You've never seen me like *what*?" Naomi turned to face Marcus, getting so close they were almost touching as she waited for his response.

Pushing his hands into his pockets, Marcus smiled. "All… breezy and laid-back."

"I'm like this all the time."

"Bullshit," Marcus declared, after a little shout of laughter. "You're always edgy."

"I'm not *always* edgy."

"You are when I'm around. I'm sure I don't need to name every example."

Naomi smiled, then reached up to straighten the collar of Marcus's polo. "Well… sounds like *you're* the common denominator, Marcus. Have you considered that?" She patted his face, then giggled as she turned to walk away — the *opposite* of the way that led back to their villa.

"Hey!" Marcus grabbed her hand. "Room is in the other direction."

Shrugging, Naomi tugged Marcus's hand for him to follow. "I know. But I hear reggae music from somewhere, and I wanna find it."

"An hour ago you were too tired for a drink, now you want to find a party?"

"That's what reggae does to you, Calloway. Once you hear it... you've gotta move. Come on."

Marcus shook his head, but went along as Naomi followed the music to a place that met her unspoken standards. The "right" spot turned out to be a little hole-in-the-wall club two blocks from their resort. Marcus's seed of doubt about the place's security was confirmed by the lack of a pat down when he paid their cover charge, which would have revealed his and Naomi's loaded weapons.

But, Naomi didn't seem to mind, and if anything popped off, he'd rather have his weapon on him than confiscated anyway, so he rolled with it. She led him to what seemed to be an emptier corner of the packed club, then turned to face him, her eyes shining bright.

"Isn't this *awesome*?" she asked, already bobbing her head and moving her hips as an upbeat reggae song began to play. Marcus's idea of fun wasn't a tiny, over-capacity club full of sweaty, energetic people, but he was glad she seemed happy. It was such a departure from what he'd seen that hell, looking at *her* was fun.

Marcus found the bar and a drink while Naomi found herself a place on the dance floor. Her natural ability as a dancer showed in every move she made, and soon, she was just as sweaty as the rest of the crowd.

"Marcus!" she said, bursting out of a group of people to find him seated on the edge of the dance floor. "You're not gonna dance?"

"Nah, not really my thing. *But*, we can stay as long as you want. Go, have a good time."

Naomi poked out her bottom lip in a pout, and Marcus was struck by how... *adorable* she looked. He shook his head, then cried out in protest as she pulled the fresh drink he'd *just* gotten from his hands. She laughed, avoiding his outstretched hand as she downed the drink in one long sip, then handed him the empty glass.

"What was *that*?" she asked, coughing into her elbow as the liquor burned her throat.

"An over-poured rum and coke. You owe me a dri—"

Marcus's protest was interrupted by a loud gasp from Naomi as the music dropped into a song with a smoother, more sensual beat than the hi-tempo reggae from before. Naomi grabbed his hands, trying to pull him up from his chair. "Come on, Marcus. Wine with me!"

"Do what?" Marcus asked, lifting an eyebrow, but not budging from his seat. "I don't know if this is the kinda place that serves wine."

Naomi rolled her eyes. "No, not *that* kind of wine. *Wine* with me," she repeated, moving her hips in a slow, exaggerated circle in front of him. Marcus watched, transfixed as her tee-shirt rose above her belly button as she danced. She bit her lip, then gave him a seductive smile as she moved lower, then rose up again, but she didn't take her gaze off his. Her eyelids hung low from the effects of the alcohol, but they sprang open a little wider when an arm — a *stranger's* arm— snaked around her waist.

Before Marcus could get on his feet to interfere, Naomi already had the guy pushed into the wall, with his arm twisted behind him in a grip that could easily break his wrist.

"*Whoa, Naomi.*" Marcus jumped up, gently breaking the two apart with a soothing hand on Naomi's shoulder. The partygoer insisted he didn't mean any harm, so Marcus sent him on his way, but preempted any other bold dance partners by positioning himself behind Naomi, who glanced at him over her shoulder with a smile and a wink.

It didn't take Marcus long to realize that *this* kind of dancing with Naomi was a bad idea. She pushed herself against him, grinding and swaying and winding and gyrating and... turning him on. He sucked in a breath as she turned around, pressing her chest against his.

"We should go…. *Not* like that," she clarified, grinning at the dazed look on Marcus's face. "I'm tired, and this is… I'm tired."

He released the breath he was holding and nodded, grabbing her hand to lead the way through the still-packed crowd. Outside, Naomi paused on the sidewalk in front of the club to repeat her quirky little move from before, lifting her hair to feel the breeze on her face. When she dropped it again, the curls fell into thick piles against her shoulders, and around her head, framing her pretty face as she smiled.

"So, you obviously had a good time tonight," he said as they stepped onto the resort grounds. He showed his id to the guards to let them into the gate, then led Naomi in the direction of their villa.

Naomi gave him a silly smile. "I did, actually."

She waited at the door while he unlocked it and stepped in first, clearing the room before he used one of Quentin's gadgets to make sure it was clear of any surveillance equipment that wasn't their own. When he was done, she unstrapped her gun from her ankle and placed it on the nightstand, then fell across the king-sized bed on her stomach, groaning as she closed her eyes.

"I need to get up and take a bath," she mumbled into the bed cover, but didn't move to do any such thing.

Marcus chuckled as he sat down beside her. "Yeah, you were working pretty hard on that dance floor, not that

I'm surprised. Why didn't you dance professionally, instead of…?"

"Instead of becoming a career criminal?"

Marcus nodded, and Naomi breathed a heavy sigh before she turned onto her back, propping her hands behind her head. "My mother, Noelle, inspired my love of dance. She was the most beautiful, graceful woman I've ever seen, and she taught me everything she knew… not just about dance either, about… *everything*. Black history, and boys, and beauty, and… everything. Best mommy a little girl could ask for."

When she didn't say anything else, Marcus prodded the side of her leg. "But?"

"*But…* you already know what happened next, Marcus. It's in my dossier."

Marcus shrugged. "Haven't read it."

"Seriously?"

"Yeah," Marcus said, with a slight scowl. "It wasn't offered to me, and when I asked I was told it was classified, so… tell the story."

Naomi chewed at her lip for a long moment, her eyes focused on the ceiling, then finally she spoke again. "She was murdered."

Jerking his head back, Marcus cursed to himself. He wasn't trying to take her to some deep, tragic place, but she was already blinking back tears. A heaviness settled in his chest as she continued.

"It wasn't quick, and it wasn't an accident. My father's half-brother…my uncle. He… *wanted* my mom, in a way that's as disgusting as that sounds… so one day, he sent people to take her. And, he had her, and then… a few weeks later, they brought her back, and left her beat up on the front door step. But… she wasn't the mommy I knew before. I was 13 when I left for dance class one day, and when I came back, the house was *crawling* with police, and the street was lit up with strobe lights from their cars, and… nobody would let me in the house. My mother put a bullet through her head to escape the demons he left her with, but… that bastard killed her long before that."

She closed her eyes, squeezing tears through her thick eyelashes as she clapped her hand to her mouth. Marcus's throat felt scratchy and dry, but he had to swallow a lump of emotion himself. He and Meagan's mother died before they were old enough to know her, but the pain of losing his father was real.

He put a hand on Naomi's knee and squeezed, then asked the question that was burning in his mind. "Did they ever arrest him? Did he go to jail?"

Through her tears, Naomi scoffed, then her face took on a hard edge as she shook her head. "Nope."

"But… they knew what he did to her, right?"

Naomi nodded, sniffling. "Yeah. But, you're an FBI agent too Marcus. You know just as well as I do... Damien Wolfe is above the law."

SEVEN
NAOMI

HE'S NOT TAKING this seriously.

That was the only conclusion Naomi could draw from Marcus's insistence on going to the beach, of all places, less than five hours before they had to complete a job. One would think that after all of their research, planning, and preparation, — not to mention their individual past experience— Marcus would understand just how critical this was. Successful completion of this task, plus a little well-planned misinformation, and Santiago Rochas would be the one that Damien Wolfe held responsible for his missing diamonds.

The Russians, the Italians, the Serbians, the Iranians, they all had their hierarchies in the US, with a terrible, powerful man at the top. Damien Wolfe was the African-American answer to that. They held counsel with each other, and there was a certain code of respect they followed, or paid the price.

Santiago Rochas and Victor Lucas were the only two men Wolfe allowed to operate under him. He was well known for violence against those who crossed him, but he doled out a special kind of torture for his subordinates. It wouldn't be quick or clean.

First, he would pull financial backing. Next, he would pull security and protection. After that, evidence of anything less-than-legal would be delivered to law enforcement with a hand-tied bow. While they were on trial, anyone they loved would get smeared and dragged through the media, with allegations both real and fabricated. And once they were convicted — because they *would* be convicted — just enough strings would be pulled to make their life behind bars hell. The right palms would be greased to ensure the right people looked in a different direction, until an "accidental" death occurred. Problem solved.

Naomi and her team knew this information because it wasn't their first time down this road. Two years ago, they'd succeeded at eliminating a third lieutenant from Wolfe's roster. It had helped that Brendan Walker was, as they all were, truly a bad guy. It didn't take much work to find a crime to exploit. They happily watched his credit cards get declined at the end of lavish shopping trips, bodyguards slowly disappear, and police start knowing on doors and raiding homes.

Pictures of his wife and mistress cavorting with a third man — Brendan's financial adviser— were splashed all across the internet. Images of Brendan in "unconventional" sexual situations played in loops on late night cable news. By the time he made it to jail, everyone in his life had absolved themselves of him, and a week into his sentence, a vicious beating left him dead.

Damien Wolfe was front and center with a smile on his face at the funeral.

None of them felt particularly good about their involvement with a man's death, but they were, in essence, simply tipping the first domino in a dangerously fragile line up that was started before they came along.

Naomi had been sorely disappointed that following the triumph, their operation — codename Silver Bullet — had to be put on the backburner while they pursued other missions. But, she understood the need for patience. It wouldn't do for Wolfe to grow suspicious of third-party involvement, so she waited.

Until now.

And Marcus wanted to go to the damned beach

"What happened to the laughing, dancing Naomi from the first night? Where is *she*? Bring *her* back out, cause you are… goddamn, why are you so tense?" Marcus asked as he leaned against the door, hands shoved in the pockets of his beach shorts.

Naomi shot him a scathing glare in return. She wished he would stop bringing up the night of their arrival, when she'd overindulged on alcohol and been a little too loose in the lips *and* hips.

"She got *serious*. She remembered that we're only *pretending* to be on vacation together. We're here to do a job, in less than five hours. We need to be ready, no mistakes."

"We *are* ready, Naomi. We've been getting that way for weeks… what the hell else can we do?"

"We go over it again."

Marcus scoffed. "We've been over this shit a million times!"

"*This shit* is the result of years of hard work. *This shit* means the possibility of taking down a major organized crime boss. If we can do this without screwing it up, it means we eliminate Rochas, which leaves Lucas as the only intermediary to Wolfe. It takes us that much closer to the home stretch. *This shit* is important!"

"I know that," Marcus said, pushing away from the door to take a few steps toward Naomi. "I've been listening, I've been training, and I've been getting ready, just like you have."

"*Not* like I have."

Marcus tossed his hands in the air. "So because my process isn't the same as yours, it doesn't count? Just because I'm not obsessing, driving myself into paranoia like you, doesn't mean I'm not ready."

"No, it means you're a gambler," Naomi shot back, standing from her seat at the desk. "We stick to a plan on this team, and we need to know it backwards and forwards; no room for mistakes. And if something does happen, we have a contingency plan, and a plan B for the contingency plan."

Marcus started to say something, then clamped his mouth shut and shook his head.

Narrowing her eyes, Naomi propped her hands on her hips. "Don't let the cat get your tongue now, Marcus. Say what you have to say."

"You sure about that?" Marcus asked, his eyes glittering with derision.

"Am I supposed to be scared?"

Marcus smirked, then took another step closer. "I was just wondering… what was your contingency plan in Paris? Cause from what I gathered, it was *luck* that your home girl was able to get you out of that one. And let's not forget that I walked right into your front door that night I took you in. What, no plan B for that? And what about when you got caught by the FBI? Cause it looks to me like the world-renowned *Jolie Voleuse* is really just a fortunate common thief with the FBI on her side."

Naomi swallowed hard. No, there hadn't been any alternate game plans for any of those times, because she'd been counting on someone else. The times that her life or freedom had been in real danger of being taken away were limited, but nearly all were the result of a betrayal or mistake by a team member — both of which were out of her control. She'd certainly made mistakes of her own, but her best work happened when she was relying on her own instinct, not letting herself get too comfortable with the supplemental assistance of others.

After this last mistake from Quentin, she didn't intend to rely on it anymore. Even now.

"Fine," she hissed, willing her chin not to tremble as she spoke. "I don't even know why I'm riding you about this, Marcus. I didn't want your help anyway. So… go to beach, get drunk, screw an island girl, whatever. I don't care."

She sat down, and didn't say anything else as she pulled the blueprints of Rochas's vacation house to the top of the pile of papers on the desk.

"Now wait a minute, Nao—"

Naomi stuffed her ear buds into her hears, cranking her reggae mix as loud as necessary to drown out Marcus's voice. She propped her head on her hand, ignoring him as she pored over the documents one more time. It didn't matter if Marcus was ready or not.

She was.

━━━━━━

DILIGENCE. Focus. Agility.

Naomi chanted her usual mantra in her head as she slipped away from Marcus, and up the stairs. There was no disguise this time. No face altering makeup, no convenient change of clothes, only a strict dependence on her ability to get up these stairs, down the hall to the third door on her left, pull up the rug under the desk, open the safe, close it back, replace the rug, and get back to Marcus's side in the next five minutes — without being seen, or arousing suspicion.

Piece of cake, really.

This party was a completely different vibe than the energetic, fun vibe of that little hole-in-the-wall club. Strobe lights, men with obvious weapons at their waists, women on poles, liquor flowing freely, pills passed around by the handful... this was very much a Santiago Rochas kind of party.

She'd had to threaten Marcus's life to get him to stay downstairs and stick to the plan. Naomi didn't appreciate his attempted deviation, but — despite the fact that she was still only counting on herself to pull this off — she was grateful that he seemed aware of the potential danger if anything went wrong.

But nothing was going to go wrong, because *diligence. Focus. Agility.*

The silver bracelet on her arm looked innocuous enough, but it was actually a timer, setting off a tiny vibration that grew subsequently stronger at 15 second and 1 minute intervals, to help Naomi keep pace. When she reached the door at the top of the stairs, she started the timer, then waited for two of the fifteen second intervals to pass before she opened the door to give the hall guard time to pass into another part of the house. Keeping her head down to avoid the cameras, just in case

Quentin failed to divert the feed like he was supposed to, she forced herself not to rush down the hall. Instead, she stumbled along on her heels as if intoxicated, pacing herself so that it took two more of the fifteen second intervals to reach her desired door.

Out of the many homes Rochas owned, this was his newest purchase, a getaway in his home country of St. James, Barbados. A flashy island mansion for a flashy island man, who thought his money was better spent bringing the décor up to his standards, instead of improving the security. With the pin she had ready in her hand, Naomi began picking the lock just as the bracelet vibrated again, and was in the office and beside the desk before it vibrated again.

Naomi slipped on a pair of satin gloves before she touched the chair to move it away, then slipped into the leg space of the huge carved mahogany desk. She positioned it so that if anyone glanced in, it wouldn't look out of place, then slid the rug away.

She pulled her wristlet from her arm and unzipped it, stashing her lock pick before she fished out her pen light, disguised as a tube of lip-gloss. Clenching it between her teeth in the dark office, she pulled up the wide, obviously mismatched plank of wood that shielded the safe. As expected, based on the scouting they'd done, it was a simple combination safe. Naomi shook her head. Rochas was the *worst*. It was his basic lack of proper security that had allowed her to steal the diamonds from him in Paris in the first place.

Santiago Rochas had been tasked with getting the diamonds from Marseilles to New York, undetected. Instead of exercising any sort of urgency, he'd stopped in to visit the girlfriend he kept in Paris, and *she* had convinced him to take her shopping. In Barcelona. So while Rochas was playing sugar daddy in Spain, Naomi was following a hunch, that instead of traveling with the diamonds, — smart — he'd left them in his girlfriend's *mostly* unsecured apartment in France. Dumb.

So, after reporting that the diamonds were stolen to a *very* angry Damien Wolfe, one of Rochas's men was "discovered" with a pocketful of the flawless black gems. And thus, the illusion of a double-cross began. Now, she just needed to finish it.

Naomi's agile fingers closed around the dial. She took a deep breath, calming her nerves as the slightly-stronger vibration against her left wrist let her know that a second minute had passed. Only three left. Systematically, she turned the dial to the right, focusing on the sensation of tiny clicks of the gears, amplified by the satin of her gloves. *There.* A slightly harder click as the first piece of the puzzle slid into place. The bracelet vibrated again, but went ignored as her adept fingers turned the dial to the left. *There.* Her breath accelerated. Only one more to go.

Willing her hand not to shake, Naomi disregarded another vibration as she turned to the right once more, carefully, *carefully*, until... *There.* The sweet, subtle sound of disengaged locks met her ears. Not allowing herself the satisfaction of a free breath or a smile, Naomi pulled the heavy pouch of diamonds free from the larger pouch strapped to her chest. Before she did anything else, she repacked her things, making sure she left nothing behind. She opened the door to the safe, dropped the pouch in, turned the dial back to where it was before she touched it, and pulled hard to make sure the lock was engaged.

She replaced the wood panel, slid the rug back into place, and pushed the chair away to leave just as she heard the nerve-shredding sound of a key being pushed into the lock. Heart pounding, she snatched the chair as close to her body as possible and held still, desperately listening as the door swung open, then slammed closed as the lights flicked on.

Naomi's adrenaline spiked, and she wished she had her gun. They'd all agreed that if she was caught in the hall, she could pretend to be a drunk partygoer, but that wouldn't work with a Glock strapped to her thigh. At least, not in her short, tulle-skirted black dress. She balled her hands into fists. If nothing else, the boxing she did as an outlet for her anger had turned her into a pretty good fighter.

She clamped a hand over her mouth, stifling a gasp as something heavy hit the desk, not moving it, but certainly making it shake like a wooden trap around her. There was a strange, muffled sound coming from somewhere, but she couldn't quite tell what it was until a woman's teasing giggle rang out into the room, followed shortly by something flirty mumbled in a low tenor. Naomi held back a sigh of relief, but it was short-lived, as the vibration against her wrist told her she only had a minute and a half left to get back to the party.

A slight hint of panic settled into her chest as she searched her mind, pulling up her plan B. She spied a door, not even three feet away. It had no lock, and according to the blueprints, led into the next room, which had access to the hall. If the lovers were distracted enough... it just might work.

Naomi got her answer for that when a bracelet-vibration later, she heard the distinct unbuckling of a belt and pull of a zipper, followed shortly by a man's appreciative groans.

Bingo.

Carefully, Naomi freed herself from the confines of the desk without making a sound, crawled over to the door and snuck it open, thanking God for oiled hinges. She closed it just as quietly, sped through the empty bedroom, and pulled *that* door open to peek into the hall. With her pulse pounding in her ears, she again forced herself not to speed down the hall. Once she reached the door that led to the stairs, she finally allowed herself to stop holding her breath. The vibration to let her know her time was up happened just as she put her foot on the last stair.

An immense satisfaction swept over Naomi as she rejoined the party. She danced to blend in with the crowd as she made her way to Marcus, feeling giddy. She was passing into another room when she was grabbed from behind. Before she could react, she was turned around, back pressed into the wall, and Marcus was in front of her. He put his hands to the wall on either side of her head and leaned close to get right against her ear.

"Stay calm. They're onto you. I overheard that they're looking for a suspicious woman. Puffy black dress. Hair in a bun. *Stay. Calm.*"

Naomi barely breathed as Marcus reached up, burying a hand in her hair to pull it free from her bun. The room they were in was crowded and dark, lit only by the strobe light. If anyone was watching, they looked like lovers sharing an intimate moment as Marcus removed his hand from her hair, letting it drift over her body and down to her waist. With his wider frame shielding her from view, Marcus used his pocketknife to cut the tulle skirting from Naomi's dress, leaving only the stretchy, body-hugging underskirt and bodice behind.

When he was done, he discretely stuffed the tulle into a nearby trashcan and led her to the front of house. Naomi's nerves were scrubbed raw, throat dry as they left the party in no apparent hurry, walked right past the stressed-looking guards, made it to their rental car, and pulled onto the street.

"So," Marcus said, breaking the silence when they were almost back to the resort. He had one hand on the steering wheel, the other one on his leg, flipping his closed pocket knife between his fingers. "I guess you ended up depending on old unprepared Calloway anyway, huh?"

Naomi wanted to slap the smug, mocking grin off his face, but said nothing, opting to stare out the window instead. She wanted to know *how*, exactly, she had been spotted. She was careful, she did everything according to plan. Even her near miss, she'd smoothed that over perfectly, so how... *Quentin.*

She was going to kill him. If she found out that he *had* somehow neglected to hack that security feed like he was supposed to, she was going to *murder* him, with her bare hands.

"What's wrong, Prescott? Cat's got *your* tongue now, huh? Little Miss Diligence isn't so diligent after all... who would have thought? I know, me!"

Naomi sucked her teeth. "Would you shut up? Fine, you did something right, *good for you*, arrogant bastard."

She crossed her arms, nostrils flared as they pulled into the parking lot of the resort. She was out of the car before he put it into park, stomping her way to the room and slamming the door in his face as he followed.

"You can be as mad at me as you want, Naomi," he droned, seemingly unaffected by her attitude as he pushed the door open. "Fact is, you wouldn't have made it out of the party without me. Hell— you wouldn't have even known they were looking for you!"

Marcus's continued smirk took Naomi's blood to molten levels. She clenched her fists, fingernails biting into her palms as she fought the urge to attack him.

Maybe a good right hook to the jaw would wipe that smile off his face.

Shaking her head, she kicked off her shoes and then went into the bathroom, slamming the door behind her. In the mirror, she splashed her face with water, annoyed that it reminded her of that *awful* day in Paris. But, she didn't have time to dwell, because voices from the other side of the door let her know that Marcus had called Agent Barnes to give a preliminary report. For a moment, she considered staying tucked away, avoiding the scolding she was due from Agent Barnes, but it was pointless to prolong it. She opened the door just in time to hear words that made her sick to her stomach.

"That was good work, Agent Calloway. Thinking on your feet, that's the kind of stuff I like to see. Excellent,

excellent work." That came from Agent Barnes, and Naomi was disgusted to see that Marcus was *still* wearing that self-satisfied grin. It widened when he saw that she was back in the room, and he leaned closer to the open video call on the laptop to give Agent Barnes a thumbs up sign.

"Well, SSA Barnes, I want to be clear that I'm a team player. Once I knew Naomi's life was at stake, I had to act fast." Marcus turned, giving Naomi a sticky sweet smile as she approached. She rolled her eyes, taking a seat beside him at the desk.

"'Preciate it, Calloway."

Oh God, not Quentin too.

She could survive Agent Barnes heaping on praise, but Quentin didn't even like Marcus. If *he* was going to be helping with the accolades, Naomi might really thro—

"But."

Thank you, Jesus, there's a but!

"Naomi wasn't the suspicious woman in black they were lookin' for. Haven't been through all the security footage yet, but another woman was there in a similar dress, slashed a guard's throat trying to get to Rochas directly."

Naomi's eyes widened. "One of Wolfe's people?"

"Don't know. But we'll find out. In the meantime, don't sweat it, cher. You were perfect, even with that little unexpected visit," Quentin said in a soothing tone. Naomi's shoulders sagged in relief.

"You guys saw that?"

"Every moment," Barnes chimed in, his voice edged with admiration. "Damn near biting our fingernails off, that's why we didn't see the throat cutting happen. Good work as always, Prescott. I'm impressed with both of you. Go ahead and enjoy your last day tomorrow, and when you get back, we'll regroup, and focus on the next step. Calloway… keep looking out for Prescott. It's good to have you on the team. Goodnight."

Barnes ended the call without waiting for a response, and there was silence in the room for a moment.

Marcus leaned back in his chair. "I should probably apologize now, but after all of your shit talking earlier about me being unfocused and unprepared…"

"I don't give a shit if you do or don't, Marcus." Naomi stood, pushing back her chair. She walked to the door, sliding her feet into the slightly-more comfortable heels she'd left there after dinner the night before. "I'm going for a walk. Maybe back to that club."

This moment alone to clear her head was something she usually did after every job, but she felt it *very* necessary tonight. Two heart-stopping scares, Marcus's smart mouth, having to hear him praised for action that, no matter how well-intended, hadn't helped her at all, plus the normal anxiety of completing a job had given

Naomi a blistering headache. Not to mention, she was still pissed off about Marcus's comments on her ability. She needed space, and without a punching bag handy, she needed the outlet of dancing. *Now.*

"You're not going anywhere."

Naomi paused, lifting an eyebrow as she glanced in Marcus's direction. "Says who?"

"Says *me.* You just heard Agent Barnes tell me to keep an eye on you."

"When we're on the job. The job is over, Marcus. We're done here."

"We're not done. We still have to preserve our cover."

Rolling her eyes, Naomi finished putting on her shoes, then shrugged. "Then I guess you're coming out with me then."

"I'm not going anywhere," Marcus chuckled. "Do you know what time it is? I'm about to shower, then take my ass to sleep. You should do the same."

Naomi licked her teeth, trying hard to think of something a little more articulate than *"I'm grown. I'll do what I wanna."* When nothing came to mind, she simply opened the door, but before she could make it out, Marcus was right there, slamming it shut as he pulled her away.

"Naomi, I'm not kidding. It's *late.* I'll take you tomorrow, but we're in for the night. I didn't go to the beach earlier when you didn't wanna go, because we're supposed to be sticking together. You can stay in."

"*Let. Me. Go.*" Naomi hissed through clenched teeth, trying to pull her arm from Marcus's grasp.

"Are you gonna stay in?"

"*No.*"

"Then *no.*"

At that, every other emotion Naomi felt turned into anger. Marcus didn't want to let her go dance it off? Fine. She had another way to disperse her anger, and since no punching bag was available... *he* would do just fine.

She aimed for his jaw, sending a swift punch that he *barely* dodged, but he let her go.

"What the hell, Naomi?"

"I told you to let me go," she snapped, ending her statement with a smirk as she turned for the door.

"And *I* said we're staying in."

This time, he grabbed both arms, to keep her from swinging, but Naomi was prepared for that. She jerked her head back as hard as she could, and tried to ram him, then grinned in satisfaction when he shoved her away to avoid the blow to the face.

She turned around, hiked her dress up around her thighs and got into a boxing position, heels and all. "We're dancing or we're boxing, Marcus. Your call."

He sucked his teeth. "I'm not afraid of you, Naomi, I'm trying not to kick your ass."

"Yeah... how about you try not to get *your* ass kicked instead?"

And... she attacked. At first, Marcus easily dodged the lazy blows she aimed at him, but Naomi could tell he had to work a little harder the fiercer she got. She handed out body punches, crosses, jabs, hooks, and uppercuts until finally she landed a body shot to his stomach.

"Goddamnit, Naomi, will you cut this shit out?" He asked, slapping her fist away as she tried to catch him with another jab to the jaw.

"No. I'm sick of your face!"

She screamed, shocked when he caught her wrist with the next blow, pulling her close to try to grab the other.

"I'm gonna handcuff your ass to the toilet if you don't *stop*."

"You'd have to catch me first, asshole!" She slammed her heel down over his bare foot, but had the modicum of mercy it took not to grind it in as he let her go. She scrambled across the bed, determined to go, but Marcus caught her ankle and pulled her back.

The impact of her body against the mattress took her breath away, giving him the necessary time to flip her over, climb on top and pin her to the bed.

"Will you *stop*? Please?"

Chest heaving, Naomi pulled the last of her energy into a head-butt attempt, making Marcus swear as he reared back. "Naomi!"

"*Kiss my ass!* I'm sick of looking at you, sick of hearing you, sick of hearing about you, sick of smelling your cologne, sick of being around you!"

What she *didn't* mention was the illness she'd started developing over the days he *didn't* come by the gym, the times he *didn't* touch her when he flirted with her in front of the parents, and she didn't admit she was positively *unwell* over the feeling of his lips on her forehead that day at the gym, wishing he would kiss her lips instead.

Instead, she hardened her expression into a fierce scowl, wishing her eyes could set his hair on fire as he hovered over her, keeping her immobile. In the meanest, most scornful tone she could muster, she asked, "Why won't you *just fucking go awa*—"

Marcus must have heard something else in her voice. Before she could finish her statement, his mouth was on hers, swallowing those harsh words as teeth clicked and tongues wrestled in a passionate kiss that Naomi wouldn't have stopped if she could. He dominated her mouth, teasing, and tasting and dipping and sucking until moisture began to pool between her thighs.

Naomi whimpered as he released her wrists, grabbing her chin to angle her face for better access as he explored. He kissed her like a man starved, and *she* was the last source of nourishment on earth.

Now free, Naomi's hands frantically found Marcus's belt and zipper. His lips never left hers as she freed him from his boxers and hooked her legs over his thighs. Balancing on his elbow, he slipped her panties to the side and plunged in, groaning as he buried himself in her wetness and warmth. Naomi gasped at the two seconds of pain before it turned into all pleasure as he stroked her in a steady rhythm.

She wasn't sure how long they stayed that way, creating a melody of moans and grunts, but too soon, he pulled away, instructing her to turn over.

She stayed where she was.

Marcus was the *last* person Naomi wanted making demands and telling her what do. That was the problem as it was, his damned *arrogance.* True, he was well-equipped and thus far, well-versed in proper usage, but—

"I don't have time for this shit." Marcus pulled her panties down her legs and turned her over himself, plunging back in before she could protest. Despite her annoyance, Naomi couldn't help the squeal of pleasure as he began stroking again. "Does *everything* have to be a fucking battle with you?" he mumbled against her ear as he leaned over her, pushing her hair to one side.

Naomi didn't answer— *couldn't* answer— because he was taking her breath away with every deep, powerful stroke. She closed her eyes, relishing the blissful feeling of his body slamming into hers.

"Stay up," Marcus said, hooking an arm around her waist as her arms started to go weak.

She tried, but minutes later, her knees were giving out too.

Again, he pulled out, to Naomi's chagrin, but that annoyance turned to apprehension when she heard the sound of Marcus's belt buckle as he slid it from his pants, then felt the thick leather through the thin fabric of her dress as he draped and fastened the belt around her waist.

"What are you doing?" she asked, unable to keep a tinge of nervousness from her voice as she spoke.

With the belt tight around her waist, Marcus pulled her to edge of the bed. He prompted her to put one foot on the floor, but kept her other knee propped on the mattress as he positioned himself behind her.

"Since you can't seem to follow instructions, and stay up…" Marcus grabbed the belt as he buried himself in her again, and Naomi gasped, half pleasure, half realization.

"Marcus, is this really necessary?" she asked, looking at him over her shoulder.

He paused. "Yeah… is that a problem?"

Naomi hesitated, staring at him before she bit her lip, and shook her head. "No."

Marcus smirked, flashing his dimples as he used the belt as leverage to yank Naomi onto him, over and over as she bit her lip in a desperate attempt to not moan his name. He was so deep, and it was *so* good that she almost drew blood from the effort.

With one hand clenching the belt, Marcus reached around with the other to stimulate her with his fingers. She closed her eyes, pushing away thoughts of anything except how amazing he felt inside her, stroking, and stroking, and *stroking* as he pushed her closer and closer to the edge of release.

Her anger was long gone. With each thrust, every flick of his fingers, every resounding slap of his skin against hers, the tension moved from her head to her core, where it built and built until it shattered, and the only thing Naomi felt, heard, or saw was pure euphoria. Distantly, she understood that Marcus was still behind her, still stroking until his own release came, but Naomi was on a whole other plane. Tingling pleasure, all over her skin, from her head to her toes as white noise filled her ears, her vision fading to black as she closed her eyes.

When she opened them again, Marcus was on top of her, holding a warm, wet towel between her legs. She got the distinct impression that he'd been waiting on her to open her eyes, because he smiled, and… dear God, why was he smiling at her like that?

"You okay?" he asked, leaving the towel between her legs as he gently removed his belt from her waist, tossing it over the side of the bed.

Naomi felt vaguely embarrassed over how she must look, with her dress twisted around her body and hiked over her hips, but she nodded, fighting the ridiculous urge to smile. "I... um... I'm gonna take a shower."

Avoiding his eyes, she hopped up from the bed. In the "hers" side of the resort bathroom, she took a deep breath, overwhelmed by how... *good* she felt. It wasn't that she hadn't had good sex before — Quentin was top-tier — but *this* was different. Her shoulders were light, and her mind was free, and between her thighs she was already pleasantly sore. But, what was scary was that she wanted him again.

Now.

"It can't happen again," she told her reflection, shaking her head.

And why the heck not?

Because... because it was *Marcus*. He was infuriating, and overconfident, and the *ego* on the man was out of this world, and he was... protective, and reliable, and self-assured, and — she sighed — incredibly sexy. And a good kisser. And good with his di—

"Just don't think about it, Naomi."

She tried not to. She *really* did. But, the entire time she was in the shower it was all she *could* think about. Naomi would have expected herself to be angry and turned off by his commanding attitude, but not-so-deep down... it *excited* her.

After her shower, she toweled off, lotioned her skin, brushed her teeth, then wrapped herself tightly in one of the resort's extravagantly plush towels to retrieve her bag from the main area of the spacious luxury room. When she opened the door, the first thing she saw was Marcus, water from his own shower still clinging to his skin as he passed with his toothbrush in his hand. Seeing her there, he paused, and their eyes met again.

For what seemed like a long time, he just stared, then finally, he turned to face her straight on. "Take off your towel."

Naomi rolled her eyes. "*No.*"

What, so now he thought he could just tell her what to do, and she would jump to do it?

"So... the answer to my question earlier was yes, it *does* always have to be a battle with you." He grabbed the end of the towel, and one quick yank left Naomi exposed. She sucked in a quick breath, ready to launch into a verbal attack as he tossed the towel aside, but the unabashed desire in his eyes kept the air restricted in her lungs.

Marcus's voracious gaze swept over her, but he didn't touch. Her nipples grew rigid, and moisture built between her thighs as he circled her. He drew close, so close that the erection tenting his towel grazed her butt as he passed behind her, but still — he only looked.

"Wait for me on the bed."

And then he was gone, back to his side of the bathroom with the door closed. Naomi sucked her teeth.

Really, who did he think he was, that she should just accept his commands? He wasn't gone long, and when he came back he was towel-free, with his beautiful erection bobbing in front of him. Marcus was breathtaking, with the broad-shouldered body of an athlete, dipped in the richest, smoothest, red-brown skin Naomi had ever seen.

Naomi allowed herself a moment to admire him before she looked away, pretending to be busy with her bag on the table. Purposely, she'd left the towel exactly where he tossed it on the floor, and her nakedness had exactly the effect she hoped it would. He couldn't keep his eyes off her. *Now* who was in control?

She could feel the intensity of his gaze on her again, boring into her, undoubtedly wondering why she wasn't waiting on the bed. Excited goosebumps ran over her skin as he padded to her across the carpeted floor. Was he mad? Was she about to... get in trouble? Did she *want* to be in trouble?

"I thought," Marcus said, his voice dangerously low as he spoke into Naomi's ear, "I told you to wait for me on the bed."

Naomi's eyelids fluttered as he pressed his erection against the small of her back. Drawing her lip between her teeth, she stifled a moan, willing her body not to betray her. "I don't follow orders from you, Marcus. You don't *own* me."

With no warning, Marcus reached around her, just barely brushing his thumb over the exposed flesh between her thighs. Naomi whimpered as he slid further, annoyed by how quickly his skilled fingers stoked a desire that had her ready to do whatever he said... as long as he kept touching her. He lowered his head to nip her earlobe, then pushed his fingers inside her. "Your body seems to recognize its owner, even if you don't. I bet you can't make *yourself* this wet."

Naomi gasped, but didn't have a chance to respond before he withdrew his hand from between her thighs and picked her up, carrying her to the bed. Once there, she clamped her legs shut, staring at him with a challenge in her eyes.

But... Marcus stared right back, arms crossed, shoulders squared, and authority in his voice when he spoke again. "Open your legs, Naomi."

Ugh. She hated herself a little for the way that command made her heart race. But, inexplicably... she did it anyway. As annoyed as she was, she was also anxious for *whatever* he was about to do.

He tossed two foil packages onto the bedside table, then stood between her open legs with his lip pulled between his teeth, staring. Her chest heaved as the anticipation grew, exciting her to the point of breathlessness by the time he climbed on top of her and leaned down, grazing his lips over hers.

"Do you understand how fucking gorgeous you are?" he asked, not waiting for an answer before he took her mouth again in a kiss that snatched the air from her lungs. "Your face, your body, your *skin*... goddamned work of art." He let his teeth graze her bottom lip, then sucked it into his mouth, massaging it with his tongue before he kissed her again.

Then, he drifted lower. His lips and tongue found her neck, then collarbone, then lavished attention on her breasts before he kissed his way over her bellybutton. He made his way down to the apex of her thighs, and he didn't stop there. Marcus kissed Naomi from her forehead to her toes before he finally settled between her thighs again, covering her with his mouth. She arched her back in pleasure, tried to pull away from the intensity but his arms locked around her thighs kept her close. He pampered her with his tongue, licking, and flicking, and swirling and teasing until her trembling body shook the entire bed as she came.

Marcus rose up so that they were eye level, then kissed her deep. He swallowed Naomi's moans as he fingers skirted her sensitive flesh, then plunged inside, stroking her into another body-wracking orgasm before she'd come completely down from the first.

Only then did he reach for one of the packages he'd tossed onto the bedside table. Although Naomi was weak with pleasure she happily spread her legs for Marcus, but he shook his head. He sat down against the headboard, and Naomi got a sudden burst of energy as she realized he wanted her on top.

Naomi straddled his lap, wasting no time in sinking down on him with a moan of appreciation. He pulled her close, so that her breasts brushed his chest as she began to ride him. Marcus caught her hips, stilling her movements as he captured her gaze and smiled.

"What is it?" she asked, unable to keep herself from smiling back.

Marcus drew her mouth to his, then trailed kisses over her jaw until he reached her ear. "Show me again how you   wine."

EIGHT

MARCUS

"IS YOUR FOOD OKAY?"

Marcus watched as Naomi continued picking absently at her food, seemingly oblivious that he'd asked her a question. After everything they'd done the night before, he was expecting the giggly, sexy Naomi from their first night. Instead, for unknown reasons, she was subdued. All day she'd been like this, quiet, contemplative, and Marcus couldn't stand it.

This was their last night in Barbados. When he and Naomi passed out the night before, his mind had been running with plans to spend the day in bed. Sex and room service sounded like a perfect way to end a fake vacation, and Marcus was looking forward to it. Naomi... had different plans.

When Marcus woke up, feeling well-rested and tension free, the first thing he noticed was that Naomi was no longer in the bed. That in itself wasn't surprising, because along with many other things he'd learned about her on this trip, Marcus knew that Naomi was an early riser. What he *didn't* expect was for her to come through the front door of their villa a few moments later drenched in sweat.

He'd teased her before about neglecting her workouts because she was on vacation, but she'd explained that she didn't want to chance an injury. Evidently, that was no longer a concern, because from the looks of it, she'd run the perimeter of the whole island.

"Good morning," Marcus said, sitting up as Naomi closed the door behind her. She returned his greeting with a nod, then practically sprinted for the bathroom, grabbing her bag on the way.

Apparently, avoidance was the theme of the day, because Naomi made it a point to keep her headphones on while she obsessed over files, wrote out her reports for the last job, and pored over the blueprints of another house.

Now, they were at dinner, their last in Barbados, and Marcus was over it. What was the problem *now*? There was no way she was still angry at him for teasing her before the job. She *couldn't* be, not after the seemingly life-altering orgasms she'd experienced under his care. All of that moaning, and screaming, and wetness couldn't be faked.

"Naomi?" he asked a little louder, and this time she flinched, wearing a distant expression as she met Marcus's gaze. He smiled, hoping she would reciprocate, but instead she swallowed hard, averting her eyes.

"Did you need something?"

Subtly, Marcus reared back his head then reached for his glass and sipped, letting the warmth of the rum leave his chest before he spoke. "Nah. Not really. Was just wondering if your food was okay, since you seem to be just picking at it."

"Oh." Naomi glanced down at the plate of food as if she hadn't even realized it was in front of her. "I guess I wasn't that hungry."

Marcus nodded, then drained his glass before placing it back on the table. "Ready to go then?"

"I am."

After paying for their food, Marcus escorted Naomi out of the restaurant. When they reached the point where they'd broken away from the path on that first night, opting for dancing instead of the quiet of their room, Marcus held back.

"Hey... last chance. You wanna go get into some authentic Barbadian partying while you still have the opportunity? That little club we went to is right up the street... "

Naomi shook her head. "Thank you, but... I'm gonna pass."

He wanted to take her by the shoulders, shake her, ask her what was wrong, but instead, he nodded his assent, and led the way back to their room. Inside, Naomi slipped off her shoes by the door, and headed back to her post at the desk. Marcus caught her at the elbow, holding her still while he wrapped his arms around her from behind, pulling her close.

Naomi's hair was pulled into a neat bun, high on her head, leaving her neck exposed to Marcus's lips. He placed a kiss there, then trailed over to her ear.

"Stop, Marcus."

He chuckled. "Still, you wanna play that game?" Marcus asked, lifting his hands to cup her breasts through the thin, silky fabric of her dress.

Her nipples beaded in response to the stroke of his thumbs, and he could have sworn he heard a little gasp of pleasure, but Naomi said, "I'm not playing. Stop."

His fingers stilled.

"Oh... sorry," he said, releasing her from his grasp. He studied her as she stepped away, crossing her arms over her chest. "It's our last day here, and I thought maybe we could..."

Naomi shook her head as she backed away, flinching when the backs of her thighs hit the desk. "Probably not a good idea."

"Why?" Marcus questioned, forcing himself to stay where he was and give her space. "What... you didn't have a good time?"

Rolling her eyes, Naomi lowered her hands to grip the edge of the desk. "Don't be a smartass, Marcus, you know I did. We *both* did. But it doesn't change the fact that last night was –"

"Last night was what, a mistake?"

"I was going to say unrealistic. Calling it a mistake would be pretending that we aren't both intelligent, consenting adults who made a conscious decision to... take on a different reality. Last night was gratifying, yes, but it was also a lost grip on the actuality of who we are, and what we're doing here."

Chuckling, Marcus scratched his head. "Naomi... I don't mean to be insensitive here, but I'm neither suggesting nor expecting some type of secret love affair here. I'm talking about sex – that's all."

"Then we're on the same page. I'm not some naive, shallow girl whose gonna get lost in the charm of your pretty eyes, and pretty dimples, and pretty smile. I'm a grown woman, capable of understanding that sometimes, sex is just sex."

"If we're on the same page, both recognize that this is just the pursuit of good sex, what's the problem?"

"The problem," Naomi said, taking a seat on the desk and crossing her legs, "Is that a sexual relationship between us creates a distraction, and the case that brought us together is too important for me to be distracted. *Nothing* takes precedence over eliminating Damien Wolfe. Nothing, and no one."

Marcus lifted an eyebrow. "Nothing? No one?" There had to be *someone* in her life that she would sacrifice everything for. With Sophie and Meagan on his mind,

Marcus couldn't fathom that. They were *absolutely* more important than any job.

"Nothing. No one."

Marcus scoffed. "Not even your boy Quentin?"

"I would put a bullet through his head without a second thought, and then I would mourn him the same way I've mourned everyone else that bastard has taken from me."

Well, damn.

"Does *he* know that?" Marcus asked. Contrary to what he'd expected, he hadn't picked up a vibe of anything more than friendship between the two of them, but he could tell they were close.

Naomi gave a dry laugh. "He would tell you the same thing. See... Quentin and I didn't just grow up together – we share a very particular grief, delivered by Damien Wolfe's hand. We agreed a long time ago – whatever it takes to avenge our families, even if it means sacrificing a friend."

Marcus nodded. "So I know you blame your uncle for your mother's death... but who did he take from Quentin?"

Tension sprang to Marcus's shoulders as Naomi hopped down from the desk and shot across the room, getting right in his face. After the night before, he knew her hands were quick, and she was stronger than her appearance said.

"No matter how *technically* true it is, don't you *ever* again refer to that scum as my uncle. We may share blood, but he is *not* my family," she snapped, punctuating her words by jabbing a pointed finger.

Marcus lifted his hands in a conciliatory fashion. "My bad. I was just –"

"Don't," Naomi interrupted. "And I don't "blame" him for my mother's death, his ass is guilty." She turned away in a huff, then turned back, approaching him again. "And fyi – my mother isn't the only one he took. My father *and* Quentin's – both of their blood is on his hands. He pulled the trigger himself."

"How do you know that?"

"I just do." She swallowed hard, then averted her gaze. "I'm done talking about this, we're getting too far away from the point."

Crossing his arms, Marcus cocked his head to the side. "And what *is* the point?"

"That last night should remain last night," she said, lifting her chin. "Sex makes things complicated, and I can't afford to lose focus. Are we gonna have a problem?"

Marcus shook his head. "Nope. Not at all."

He should have felt lucky. He was, after all, dodging the whole "explaining that he wasn't looking for a relationship bullet" that he so hated getting hit with. This situation was ideal – one-time sex with a beautiful

133

woman who wanted nothing more than to be left to herself when they weren't engaging in the act – but for some reason, Marcus was bothered by Naomi's resolution that last night would be a one-time-thing.

First of all, women *always* came back for more with Marcus. They talked a big game about getting *him* sprung, but it was usually the other way around. What the hell made Naomi so different?

Second, the constant diligence, unshakable focus, and unwavering seriousness she prided herself on was an anxiety attack waiting to happen. But... that wasn't really Marcus's problem. If she wanted to drive herself to an early grave seeking vengeance... that was fine by him.

So, he left her alone.

Marcus got the distinct impression that she appreciated the quiet, preferring the solitude of her mind to his company, so her left her to it. All the way into their early morning flight, up until the point he pulled up in front of her building back in the US, few words were exchanged between them. Naomi protested Marcus's insistence on taking her bags up for her, but grudgingly agreed when he reminded her that they were still supposed to be maintaining the appearance of a relationship.

Marcus tucked her bags under his arms and followed her up to her condo. Inside, he placed them beside her couch, then went to stand at the door, hands shoved in his pockets.

"Um... did you need something, Marcus?" Naomi asked, lifting an eyebrow as she pulled a bottle of water from her refrigerator and took a swig.

Marcus shrugged. "Not *really*, I guess."

"But?"

"What's gonna happen when you finally take Wolfe down? What then?"

"I pop open a bottle of champagne and pour it over his grave."

Chuckling, Marcus shook his head. "Okay... so you pop bottles, and you feel good for what... that one moment? What about after that?"

"What do you mean, after that?" Naomi asked, putting her water down on the counter.

"When you have to contend with the fact that you've spent a good part of your life focused on avenging your parents. I mean... getting rid of Wolfe doesn't bring them back, but you've put your whole life on hold for it."

Naomi propped a hand on her hip. "What's your point, Marcus?"

"That this shit isn't healthy. Your life has to be about more than just *revenge*."

Closing her eyes, Naomi pushed out a breath, then shook her head. "You don't get it, do you? This isn't "just" about revenge. Every day of my life, I wonder if *this* is going to be the day that just like he decided to destroy my father, Damien Wolfe is going to decide to destroy *me*. Constantly looking over my shoulder, in case he decides that he has to do to *me* the same thing he did to my mother. I'm alive and well because he allows it to be so. You think I *want* to be on constant alert? You think I enjoy avoiding friends, not dating, not being able to have a family? This isn't all about my revenge – it's also about my *freedom.*"

Marcus swiped a hand over his head. "Wow... I didn't think about that. That's... one heck of a personal hell to live in."

"Trust me – I know."

"Yeah... even more reason to allow yourself to escape sometimes."

Naomi looked away, focusing on the label of her water bottle in a way that let Marcus know their conversation was over. He didn't even know why he was still there anyway, other than an errant desire to see her lighten up a little.

He understood being serious about the job. Despite Naomi's belief that he was reckless, Marcus rarely made a flub on the job. His methods of completion may have put the wrong kind of attention on his career as an agent, but his talent was without question. His team knew him as a fearless, dedicated, case-closer, but Marcus knew when it was time to push the harsh realities of the job to the back of his mind. He knew how to let go, how to have a little fun – and Naomi did too, because he'd seen it himself.

But... apparently that rare moment of weakness had reminded her of what was at stake, and their little sexual escapade had driven the stake further.

"I'm gonna head out," he said, reaching for the doorknob. "I guess I'll see you tomorrow."

Naomi looked up from her bottle to nod, and tightness bloomed in Marcus's chest when he realized she had tears in her eyes. He quickly shook the feeling away, pulling open the door as she approached to close it behind him.

"Thank you for dropping me off."

The glossiness of her eyes pricked at Marcus, but he pushed it away. There was no point in feeling sorry for her, not when she'd made her decision clear. But... she looked so damned *sad*. "No problem, *sweetheart*," he said with a wink as he stepped out. "Goodnight."

She smiled, just a little, and Marcus smiled back, glad that he'd accomplished his mission. He started down the hall, stopping just before he reached the elevator to turn in response to Naomi calling his name.

"Yeah?"

Naomi shifted uncomfortably in the doorway, taking a deep breath before she finally spoke up again. "Um... maybe, we..." She stopped, cleared her throat, and then took another long breath. Just like that, the tears were gone, and the tough-girl Naomi from before was back. "Let's *escape* one more time."

Narrowing his eyes, Marcus took his time getting back down the hall. When he was standing in front of her, he said nothing, but looked at her for a long time. What had changed? Why the sudden shift in stance? Not even 24 hours ago, she was swearing that it was best not to do it again... now she wanted to christen her place?

"Don't be an asshole, Marcus. Say something." She crossed her arms, glaring up at him as she waited for a response. When he didn't give her one, she sucked her teeth. "Or... say nothing. You probably can't perform again like you did in Barbados anyway. It was probably just a fluke, so –"

For the second time in two days, Marcus kissed the unpleasant words out of Naomi's mouth. If she wanted to taunt and tease, so be it. He was available to teach a lesson. Her response was eager, pressing her body against his as he pushed her inside and slammed the door behind them. Marcus cupped her butt, squeezing and kneading as he picked Naomi up and pressed her into the wall.

Her approving moan sent blood rushing to Marcus's groin. He rocked against her, prodding his erection against the space between her thighs, which earned him another groan of appreciation.

Marcus dipped his tongue deeper into Naomi's mouth. The more he took, the more she gave, tit for tat as the kiss grew ravenous, more fervent, and more... necessary. Marcus intended to turn up her thermostat, then leave her hot and bothered, but he was having the hardest time pulling away. Her lips were too sweet, body too soft, and the heat of her arousal was calling too loudly to be ignored.

He shoved the straps of her dress over her shoulders, letting it pool around her waist. She was bra-less underneath, exposing two perfect handfuls of breast. Marcus propped her higher on the wall, inhaling the sweet scent of her skin before he took her nipple in his mouth, using his tongue to stroke it to a hardened peak before he kissed his way to the other side. When he'd worked that one into a similar sensitive state, he made his way back to her mouth.

Naomi greedily sucked his tongue as he cupped her breasts. Her enthusiasm was magnetic, and the heat between her thighs was damn nearly *heavenly* as Marcus pressed himself against the thin fabric of her panties. She whimpered, rocking against him in an attempt to get closer, and Marcus grinned.

She squeezed her eyes tight, moaning as Marcus slipped a finger underneath her panties and against the wet, silky warmth between her thighs. "That feels good to you?" he asked, his voice rough with his own excitement as Naomi moved impatiently against his hand. "I can't hear you."

"*Yes*," she murmured, gripping his biceps.

"Yes *what*?"

"Yes, it feels goo– *ah*!" Naomi cried out in pleasure as he slid a finger inside her. With his mouth against her ear, he pushed deeper, stroked her harder, until she seemed barely able to catch her breath as she gasped with pleasure.

"Now... tell me Naomi... what happened to that shit you were talking a few minutes ago? Tell me again how I can't put on a repeat performance."

Marcus pushed a second finger in, burrowing deeper as she opened her mouth to respond, and Naomi fumbled her words. She was *so* wet, and looked *so* sexy with her lips parted, that Marcus had to bite down on his *own* lip not to kiss her.

"What was that?" he asked, dragging his thumb across her clit. Naomi's legs began to shake as he repeated the action, moving his thumb in deliberately slow circles. Again, Naomi tried to answer, but he increased the pressure of his thumb, adjusting to a side to side movement that made her toss her head against the wall, eyes rolling back as she pulled her lip into her mouth. She rolled her hips against his hand at a frantic pace, and Marcus took it as her non-verbal way of asking, "Faster please".

Marcus smiled. "Did I hear you say this wasn't good for you? Is this better?" he asked, moving into a deep, rapid stroke as Naomi clenched around his fingers. Her whimpers grew faster, louder, legs quaking until she tensed, digging her nails into Marcus's arm desperately as she came.

Marcus waited until she could breathe normally, then slowly removed his hand from between her legs. "I know that was probably really disappointing for you," he said, meeting her sex-drunk gaze with a satisfied smirk. "But... your *pussy*... seems pretty happy to see me."

Naomi narrowed her eyes, then unlocked her legs from his waist to drop to the floor. "Fuck you," she said, shoving him away.

With one finger, Marcus tipped up her chin. "Isn't that why you invited me in?"

Marcus's snide grin turned into a bark of surprise when Naomi grabbed a handful of his shirt and yanked him along, pulling him behind her as she went deeper into her apartment. He was so caught off guard that he went along with no complaint, allowing himself to be escorted into the bedroom, then shoved across the bed.

He was honestly impressed by the speed with which Naomi yanked his sweats and boxers from his waist, tossed her dress and panties across the room, rolled a condom over him, then climbed on.

"You talk *way* too much," she said, positioning her hips over his. Mouth ajar, Marcus watched through half-lidded eyes as Naomi sank onto him until he was buried deep. He groaned as she began moving her hips, biting her lip while she gyrated against him.

Goddamn it, girl.

This was the Naomi he preferred best, and it had *everything* to do with the fact that she was hot, tight, wet, and riding him like her life depended on it. Fluidity of movement was the only constant. Up, down, in a spiral, a slow grind, a fast bounce – Naomi was always doing something different, never giving Marcus a chance to get too used to one motion before she was transitioning into another, and he enjoyed *every* second. He was perfectly happy to serve as Naomi's stage as she performed.

He reached up to cup her breasts, but she smacked his hands away to cup them herself, kneading and squeezing as she rolled her hips. "Do you like this, Marcus?" she asked in a low, sexy murmur as she pulled her nipples between her fingers.

"Hell ye – *ohh*," he growled in appreciation as she sank lower, so low that her ass rested against his thighs as she ground her hips.

She giggled, putting her hands on his chest for balance as she leaned forward. "What? What was that, Marcus? I can't hear you."

Marcus chuckled, then buried a hand in Naomi's hair to pull her into a kiss. "So *you* wanna talk shit now, huh?" he asked, smiling against her lips. "Okay. Let's go."

Grabbing her hips, he rolled them over and then plunged back inside, pulling a loud gasp from Naomi's lips. He gripped her by the shoulders as he thrust deep, then deeper in response to Naomi's vocalizations of pleasure. Marcus buried himself as far as he could, as hard as he could without causing her pain.

"Hey, Naomi," he said, propping her leg over his shoulder and nuzzling his face against her calf as he pushed deeper. She squeezed her eyes shut, clamping her lips together to stifle a cry. "The last time I was in your apartment, I was taking you in, remember?"

Naomi's eyes flew open, and she slapped him, but Marcus didn't lose rhythm, only grinned as she said breathlessly, "Hey, Marcus. Remember what happened last time I slapped you like that? I walked out right out of your grasp."

His response was to go harder, but Naomi gave as good as she got, meeting him stroke for stroke until they came. Marcus collapsed beside her on the bed, his arm draped around her waist as they caught their breath.

"Marcus?" Naomi said, looking at him over her shoulder when her chest finally stopped heaving.

"Yeah?"

"Lock my door on your way out. Goodnight."

[COMMAND: open private chat]

CRAWDADDY: who dat?

    painted_pixel: hey

    CrawDaddy: hey yourself. news?

    painted_pixel: yes. they want me to do something I can't do.

    CrawDaddy: can't physically or mentally?

    painted_pixel: morally.

    CrawDaddy: what is it?

    painted_pixel: can't answer that.

    CrawDaddy: why?

    painted_pixel: you'll get involved.

    CrawDaddy: thanks to you, i'm already involved.

    CrawDaddy: we should meet.

    painted_pixel: don't be silly.

    CrawDaddy: how is that silly?

    painted_pixel: i took enough of a chance reaching out to you for help in the first place. you really think i'm about to show you my face?

    CrawDaddy: you don't trust me?

    painted_pixel: i don't KNOW you. you're a username on a screen.

    CrawDaddy: a username you've known for 15 years. you trust me enough to put me and the people i care about in danger by involving me in this, but i can't even see your damned face?

painted_pixel: do I really have to remind you that your people aren't the only ones in danger?

CrawDaddy: no. but you're asking me to risk a lot. is it too much to want to lay eyes on you, in case this shit goes south – which it probably will?

painted_pixel: this was a mistake. forget i asked. please keep this to yourself.

CrawDaddy: really, p?

[USER: painted_pixel no longer exists. aborting chat.]

naomi

"Okay, Naomi. Back to business we go. Diligence. Focus. Agility. That's all that matters."

In the mirror, Naomi took a breath, briefly closing her eyes before she pulled the zipper of her thin yoga jacket all the way up to her neck. She didn't want anyone – meaning Quentin – asking questions about the obvious love bites covering her collarbone and throat. In the moment, she had enjoyed receiving them, but now that it was time to rejoin the real word, every single one was a maroon-colored reminder that she'd crossed a line. Majorly.

Pulling her phone from her pocket, Naomi glanced at the time.

7:22 AM.

Marcus had only been gone a few hours, and when Naomi closed her eyes, the sensory memory of his weight between her legs made her clench her thighs. He'd ignored her attempt to kick him out, opting instead to flip her onto her back, doing things with his tongue that made her not really want him to leave. Then, he was inside her again, and they did it over, and over, and *over* until it was the wee hours of the morning and they were both exhausted and completely spent.

He did leave then, with a parting kiss on Naomi's forehead, then lips that made her practically vibrate with excitement. "Anytime you wanna "escape"... you let me know." And with those words, he was gone. Naomi laid there for a long while, naked and too tired to move, until she finally gathered the strength to get up and deadbolt her door, activate the security alarm, and take a shower. She did a sloppy job of changing the sheets, then collapsed into the bed for a few hours of dreamless sleep.

Now, it was officially morning, and as she'd already told herself, time to get back to business.

"GOOD MORNING QUENTIN," she chirped thirty minutes later as she breezed through the door of their office at the gym.

He looked up from his screen to shoot her a smile. "Mornin' cher. You enjoy your time in Barbados?"

Naomi gave a noncommittal shrug. "It was work. Nothing to enjoy, really." She turned her back to him to put her bag down behind the desk, and when she turned back, he was right in front of her, wearing an incredulous frown.

"You get ya'self plenty of rest?"

Naomi swallowed hard as she bobbed her head, trying to avoid Quentin's searching gaze. "I got enough. Why? Do I look tired?"

"Nah," Quentin said, using a finger to tip up her chin, then turn her head to the side. "You don't look tired, but you *do* look like you got attacked by something." He ran a finger along the bruises on the bottom of her jaw, which she couldn't hide with the collar of her jacket.

"Oh, this?" she asked, covering the bottom of her face with her hand. She was gonna *kill* Marcus for this. "I think it's just an allergic reaction to something."

"Or some*one*... named Marcus Calloway."

Naomi narrowed her eyes and shoved Quentin away, crossing her arms over her chest. "Okay, fine. Marcus and I... had a thing. Is that a problem?"

"Be easy. Why you pulling that tough-girl shit with me? You don't *have* to pull that shit with me, cause remember, I know different, yeah? Mimi, I'm not judging, or scolding you, my only concern is that you're looking out for ya'self, and I'm still not sure about this dude."

"There's nothing to be sure about, Q. It was sex. That's all. Besides, two days ago, you and Agent Barnes were praising Marcus for "saving my life". What changed?"

Quentin held up a finger, motioning for Naomi to follow him to his desk. Once there, he powered on his computer screen, minimized what appeared to be a basic chat, and opened a folder named "M. Calloway" which held a long list of files. Arrest record, psyche profiles, high school report cards, frat party photos, sub-folders on his exes – Quentin had Marcus's entire life pulled into one convenient place. He opened a file labeled "finances" and maximized it on the screen.

"*This* is what changed," he said, pointing at the screen. "Did a little diggin' on your homeboy. He has his main bank accounts, checking and savings like everybody else, but look here. You see this group of deposits? They're small, so they don't raise suspicion, but look at the pattern. Look at the *total* amount in this account – this *extra* account, that I had to pull out the big guns to find. These are payments for something, and I bet you that

148

pay-stub doesn't say FBI. And now look at this," he opened a folder that said "communications", then double-clicked one of the files, "his phone records. These text messages are coded. These 10-second long phone calls... it's kinda suspect."

Naomi nodded, still peering over Quentin's shoulder. "Does Barnes know about this?"

"Just got into the account this morning," Quentin replied, shaking his head. "It could be nothing, ya' know? Maybe the coded communication is something he does with his team. I'm not saying anything to Barnes until I know for sure, but... I want *you* to watch out. Keep a clear head."

"I know. One of us has to be around to take out Wolfe. That's still the goal, right? Payback, over everything, even if one of us has to go."

He sighed, scrubbing a hand over his face. It reminded Naomi of Marcus's question about whether Quentin was on the same page with her regarding their plan. For many years, he'd claimed to be, but Naomi knew, deep down, that if it came to a choice between her life and Wolfe's, Quentin would absolutely spare hers. Naomi loved Quentin – he was her oldest friend, and like a brother if they hadn't crossed the line to sex – but she was resolute. Just like she'd told Marcus, Wolfe's death was her primary motivation. She would risk anything and anyone – including Quentin – for that goal.

"Not about to talk to you about that, Mimi, but it reminds me of something else I need to show you." Quentin closed the other two files, then opened one from a file labeled "personal".

Naomi's eyes darted over the screen, trying to piece it together until Quentin pointed, giving her a vital context clue. "Look at the date."

She did, focusing on numbers that always made her blood run cold. "What is this about, Quentin?"

Instead of answering, he pointed at a short list of three names. She'd seen those three names together a thousand times, had read the information on the homicide report on the screen even more than that. But, it wasn't until now that the third name on the list rang a haunting little bell.

"Does... does Marcus know about this?" she asked, gripping the back of Quentin's chair for balance as a wave of nausea rocked her stomach.

Quentin shook his head. "If you're asking what I think you're asking... no. I don't believe so."

"Good. Good." Naomi stood up straight, swallowing the urge to throw up.

"You don't think we should tell him his –"

Naomi held up a hand, urging Quentin not to speak. "No, as a matter of fact. I don't. What would it accomplish?"

Other than screwing up our plans...

"Maybe it will help him be all in," Quentin shrugged. "You said you felt like he wasn't focused."

"I was wrong. Agent Calloway is already all in. Besides – weren't you *just* trying to convince me not to trust him?"

"Didn't say I didn't trust him, cher. Said I wanted you to watch your back. There's a difference, now."

"Okay, Q. I got it."

Quentin turned in his chair to face her, then grabbed Naomi's hands. "Do you?"

"Yes, damn. What is this about?"

"I'm just asking... things have been different with us lately, so... I gotta make sure. I'm just tryna make sure you still consider me a friend, Mimi."

Naomi shook her head. After his multiple fuck-ups, she'd been close to severing that thread, but the fact remained that Quentin really was a dear friend. "Of course I do, Quentin, you know that. Remember... you hold way too many of my secrets for me to ever let you live if I decide we're no longer friends."

"Yeah, yeah," Quentin chuckled, pulling her down to kiss her forehead. "What'd I say about that tough-girl shit?"

"I wasn't listening, I have no idea," Naomi called across the room as she headed for the door. "I'm going to go check on my classroom."

Her hand was already on the doorknob when Quentin called out for her to wait a moment. "One more thing, cher. The woman on the video, who slit the security guard's throat in Barbados... I've identified her."

Naomi glanced back, waiting on him to finish. When he didn't, she waved her hand, urging him on. "Okay, so.... who is it?"

Quentin sat back in his chair, a somber expression riding his handsome face. "It was *her*, Naomi. It was Royale."

NINE

MARCUS

"SO... about this new little... *girlfriend* of yours..."

Under his breath, Marcus groaned as Tomiko Oshira sauntered into the lushly decorated foyer, her caramel skin glowing like she was fresh from the spa.

"Miko... it's been a while," Marcus said, shying away from her touch. He hated that she was always touching, teasing, and flirting – the kind of shit that would get a bullet through Marcus's head if the wrong person saw it.

She slid into the empty space on the couch beside him, not bothering to pull down the hem of her dress when it hiked up around her thighs. "I *know,* which brings me back to my question. I guess Naomi Prescott is the reason you've been treating me like a stranger? You never call, you never come by...." She placed her hand high on his thigh, "I'm starting to think you don't like me, Marcus."

You're on the right track.

"I don't call or come by because we wouldn't want your old man getting the wrong impression about us, now would we?" Marcus asked, pushing her hand away as he moved over, putting a decent amount of space between them. "You know how he is about his... possessions."

Tomiko smirked, then shrugged as she bit down on her fingernail. "What he doesn't know, won't hurt him."

"I'm sure that's the same thing your boy Devonte thought," Marcus countered, reminding her of the bodyguard who had been caught with his hands in *her* cookie jar. Marcus wasn't the least bit interested in a similar "stuffed in a trunk alive, car set on fire" kind of fate. Her exotic mix of Asian and Black features were certainly attractive, but nobody was *that* fine. "Anyway... how do you know Naomi?"

"Oh, Mimi and I go *way* back. You *do* know whose niece she is, right?"

Marcus narrowed his eyes. "What are you talking about Miko? And don't start making shit up to start drama. I know how you like to do."

"*Me?*" Tomiko giggled. "I would *never* do anything to purposely cause confusion... but, from the look on your face, I'm guessing your new sweetheart didn't tell you about her family ties... *or* her criminal record."

Chuckling, Marcus shook his head. "Naomi does *not* have a criminal record."

At least not a public one, he thought, making sure he wore skepticism on his face. There was no doubt about the veracity of Tomiko's information... the question was: how did she get it?

Tomiko grinned. "Well, I guess you would know, wouldn't you, Mr. FBI? What did you do, run a background check on her?"

"I did."

And that was a verifiable fact. He'd talked Renata into working a bit of covert techie magic, but now, anyone looking for it would see that the same day Marcus saw Naomi at the gym for the first time, he'd used his ID in the system to look her up. No criminal record, and *no* mention of Damien Wolfe as a relation.

"And it was clean?"

Marcus nodded. "Yes, it was clean, because she's not a criminal."

"If you say so."

"Well what do *you* say, since you two go "way back"...or so you claim."

Tomiko shook her head. "Not my story to tell. I'm sure she has her reasons for selling you whatever lie – oh, excuse me – for presenting her past in whatever light she chooses. But I would *love* to know how you met her."

"She teaches my niece's ballet class. I had to go pick her up one day, and... the rest is history. I mean, you claim to know so much about her, I'm sure you've seen her. She's gorgeous."

"She's *alright*-looking."

Marcus didn't miss the flare of her nostrils or the eye roll she gave. "Do I sense a little jealousy?"

Tomiko sucked her teeth, flipping her thick hair over her shoulder. "I never have and never *will* be jealous of Naomi Prescott. She has *nothing* on me – in any area."

Marcus disagreed, but kept it to himself. There was no point in sharing his opinion that Naomi, with her perfect mahogany skin, was definitely the more attractive of the two. Tomiko had flown into a rage before over much less.

He'd initially written her off as the conniving, money-hungry girlfriend of a criminal, but now he realized he'd been hasty with that assessment. Tomiko's goal may have been to cast suspicion on Naomi, but Marcus was more interested in what *she* was hiding.

"You still haven't mentioned how you know her," Marcus said, stroking his thumb over his chin. If he could just get her to drop another little hint...

"And I won't. Not yet. I wanna see how serious you two get before I play my hand. Although... taking her to Barbados... that was pretty damned serious, right?"

Who the hell is this woman?

Marcus shrugged. "Maybe... maybe not."

"Mmhmm. You know one of Rochas' guards was killed at his house down there – I think you were there at the same time." Tomiko picked at her nails as she said this, giving the appearance of boredom, but Marcus was no fool.

He pulled his face into a scowl. "And why the fuck am I just now hearing about it? Nobody thought that was some shit I should know?"

Tomiko flinched, lifting an eyebrow in alarm as she subtly scooted away, putting an extra inch of space between them. "Chill, Marcus. I guess the boss-man didn't think it was worth interrupting your little vacation."

"But it was fine for me and my girl to be in danger. Got it."

"That's not what I said."

"Sure the fuck sounds like it to me," Marcus said, straightening the collar of his crisp white button-up. In a scornful tone, he continued, "I guess I need to discuss the terms of *my* participation here. I was under the impression that safety was one of the perks, since I'm risking my freedom and my job."

"Relax," Tomiko hissed in a whispered plea, her gaze darting around the empty room. "I'm messing with you, the hit was sanctioned. Unsuccessful, but sanctioned. It was supposed to be Rochas, but... shit happened. And anyway – it's that girlfriend of yours you need to be worried about."

Marcus chuckled. "And you expect me to believe *that,* after you just sat here and proved you'll lie to get a reaction out of me?"

"Mr. Calloway?"

Marcus looked up to see an attractive older woman standing at the sitting room door.

"Yes?"

"He's ready for you."

With a slight nod, Marcus stood, and Tomiko did as well.

"You can believe what you want, I don't really care, as long as it doesn't affect me." She turned to leave, giving Marcus a full view of the open back of her dress, and inky-black top of a tattoo of tied ribbons. "Oh, and I forgot," Tomiko said, smiling as she turned back to face Marcus. "Congratulations... you couldn't choose a better family to get involved with. Enjoy your meeting."

"OUCH, MAN. LOOKS LIKE IT HURTS," Marcus said, cringing as his other team member, Kendall Williams, pulled a fresh tee shirt over his head. They'd just finished their yearly fitness assessment, and had stopped by the training facility to shower and change before heading home. Kendall's skin was a deep brown, but the dark purple bruise across his ribs was still a stark contrast.

Kendall shrugged, and Marcus knew it wasn't a "tough-guy" act. There was no one he'd rather have by his side if an operation went south, and it came down to physical combat. Conversely, Kendall was also the person he'd least like to be on the opposing side of a fight. Well... maybe Naomi.

Marcus lifted an eyebrow. "Man... don't tell me you're still doing that MMA shit as a hobby?"

"Come on, Marcus," Kendall said, shaking his head as he grabbed his bag to follow Marcus out of the locker room. "First rule of fight club..."

Marcus let out a shout of laughter as they stepped into the hall. "You need your head checked Ken."

"I've been saying that for years. Am I finally gonna get somebody to agree?" Renata asked, joining them in the hall as she exited the women's locker room. All three had stayed late to complete their assessments.

Kendall chuckled, playfully tugging one of Renata's braids. "Whatever. How did you do on the physical, Cleopatra Jones?"

"I aced it, *duh*. What did you expect?"

"Nothing less than perfection, Ren," Marcus chimed in. "You're the most kick-ass, pacifist computer-geek I know."

Renata paused in the hall to curtsy. "Why thank you. What are you guys about to get up to?"

Scratching the back of his head, Kendall gave a sheepish grin. "First rule..."

"So you're gonna be purposely getting your ass kicked," Renata giggled. "What about you Marcus?"

He shrugged. "Probably see what Naomi is up to."

Kendall shook his head, directing his attention to Renata. "Yo, I'm not sure about this "new Marcus", with this lovey-dovey stuff. Is he *ever* not seeing what Naomi is up to?"

Renata laughed, giving Marcus a teasing poke in the side. "I don't think he is! They *just* got back from Barbados like two weeks ago. He's not even giving the girl time to miss him! I guess you two are pretty serious?"

"Uhhh..."

"Don't be shy about it, Marcus, Naomi is beautiful. *And* I'm sure she keeps you on your toes. You don't have to be embarrassed to tell *us* you really like her," Renata insisted, a big smile on her face as she waited for him to answer.

Marcus would have *loved* to deny her assessment about "really" liking Naomi, but two things prevented that. First up, it was part of preserving their carefully laid cover. Secondly... he maybe... sort of... kind of... *did* like her, despite the fact she was exactly opposite the kind of sweet, easy-to-get-along-with women he usually appreciated. Naomi was stubborn, temperamental, brazen, and had the kind of smart mouth that made Marcus unsure if he wanted to tape it shut or kiss her. As infuriating as those qualities were, they simultaneously made her more attractive. And the *sex*...have mercy.

"I guess that's our answer, Ren. Do you see how he just zoned out, with this damned blissful look on his face?"

"Right! And is that... is that *drool?*"

Laughing, Marcus brushed his hand through the air, waving them off. "Man, whatever. What about you Ren?"

Looking at her as he waited for an answer, Marcus noticed again that even though Renata seemed her outwardly perky self, there were bags under her eyes, and her face was creased like she hadn't been getting a lot of sleep. The usual brightness in her eyes was dim, but she maintained a happy expression. "Oh, just gonna get in some quality time with my oils and canvas," she said, smiling between Marcus and Kendall. "Oh yeah? What are you working on now?" Kendall asked, reaching for the door that would lead them back through the field office – their quickest route to reach the parking lot.

Renata's smile faltered for a moment, and there was a hitch in her voice when she answered. "My daughter. A portrait."

"Cool." Marcus clapped her on the shoulder. "I'm sure she'll be excited to see it when she gets back."

Marcus lifted an eyebrow at Renata's subtle intake of breath before she nodded. "Yeah. When she gets back."

If he had the time, he would have asked Renata why the hell she was acting so bizarre about her daughter, but he was due at the gym for another meeting with SSA Barnes, Quentin, and Naomi.

WHEN HE ARRIVED, it was just he, SSA Barnes, and Quentin in the office.

"Ms. Prescott won't be joining us today," SSA Barnes said as he looked up from Quentin's computer screen, answering the unspoken question in Marcus's eyes. "We'll actually be brief today – I have a date. Besides that, we're at a bit of a standstill until we get this figured out." He motioned at the screen, and Marcus noticed that Quentin's usually laid-back vibe seemed to have been replaced by stress.

"What's going on?" Marcus came around the desk to look at the screen with the other two men, and immediately shook his head. "What the hell am I looking at?"

"Code," Quentin drawled. "Three levels of encryption, traps everywhere, mirrors and mazes to get lost in... this is impressive shit."

SSA Barnes's tone was dry when he spoke up. "Well, I'm glad you're impressed... but how do we get past it?"

"Your guess is about as good as mine right now, boss-man. I'm gonna need some time with one." Quentin sat back in his chair, stroking his beard.

"We don't *have* time. Today, I received intel that somehow, when Wolfe confronted Rochas about those diamonds, they *weren't* in the safe."

Marcus and Quentin both lifted eyebrows at Barnes.

"Say what now?" Marcus said, crossing his arms. "We all know Naomi put those diamonds in that safe."

"Right," Quentin agreed. "Barnes, we *watched* her do it."

SSA Barnes held up his hands. "Nobody is disputing that. We think that someone came behind her – stole the diamonds back."

"Well, isn't that fucking great?" Marcus rubbed his temples. "So... the whole job in Barbados... wasted?"

"Maybe... maybe not." Barnes tapped his chin with his finger as he began pacing. "I have good intel that Victor Lucas – Wolfe's other lieutenant – stole those diamonds from Rochas. I don't know who he hired for the job, or what his motivation was, but we can pretty safely assume that he's not interested in those diamonds getting back to his boss."

Marcus pulled up his shoulders, confused. "And why is that?"

"Well... think about it," Quentin said, turning in his chair. "If he wanted Wolfe to get the diamonds back, he could have left them with Rochas. It wasn't a secret among them that Wolfe was suspicious. So... the only reason to take the diamonds would be if he wanted them for himself."

Scratching his head, Marcus ran it over in his mind. "Or... he's trying to save Rochas' ass. Why?"

SSA Barnes answered. "So Rochas would owe him"

"But why would Lucas need Rochas in his debt?" Quentin asked.

Smiling, Agent Barnes came back to stand in front of the desk. "That's why I need you to get into his security. If we can get eyes inside his house, access to his computer, access to his files, we can dig around, see what's going on. But until then, we're flying blind. And, we still haven't identified the party attacker from the video."

"Sounds good," Quentin said, "But again... it's gonna take time. Lucas isn't the same kinda guy as Rochas. He has top notch security, and if I mess up, his system could get into mine before I even know it. Then.... he knows exactly what we know, who we are, *where* we are. It won't be pretty."

"Would having another hacker help?" Marcus asked.

Quentin nodded. "Absolutely."

"Who you thinking about Marcus?"

"Renata Parker, sir. She's on my team, and she's pretty bad-assed with this techie stuff. Easy to work with, loyal." Marcus thought about her reaction to his asking about fourteen-year-old Taylor. "And I think she could use some extra distraction."

"You trust her?" Agent Barnes gave him a stern look, which Marcus met without backing down.

"Implicitly."

Barnes nodded. "Okay. I'll talk to SSA Black tonight about bringing her in."

Marcus lifted an eyebrow. "Tonight?"

"Tonight," Barnes repeated with a wink as he headed out the door. "I told you I had a date."

Marcus laughed as Barnes left the room, then turned back to Quentin, whose attention was already back on the computer. "So... what's up with Naomi? She sick or something?"

With his chin cupped in his hand, Quentin looked up. "Nah, nothing like that. She had to go to the gun range today. Yearly assessment Barnes makes us do."

"Yeah, my team did the physical today. But... what does her going to the gun range have to do with her not being here?"

For a moment, Quentin just stared, without answering, then he pushed out a breath as he rubbed his eyebrow with his thumb. "Naomi isn't particularly fond of guns. Carries one, and'll use it without hesitation if necessary, but... she just doesn't like guns. Gun*shots*, specifically. Puts her in a bad place."

"Why is that?" Marcus asked, pushing his hands into his pockets as he leaned against the wall behind him. As tough of a front as Naomi presented – and with her talk about putting a bullet in Quentin – he was surprised to hear she didn't have an affinity for guns.

Quentin shrugged. "Gotta talk to Mimi about that. She wants you to know, she'll tell you."

Marcus scowled as Quentin returned his attention to the screen. Would it really be that damned hard to just tell him what Naomi's problem was?

"Hey man... you and Naomi..."

"Just friends," Quentin answered without looking up. "Won't get no jealous lover bullshit from me. But, say man.... let me be clear." He did look up then, his expression serious as he met Marcus's eyes. "Naomi is one of *very* few people in this world I care about. I'm not interested in being in your business, not at all, but if I ever get the feeling that I *need* to be in your business... don't let the glasses and the computer fool you, man. It won't end well. No disrespect intended – just wanted to put that out there."

Marcus nodded, extending his hand in a friendly gesture, which Quentin accepted. "None taken. But... I was just asking where she was, man, you didn't have to give me the "who is this motherfucker taking my sister to the prom" thing."

Chuckling, Quentin sat back in his chair. "Whatever you say, man. She's in her classroom zoning out, but I'm about to have to go get her. Barnes isn't the only brother with a hot date, and I've gotta run home."

"Why don't you go ahead?" Marcus asked, pushing away from the wall. "I'll wait on Naomi, so she's not locking up by herself."

Quentin agreed, and twenty minutes later, Marcus and Naomi were the only people in the building. Marcus occupied himself on his cell phone for a while, but inevitably, the music pumping from the classroom drew him to where Naomi was.

As usual, she was in her "uniform" of leggings, a sports bra, and toe shoes, but this time, she was dancing to a classical piece that Marcus didn't recognize. Instead of watching her in silence like he wanted, he gave her the courtesy of knocking on the door, and waited to be invited in.

Naomi barely looked at him, which Marcus had gotten used to over the last two weeks. She wasn't overtly combative like before, but she wasn't exactly *friendly* either. The most attention she gave Marcus was in front of people, when they were still putting on their "couple" show. They went on a couple of quiet, fake movie dates, because they could mostly ignore each other while they watched, but still give the illusion of actually being together. And, somewhat to Marcus's dismay, he had *not* been invited back to her place, for activities of any kind.

After she opened the door, she went right back to dancing as if he wasn't there. Seeing her now, moving around in clothes that fit her like a second skin was a painful reminder that their last time together had been two weeks ago, and before that... it had been *months* for Marcus. Meagan's assessment that he preferred a drive-thru arrangement was correct, but it didn't mean the options were in abundance.

Marcus thrived on simplicity. He favored consistency, but the women he desired for the type of unstructured, low attention, low quality time relationship he wanted – the only kind he could balance with his job – wanted the exact opposite. On occasion, he would find someone, have a few nights of hot protected sex, then move on, rarely ever seeing them again. But Naomi, hottest of the hot, was constantly in his face, because the job made it impossible to get away.

"Did you need something?" She asked, moving gracefully across the room on her toes, with what appeared to be minimal effort.

Marcus shook his head. "Not really... everybody else is gone. Just waiting on you to finish up so you don't have to shut everything down alone."

"You must have been talking to Quentin." She stopped in front of him, looking him right in the eyes. "Who thinks I'm not capable of taking care of myself."

"That's not true," Marcus said, taking a seat in one of the empty chairs along the wall. "He's just looking out for you. Wants to make sure you're good."

Naomi scoffed. "Mmhmm. I just need a few more minutes."

"Go for it."

Marcus watched, impressed, as she ran through her routine again. When she came to a stop, panting and sweating, he diverted the blood flow from other places back to his brain long enough to formulate a question. "You know... back in Barbados, you never did answer my question really about why you didn't become a dancer. You ended up telling me about your mom."

She giggled a little, causing Marcus's eyes to go wide. He wasn't expecting *that* response.

"My ass," she said, reaching behind her to grip the soft flesh. "That, plus hips, and tits... "too distracting", too "bouncy" for ballet anyway. But..." that brief hint of a smile left, and she turned somber again. "My mother... she was the reason I danced at all. After she died, I only kept going to honor her memory. I wanted to stop – *never* wanted to look at a dance floor again, but my dad encouraged me. He liked to watch me, because I reminded him of Mommy. He wasn't around a lot when I was smaller, but after Mommy... he always was. And just like she taught me her specialty... he did too. For three really beautiful years, I thought that *maybe* I had a chance of being okay, but then... Wolfe took my father too, and as soon as I graduated high school, I... disappeared. Me, Quentin, and another girl, who I *thought* was a friend."

"Thought?"

Naomi nodded, placing her hands on her hips as she stood. "She was my friend from ballet, no family. I taught her how to steal without getting caught, and the three of us were a nice little team. We would steal stuff from criminals, sell it to their competitors, then give half the money to homeless shelters, food pantries, drug rehabs... trying to balance out some of the damage that those same criminals were doing to the communities. We kept enough to have an okay life. Quentin and I were content, but Royale – that's what we called her in class, Ballet Royale, and she kept it – she was... high maintenance. She'd never had anything, but once she got a taste of it... donating the money didn't work for her anymore, so she left and did her own thing."

"But... she double crossed you, right? Barnes mentioned the name Royale to me before," Marcus said, balancing his elbows on his knees, chin in his hands.

"Yep." Naomi turned off her music, then pulled on her yoga jacket. "But Barnes doesn't know who she really is – and if he asks you, neither do I."

Marcus pretended to zip his lips as he shrugged. Barnes hadn't been incredibly forthcoming with information that didn't directly relate to the case, so Marcus wouldn't be either.

Naomi smirked. "I was 23 when she did it. She was mad because I beat her to a score. And she knew me, from being with me all those years. She knew exactly who I would go to for the sale, but when I set it up... the FBI was waiting for me instead."

"Damn."

"Damn, indeed," Naomi shook her head. "And it didn't matter that *I* knew I was stealing from criminals – it was still stealing, and they took me down. But Barnes... he listened to what I was trying to tell him. I knew things, knew people, and knew how different events connected. So... he gave me an option.... seven years later, here we are."

Marcus sat back in his chair, watching Naomi as she walked to the door, then paused, waiting for him to follow. "So... what you're telling me is, you were never *really* the bad guy. More like... Robin Hood?"

"I guess you could think of it like that." Naomi laughed for a moment, then turned somber. "But... I don't want to give the impression that it was fun, or happy. The majority of it was actually a *really* dark time of my life... which sounds *terrible* looking at the current state of my life."

"Come on," Marcus said as he stood. "It's not *that* bad right? You've got friends, Quentin and Inez. I haven't met her yet, but she must be pretty cool, since I don't get the sense that you give people that title lightly. You've got a banging ass apartment, *and* a townhouse. You're *fine.* You own a business, and you've got your... what do you call the girls again?"

Naomi smiled. "My baby ballerinas."

"There you go. Your baby ballerinas. So... it's not all bad, right?"

"I... I guess not," she shrugged. "Now, if I can just get Damien Wolfe's shadow from looming over me... I'll really be able to breathe then."

Nodding, Marcus followed her out of the classroom, then waited while she locked the door behind them. As they left, he found himself wondering what Quentin had meant about the trip to the gun range putting Naomi in a bad place. To Marcus, she seemed perfectly fine.

naomi

Something wasn't right about it. Sixteen year old Naomi couldn't pinpoint what the problem was exactly, but... something was wrong. The feeling in the air wasn't right, and the scent blowing in off the bayou burned her nose, and she had goosebumps on her skin even though it was such a hot summer night.

She wasn't even supposed to be there. Her father, Nelson Prescott, had left her tucked in her bed, safe behind the steel reinforced doors and bulletproof glass of their apartment with instructions not to open the door for anyone. He promised he would swallow his key if he fell into the wrong hands. Naomi laughed, like she always did when he said that. He kissed her nose and left, and not even a minute behind him, Naomi followed.

At the end of the street, he'd gotten into a running car, with his best friend, Julian LaForte. Quentin's dad. She could never *get Quentin to come with her. He wanted to spend his time chatting with some girl he'd met online, who was probably actually a fat white guy. So Naomi pulled her bike from the side of the house, and went alone.*

Naomi was good at following, good at tracking people down. Nelson and Julian had been to this little ramshackle house many times, so she didn't even have to keep up with the car. She'd found a quicker, quieter, safer way to get there without being seen, so she took her own route, hid her bike carefully in the overgrown bushes, then broke into the house and waited in the dark for them to arrive.

Usually, it was just the two friends. Naomi would listen, soaking up every word as they launched a plan to take down a man whose name made Naomi's blood run cold. The man who'd picked her up, tickled her, and placed kisses on her cheek when she was a toddler.

Her uncle, Damien Wolfe.

She hadn't understood then, and just barely understood now what he meant when he would say to her

"You should have been mine," but after he did what he did to her mother, Noelle, it made more sense.

Damien had always wanted sweet, beautiful Noelle, but she was more interested in his handsome, charming half-brother Nelson. Damien was a gorgeous man, with cinnamon-colored skin and deep hazel eyes, but he had a streak that was downright mean, *and Noelle was smart enough to recognize it. Years went on, and Nelson and Noelle got married and made a beautiful family.*

A family that Damien thought should have been his.

Of the two brothers, Damien was the more ambitious – ruthlessly so. He worked his way from a petty drug dealer, to a lieutenant, while he built a legitimate empire in nicotine. With that power in his hands, he went back to Noelle. Offered to get rid of his brother, give her a life that Nelson – who worked under him, lifting whatever tickled his fancy – could never give her. Noelle declined, but he took her anyway, and now.... Nelson was ready to have his revenge.

Problem was – or so Naomi thought – Nelson was a pacifist. She didn't understand what the problem was with kidnapping Wolfe and doing the same things to him that he and his thugs had done to her mother, but Nelson thought jail time for drugs, jewelry, and sex trafficking was the better course of action. He'd talked Julian, who also worked for Wolfe into participating in his mutiny,

174

but the third voice Naomi heard as they entered the house... this man was new to her.

"I'm telling you, it's going to be fine. We take good care of our confidential informants. We'll get your families in witness protection, keep your kids safe. You're doing the right thing." That was the new guy, his voice way too eager. He had to be law enforcement of some kind, making those kind of promises.

"Mr. Big Shot Special Agent..."

Bingo, FBI, CIA, something.

"What guarantee do we have? I got a wife, a son... if this thing goes bad...." That was Quentin's dad, in his Cajun drawl. While he was having computer sex, or whatever he was doing with his little online friend, his dad was down here risking his life. Naomi made a mental note to rub it in his face when she next saw him.

"This really isn't your fight, Julian." Hearing her father's voice, Naomi carefully adjusted her position behind the dilapidated couch so that she could see underneath. The only thing she could see were shoes, and her dad's were pacing the worn carpet. "You got involved with this to help me out, but I understand you need to look out for your family."

"You are family," Julian argued. "Noelle was like a sister to me, and you know Quentin and Mimi are best friends, may even be sweethearts someday. I don't feel they're safe as long as Wolfe is around."

The agent chimed in again. "I wouldn't have flown down here alone if I wasn't confident. My partner's wife went into labor, so he stayed behind, but I came on anyway. Because I believe you guys can do this. We've been trying to catch up to Damien Wolfe for a while. If we can get him on tape, admitting to even one –"

BANG!

Naomi's first instinct was to cover her ears in response to the loud, reverberating sound that rang through the air as a passing car backfired on the street. But then, the resonant thud of a body hitting the floor met her ears. The new man, the FBI agent, he was first, sending ripples of dust into the air as he fell, just out of view except for his shoes.

BANG!

Julian LaForte, who was closest to Naomi's hiding spot fell next. A gun clattered to the floor beside him, close enough that Naomi could reach it if she stretched a little, if she wasn't so busy keeping her hands clamped over her mouth so she wouldn't scream about Julian's blood creeping toward her in a slow puddle.

BANG!

Nelson Prescott was last, and he fell in full view of where Naomi was crouched. Their gazes met, and Nelson's mouth dropped open a little as recognition lit his eyes. Blood spilled from an open wound at his side as another pair of shoes came into view.

"Well... this was cozy, wasn't it?"

Naomi recognized his voice as soon as he spoke. Her eyes left her father, landed on the gun Mr. LaForte had dropped. It was so close. Maybe if she could just... movement caught her eye, and she looked back to see that it was her father. He was shaking his head, pleading with his eyes: Don't touch that gun.

Nausea made Naomi's stomach roil as Damien Wolfe knelt beside her father.

"Did you really think you were gonna what... turn me in to the Feds? Really, Nelson? Your own blood? You would do that to me... over that slut?"

He spat out that ugly word about her mother like it was nothing, and tightness pulled at Naomi's chest. Nelson opened his mouth to speak, but all that came out was a dry, desperate rattle.

Damien laughed. "You're done for, man. You know I've been expecting something like this from you, right? I was wondering when you would show a little heart, retaliate about Noelle, but it took you three years, man? Three damned years. You're just as much of a nobody as I thought you were, and that stupid bitch chose you over me? I've had your lines tapped for the last year, dummy. LaForte's too. I saw this shit coming a mile away... but I had to let you think you could do it.

You called the FBI, so this innocent man is another death on your hands, Nelson. You could have prevented this shit by giving me Noelle when I asked for her. But now," He cocked his gun again, and Naomi stifled a gasp as the barrel appeared against Nelson's temple. *"You've gotta be eliminated. How's that pretty little girl of yours? Looks just like Noelle, doesn't she? She's what... sixteen now? Tight little body... pussy is probably still brand new... yeah... perfect time to pay her a little visit. Maybe she'll behave better than her momma."*

Damien pulled the trigger, and Naomi squeezed her eyes shut, not wanting to see the light leave her father's eyes, or worse. She kept them closed, relishing the darkness as footsteps vibrated throughout the room as men moved around, presumably taking information from the three men's bodies.

"Gonna have to change my motherfucking jacket before we hit this party. Leave the bodies here. I wanna make an example," she heard Damien mutter, just before the footsteps exited the room, and then the house. This time, Naomi heard the hum of an extra car engine as it came to life, then pulled away, speeding off into the night.

For a long time, Naomi just lay there, in a derelict house, behind a dilapidated couch, in the darkness and silence and odor of the bayou, screaming in her head because she was afraid to do it out loud.

Daddy.

Daddy.

Daddy.

TEN
NAOMI

"DADDY!"

Naomi sat up in bed, sweat pouring off her as if she'd just finished several miles on the treadmill. She pushed her hair back from her face, looking around frantically to ensure that she was *not* back in that raggedy little house near the bayou.

She felt sick to her stomach, her head was pounding, but perhaps worst of all, she felt overwhelmingly *alone*. Quentin was off on a date, and Inez was halfway around the world, doing secret CIA shit that required her smartphone be left at home.

Shoving her covers back, Naomi swung her feet over the edge of the bed. She didn't even bother with her slippers, just pulled her nightgown over her head and tossed it into the hamper, then got into the shower. The hot water did nothing to wash away her seemingly unstoppable tears, the feeling of Julian LaForte's blood soaking the knees of her jeans, or the sight of her father, unrecognizably mangled from the bullet Wolfe had put through his head. Quentin's dad... and Kenneth Calloway, the man she now knew to be Marcus's father – three men dead, at the hands of one.

Damien Wolfe *would* pay for what he'd done, Naomi was determined to make that happen. For now, she would settle for a dreamless sleep, the kind she was unlikely to get after a trip to the gun range. Gunshots *always* triggered these nightmares, and eventually they went away, but that didn't help her *now.*

Out of the shower, she toweled off and put on a fresh gown, then changed her bed to non sweat-soaked sheets. She climbed in again and closed her eyes, but behind her eyelids, that horrible, bloody room, reeking with the aroma of death, was all she could see.

Sleep wasn't to be had tonight.

Her gaze, still blurry with tears, fell on her phone, and she remembered an offer made to her just a few weeks before. She picked it up and started to dial, then changed her mind. Naomi climbed out of the bed, got dressed, and grabbed her keys.

WHAT THE HELL am I doing here? I look so stupid right now, Naomi thought, as her second knock went unanswered. Unwilling to knock again, she wiped errant tears from her eyes and turned away from the door.

What would her life have been like if it weren't for that night? If Wolfe *hadn't* known about the meeting that night – or if the meeting had never happened. If her father had just been strong enough to eliminate Wolfe. Or, perhaps, if she had taken that gun... what then? Chances were that she would be dead too, but maybe she could have taken Wolfe out along the way. At least then, she wouldn't be the only one in hell.

Maybe instead of being in someone else's hallway after midnight, she would be in her own bed, cuddled close to a husband, with two kids tucked between them. Maybe she could have a normal life, free of looking over her shoulder, free of the fear that one day Damien Wolfe would make good on that final threat to her father. Maybe one of her baby ballerinas would really be *her* baby ballerina.

Naomi cupped a hand over her mouth, choking back a fresh round of sobs. She suddenly felt tired. *Exhausted*, from having to constantly be in control, constantly be strong, constantly put up this front that she was the toughest girl in the world, when she really... *wasn't.* Shaking her head, Naomi sat down against the wall, draping her arms over her knees for a place to rest her head.

"Naomi?"

Her breath hitched in her throat. Before she looked up, she frantically wiped the tears from her face with her hands. Swallowing hard, she stood to face Marcus, who was standing in the hall just outside his door, looking confused.

"Naomi," Marcus said again, taking a step forward. "It's almost two in the morning... what are you doing here?"

Naomi's eyes drifted over his shirtless chest, then back up to his face, but she couldn't get her mouth to open and speak. When she didn't respond to his question, Marcus narrowed his eyes for a moment, then smiled.

"*Ohhh*," he said, pushing his hands into the pockets of his sweats as he sauntered closer, biting his lip. "Two weeks is as long as you could hold out, huh? I knew it wouldn't be long."

Naomi rolled her eyes, shaking her head as she took a step away from him. "You know what? *Never mind*."

"Wait a minute..." Marcus grabbed her arm, stopping her as she headed down the hall. Brushing her thick curls away from her face, he studied her for a moment. "Have you... have you been *crying*?"

"I said never mind. It's not your concern," Naomi snapped, trying unsuccessfully to pull away.

Marcus shook his head. "It *is* my concern. You brought it to my place, at booty call hours. Come inside."

"I'm not here for a booty call."

"Then why are you here?"

Naomi squeezed her eyes tight, trying to stem a fresh round of tears from falling. She shook her head. "I don't know. I have no idea," she said, her voice choked with the effort of trying not to cry.

Lifting an eyebrow, Marcus stared at her for a moment before he nodded. "O-kay. Come on."

Wiping her face with the back of hand, Naomi didn't resist as Marcus pulled her into his apartment, closing and locking the door behind them. She really *didn't* know why she was there. Sex wasn't on her mind, especially not the high-energy, combustive kind she expected from Marcus, but... the thought of being alone made a situation she was barely enduring seem outright unbearable. Even having her nerves run into the ground by Marcus was a better alternative.

"You thirsty? Hungry?"

Naomi declined. Her throat and stomach were on fire, but the thought of eating or drinking made them contract in pain. Marcus nodded, and kept pulling her along, leading her to what she quickly realized was his bedroom. Sophie had told her after class a few days ago that she and her mother would be out of town, so privacy wasn't a concern, but *still*. This wasn't what she came for.

"Marcus, I –"

"You said that already. Relax."

Fists clenched, Naomi stood still while Marcus unzipped and removed her jacket, then draped it over a chair. He directed her to sit down, and her eyes narrowed in confusion when he knelt in front of her to take off her shoes, then pulled her up again to lead her to the bed. He pulled her in, then turned off the lamp, drawing her close as the room dropped into darkness.

Naomi felt strangely comfortable, with her face tucked into Marcus's neck. In what seemed like moments, he was asleep, leaving her to puzzle over what exactly was happening. Why was he being so.... not an asshole?

Soon, Naomi's eyelids grew heavy again. She moved closer to Marcus, pressing herself against his chest, and he unconsciously draped an arm over her. The weight of his arm wrapped her in an oddly gratifying sense of security and calm. Cautiously, she closed her eyes.

This time, she only saw darkness as she drifted into untroubled slumber.

GOD HE SMELLS GOOD.

With her face still burrowed against Marcus's neck, Naomi inhaled deep, breathing in the clean, earthy, masculine scent of his skin. Propping herself up on her elbow, she surveyed his handsome face. Marcus was *beautiful* to her. Male perfection in all its glory.

For a brief moment, she allowed herself a little fantasy in which they were a different Marcus and Naomi, ones who weren't orphaned in the world. Alternate versions of themselves who got to live peaceful lives, free of the burden of nightmarish memories. How different might their dynamic be then, if their first meeting had simply been Agent Calloway, picking up little Sophie from Madame Mimi's class?

With a doleful smile, Naomi stroked his chin with the back of her hand, letting his facial hair rasp over her skin. In the semi-darkness, she allowed her hand to drift over his muscled chest, down to the ridged plane of his stomach. She wandered lower, past his navel, down to the waistband of his boxers and then slipped her hand inside. With no moisture on her hands, she couldn't stroke him like she wanted, but her fingers danced over his smooth, velvety skin. She watched Marcus, marveling at the way his face came to life at the same time he came alive in her hands, thicker, heavier, longer, and harder, in a way that made moisture pool between her legs even though that wasn't even why she was touching him.

So why are *you touching him?*

Naomi didn't know the answer to that. All she knew was that now that she'd woken Marcus up at four in the morning with her hand in his boxers, barely two hours after her surprise arrival that she insisted *wasn't* a booty call, she was going to have to say *something*.

Or... not.

Marcus watched silently, through half-lidded eyes as she pulled him free of the restrictive fabric. His breath hitched when she touched him again, gripping him in her hand, running her thumb over the pearl of moisture that beaded at the tip, attesting to his arousal.

Pushing everything else from her mind, Naomi used her hands and lips together as she took him in her mouth. His muscles jerked and jumped in reaction to the gift of the wet heat of her tongue, and a wave of satisfaction washed over Naomi as he took a handful of her hair in his hands. He didn't push or guide her, just let it rest there as Naomi savored him, encouraged by his soft grunts, groans, and growls of pleasure.

He moved his hands in her hair, gripping then releasing like he was trying to restrain himself as he lifted his hips, almost imperceptibly stroking into her mouth. Naomi tightened her suction, used more tongue, made it wetter, went faster, then slower, then faster again until Marcus gripped a fistful of her kinky curls, dragging his fingers across her scalp as he groaned.

"Goddammit, girl."

She got a short burst of delight from the knowledge that she was in control. *She* was in charge of *his* body, but it was immediately followed by a strong urge to *not* feel that way. Naomi was tired – *drained*, even – of the constant desire to be in control. Worn-out of being powerful, and strong, and controlled. She just wanted to *feel*.

She released him from her mouth, using her hand to continue stimulation as she looked up, meeting Marcus's intense gaze.

"I wanna feel you."

Naomi wasn't sure which of them spoke first, but the sentiment left their lips at the same time. She briefly closed her eyes in relief, and when she opened them again, she slid off her leggings, panties, and tank top while Marcus watched. His strong, hot hands cupped her breasts as she climbed on top of him to straddle his waist, leaving his erection pressed between them. For a long moment, neither moved, just stared. Naomi's chest was heaving, heart racing, as he got harder and she got wetter, waiting to see what Marcus was going to do.

When he kissed her, it was a deep, passionate kiss, so unlike the way he'd kissed her before that it made her heart race. She parted her lips to invite him inside and draped her arms over his shoulders as he accepted, stroking her tongue with his. It wasn't bruising, but insistent, hungry, but not impatient. Marcus was *giving* with this kiss, not taking, and Naomi eagerly accepted what he was offering.

Gripping her hips, he pulled her closer, so that her wetness was pulled tight against his hardness. She moaned, subtly rolling her hips as he kissed her deeper still. Marcus reached around her to grip handfuls of her ass, kneading and massaging as she rocked her hips harder, creating a sweet, pleasurable friction between them. Marcus dipped his head, gently catching one of her sensitive, hardened nipples between his teeth before he pulled it into his mouth.

Naomi cried out in pleasure, arching her back. Balancing on her hands, she leaned back, giving him better access to lick, suck, kiss, and nibble her into a trembling mess, even as she continued to move her hips, sliding against his hardened arousal.

"Marcus...?" she said, her voice almost a whisper as he looked up and their eyes met. "Are you sleeping with anyone else?"

His eyes widened in surprise, before he shook his head. "No. Why?"

Yet another question for which Naomi had no answer – at least, not one that she would verbalize. Not to Marcus, not right now. They'd already gone further than the point that wearing a condom mattered for STD protection, and pregnancy prevention wasn't a problem, thanks to her IUD. She wanted to know if he was sleeping with anyone else because she realized, in that moment, that she *just didn't want him sleeping with anybody else*. But she had no "good" reason for that, she had no claim on him.

"Cause, I wanna... *feel* you. *Now.*"

Using his shoulders for leverage, she lifted herself up, then sank onto him, briefly closing her eyes as her body adjusted to the weight and fullness of him inside her. They'd only felt each other like *this* once, that very first time in Barbados, and from the expression on Marcus's face, Naomi could tell that the hot, slick feeling of flesh against flesh had been mutually missed since then.

His fingers dug into her hips as she began to move in slow, undulating waves that only lasted a few minutes before the pursuit of pleasure had her riding harder, faster, taking him deeper until he wrapped an arm around her waist, pulling her tight against him to keep her still.

"Slow down, Beautiful." With his free hand, Marcus pushed her hair away from her face, giving her a kiss that made chills run up her spine. He released his hold on her, and Naomi obliged his request to take her time. She rolled her hips in deliberate circles, clenching around him as she rode him in carefully measured strokes.

Marcus's hands were greedy, but gentle as he explored her skin, gripping, and kneading, and squeezing and massaging whatever he could reach as he kissed her. "This is... the *best* birthday gift a man could ask for," he murmured against her lips.

"It's your birthday?" Naomi asked, pulling back slightly, eyes wide as she tried to remember if she'd seen that in his file.

One hand between her legs, the other cupping her breast, Marcus grinned, flashing his dimples. "Nah."

Naomi rolled her eyes, giggling as he leaned forward to kiss her neck. "Silly ass," Naomi whispered, closing her eyes in response to the warmth of his tongue. He wrapped his arms around her waist, and she draped her arms over his shoulders, resting her hands at the base of his neck. The closeness filled Naomi's chest with an unfamiliar warmth, making her feel lightheaded, and almost giddy as Marcus met the roll of her hips with upward strokes of his own, deeper, faster, harder, mounting the pressure at her core until it shattered and spilled. She clenched around him, milking a powerful release from him as well, and they stayed like that, clutched together, until Naomi finally extracted herself from Marcus's arms, lifting herself from his body.

"Shower?"

Marcus lifted an eyebrow, but pointed the way to the bathroom. Naomi closed the door behind her, peed, and then got right into the shower, trying to rid herself of the confusingly pleasant sensation she couldn't identify. She should have known it would happen – it had happened *every* time with him so far, a strange feeling of … *contentment*, which she really couldn't afford. Not with a coworker. *Not* with Marcus.

She said nothing when he came into bathroom to handle his own business. Closing her eyes, she prayed that he wouldn't join her in the shower. Her body said yes, but her brain said *no, you've done enough.* She heaved an inaudible sigh of relief when the opening door indicated that he didn't plan to stay.

Naomi's only reply was a quiet thank you when he announced that he was leaving a tee shirt for her to wear. She turned off the water, toweled off, and pulled the over-sized tee over her head, then snuck through the darkened bedroom into the hall to get to the kitchen they'd passed on the way in.

She poured herself a glass of water and stood at the counter to drink it as she lost herself in thoughts of what the hell she was doing there, and why. She had no idea how long she stood there, but the next thing she knew, the first signs of sunrise were coming in through the big front window of Marcus's apartment.

Naomi felt him coming before she saw him, and closed her eyes to the warmth of Marcus's hand against her back. Despite herself, she moaned as his arms closed around her, enveloping her in warmth, and strength, and delicious clean smells from the shower she assumed he'd just taken, based on the slight dampness of his skin.

She forced herself to pull away, turning to face him in the growing light of daybreak.

Marcus looked to the ceiling, running his tongue over his teeth as he shook his head. "What is it this time?" he asked, leveling her with a gaze that made her look up to meet his eyes.

"What are you talking about, Marcus?"

"Why are you doing this again? We have... *excellent* sex, then you push me away like you're... I don't know... *ashamed*. Is that what it is?"

Naomi's eyes went wide. "*What?* No, I'm not *ashamed*, I'm... I'm *scared*." As soon as those words left her lips, Naomi wished she could take them back. This was... too much. She hated feeling so open and exposed, hating feeling so vulnerable, and the confused, slack-jawed expression on Marcus's face didn't help. Taking a deep breath, she squared her shoulders, admonishing herself to tuck her emotions away. They'd never served in her favor before, and it didn't look like that was changing now.

Shaking her head in an effort to clear her thoughts, she shut Marcus out of her head and started toward his room to get dressed. Pretending to be unaffected had worked – somewhat – the day after their little encounter in Barbados, so she had to hope it would work now.

"Wait a minute," Marcus said, grabbing her arm. "Scared of what?"

She shrugged. "Nothing. Never mind."

"No. We're not gonna do that "never mind" shit. You came here for a reason that you claimed *wasn't* sex, but that's the only thing we've done. So I need you to tell me why you showed up at my place in the middle of the night, crying, and now you're talking about you're scared. What the hell is going on here?"

192

"I had a bad dream, okay?" Naomi yanked her arm from him grasp. "I had a bad dream, and I needed to not be alone, but... I shouldn't have come here, to you. I'm sorry for.... interrupting your night."

Marcus scoffed. "Okay. A bad dream. Yeah right, Naomi. You run around like Little Ms. Big Balls, and I'm supposed to believe a bad dream made you drive over here in the middle of the damned night. Cause you're a little girl now. *Sure.*"

"You don't get it, Marcus," she said, with a dry laugh. "I *am* just a little girl, because that's where my life stopped. You wanna know what my dream was about? *Bang.* One man dead. *Bang.* Another. *Bang.* My *father* falling to the ground not even ten feet in front of me, bleeding out while I watched. *While I watched.* I *watched* Damien Wolfe shove the barrel of a gun against his temple and tease him. My father died thinking that his *brother* was going to do the same disgusting things to *me* that he did to my mother, and I live every single day wondering if that was just a taunt, or a promise he plans on fulfilling. So, yeah, I'm still a kid, stuck in that moment unless I scrub him off the earth.

"So... excuse the hell out of me if I seem obsessed. Excuse me for not being the carefree girl that *trust me*, I would *love* to be. And please... fucking *pardon me* if I have sex that's *only* supposed to be sex, but it doesn't feel like *just* sex, it feels like more. And even though the guy infuriates the hell out of me, I like him anyway, but I *can't* like him, because that leads to more, and more leads to love, and I can't do love, because I'm terrified that's just another thing Wolfe might decide to take from me."

Naomi covered her mouth, choking back a sob as she headed for the bedroom again. She didn't resist when Marcus caught her around the waist and turned her around, pulling her into a hug against his chest. Wrapped again in his warmth, the dam holding back her pain broke, and tears spilled freely as she cried.

"I'm sorry," Marcus said, kissing the side of her head as he stroked her hair.

Naomi nodded, trying to push away, but he kept her held close, and eventually she allowed herself to relax into his embrace. It wasn't until she'd calmed down that he pulled back to kiss her forehead, then her cheeks, and finally her lips as he brushed her tears away. Naomi's heart swelled as he cupped her face in his hands, looked her in the eyes, then said again, "I'm *so* sorry." before he pulled her back against his chest.

"ALRIGHT KIDS. Let's welcome Special Agents Kendall Williams, Renata Parker, and Inez Araullo to our little team," SSA Barnes said, pointing out the three new people sitting at the table. Naomi gave them a once-over and a cordial smile, but she was more interested in the fact that Quentin's teeth were working overtime grinning at Agent Parker.

She'd *never* seen Quentin so... enamored, but she knew it had very little to do with Agent Parker's looks. The woman sitting next to him was undeniably pretty, with copper-brown skin, braids that Naomi knew were waist-length from that day in the interrogation room, but were currently pulled up in a bun, and thick black framed glasses. Renata Parker was adorable and curvy, two things Quentin was partial to, but her *real* appeal was in her computer prowess. She seemed a little on the shy side, but Naomi had no doubt that Quentin would use his sexy Creole charm to pull her personality out.

Naomi was pretending not to notice Marcus staring at her from across the table. She wondered if he was even listening – if *any* of them were listening – as Agent Barnes droned on about the next step in the job – getting into Victor Lucas's computer. She shook her head. She needed to focus.

"So... Quentin, we got you another hacker... explain for the rest of us what we're up against."

"Well... Victor Lucas is a very different scenario than Rochas. Believes in high-tech security, the best money can buy. Keeps personal guards with him, but other than that... it's all tech."

SSA Barnes nodded. "But the question is, is it hackable?"

"Everything is hackable," Renata chimed in, pushing her glasses up on her face. Naomi smirked as Quentin looked up from his computer to give her his undivided attention. "With the right tools, we can get far... but only *so* far. The information we need could be on Lucas's desktop computer, in his house. So someone would to have to get in there and lay hands on it in person. Quentin has already done a lot, but it's not something one person can do alone."

"Wait... how you know what I've done?" Lifting an eyebrow, Quentin tilted his head to attempt a look at Renata's laptop screen. "Did you... *hack* me?"

With a sheepish smile Renata lifted her hand, holding her thumb and pointer finger up as she pinched them together. "Just a little bit. Not too much."

"Just a 'lil bit, huh?" Quentin asked, leaning back in his chair with a smile. He ran his tongue over his lips, and didn't bother to hide the fact that he was checking her out. Renata blushed, pulling her lip between her teeth as she turned her attention back to her screen.

Staring at him until he looked her way, Naomi subtly caught Quentin's attention. With her wrist against the table she lifted her hand in a "slow down" gesture, and silently mouthed "be easy, cher", then smiled. He gave her a little nod back, and she looked away, again locking eyes with Marcus. It was Naomi's turn to blush then, the heat of his gaze reminding her of the way he'd touched her the night before.

A week had passed since their night at his place. After her little breakdown, he'd taken her back to his bedroom and made love to her with sweet, soul-searing intensity that made her eyes water just thinking about it. Against her better judgment, they'd spent almost every night together since. Naomi didn't quite know what to make of the shift in the way they interacted. Now, when he kissed, or flirted with her in public, they weren't putting on a show. They were simply... doing what felt natural.

"Naomi, are you listening?"

"Hmm?" she asked, tearing her gaze away from Marcus to look at SSA Barnes.

"I asked if you'd looked over the schematics for Lucas's house yet. Quentin and Renata think there's a good chance you may have to go in there, and if that's the case, I want you prepared."

"I'll be ready."

Marcus lifted a hand. "Wait a minute... go in there? As in, in his house, by herself?"

Naomi cocked her eyebrow, scrutinizing the concern in Marcus's face. He'd schooled his expression into indifference, but his tone was slightly pitched up, shoulders tight as he crossed his arms over his chest.

Is he... worried about me?

"Marcus... you do realize I've been doing this for years, right? I'm pretty sure I've been in much more dangerous situations than sneaking into a private residence."

Something she couldn't decipher passed over his face before he shrugged. "I mean... you're the thief. If you say you've got it, I guess you've got it."

Naomi narrowed her eyes. What the hell was *his* problem? Looking around, she noticed that both Kendall and Renata were trying their best to look like their attention was somewhere other than with them at the table. They'd known him longer than the others – maybe *they* knew, and were used to, whatever the heck this reaction was.

"Thanks for the vote of confidence," Naomi said, keeping her gaze trained on Marcus, even though he wouldn't look her way. She kept her tone even, not wanting to betray the fact that his calling her a thief, after everything he knew, hurt her feelings.

"There somethin' you're not saying, Calloway?" Quentin drawled, running a hand over his stubbled chin. "What's on your mind?" There was a challenge in his voice, cluing Naomi that he'd noticed the same thing she had.

"I think it's dangerous." Marcus sat up, nostrils flared as he glanced between Naomi and Quentin. "Going in there by yourself is *not* the same thing as the party, where you had assistance less than 100 feet away if you needed it. Lucas's house is a fucking fortress. We won't be able to just bum rush the gate to get to you if something happens."

Shaking her head, Naomi leaned on the table so she was close to Marcus. "You think I don't understand that? That's why we plan, and plan, and plan some more. A--"

"Contingency plan for the contingency plan. Yeah, I've got it. But a contingency plan isn't bulletproof, and neither are you. Unless you *want* to end up like..." He stopped, pushing out a heavy sigh as he scratched his head.

"End up like who, Marcus?" Naomi's voice was quiet, and even SSA Barnes said nothing to interfere, just rocketed his gaze between she and Marcus. "Finish what you were gonna say."

"Naomi..."

Naomi fully recognized the plea in his eyes for her to stop, but she wasn't the one who took it there. *He* did. And how *dare* he?

"No. Say it. You think I want to end up like my father, right? Or wait... are you referring to my mother? Which one?"

When he didn't answer, Naomi pushed her chair back and stomped out, leaving a table full of her uncomfortable colleagues behind. She sought refuge in her classroom, but she didn't dance. She put her earbuds in, cranked up Lil Kim's *Hardcore* album, and closed her eyes while she pondered Marcus.

Sitting on the floor, with her knees pulled into her chest, head resting on her knees, she tried to figure out why the hell he was suddenly so worried about her. As if she hadn't gotten into more secure, more dangerous places before. She'd gotten into embassies, museums, *royal palaces* undetected, and no one knew anything was awry until she was long gone. Yet Marcus thought she needed what, his protection to successfully complete anything?

Yeah, right.

She already knew that their pseudo-relationship was going to be a problem, but now Naomi saw it for what it really was – a disaster. Marcus already had little professional respect for her, and now she'd gone and slept with him, shown him all of her weaknesses, *exposed* her emotionally raw self... and for *what*? Now he wanted to treat her like a helpless child, incapable of completing her assigned task.

This is exactly what you get for opening up to him.

Naomi stiffened when she felt his familiar weight, smelled his familiar scent as he approached her. Even with her eyes closed and ears plugged, she knew that it was Marcus who sat down beside her. For a while he said and did nothing, then Naomi felt a little tug as he pulled one of her earbuds out.

"Can I talk to you?"

She shrugged, but didn't look up. "Sure," she mumbled into her knees. "I'd love to hear more about how incompetent you think I am."

With a heavy sigh, Marcus pushed himself up, then pulled the other bud from her ear as he knelt in front of her. "Naomi, I do *not* think you're incompetent, I think you –"

"Can't handle myself? Can't work under pressure? Can't –"

"See the forest, because you're focused on a single tree. You're so stuck on Damien Wolfe that you can't be objective, and that's needed here, badly. You have tunnel-vision, set on killing this guy like you've been sanctioned for that, and I don't know that you're not being reckless, taking chances that maybe you shouldn't, thinking that you're indestructible and can't be caught."

"So what? You weren't concerned about me at that party."

"Not true," Marcus said, pushing her knees apart so he could get close. "I see you've got selective memory, because as *I* recall, it was a threat to "fuck up my face" that kept me from going up those stairs with you. Even when I didn't like you, I didn't want you by yourself, against men that could easily overpower you."

Naomi smirked. "So you *like* me now?"

"I'd pull you off a ledge if you were falling."

"Rescue me from a burning building?"

"No... Depends on how intense the fire was, what floor you were on... Probably... Yeah, I would."

"Why?" Naomi asked, the word coming out barely above a whisper as their eyes met.

"Because.... I don't want anything bad to happen to you."

"Because you like me."

"Because... *goddammit*, Naomi."

She held her breath as Marcus cupped her face, pulling her into one of his panty-wetting kisses before making his way to her ear. "This is your fault. All I wanted was to arrest a criminal, and you just *had* to be all bad-ass, and sexy, and smart, and interesting, and great in bed, and complicated... not at all what I thought you were. You're *worse*."

"Shut up," she said, shoving him back even though a smile played at the corners of her mouth. "You're no walk in the park yourself."

Marcus scoffed. "*Please.* I'm awesome."

"You're *awful*."

"You like it."

Naomi dropped her gaze, running a fingernail over the edge of her phone before she looked up again, chewing at her lip. "I do."

She closed her eyes as Marcus's lips grazed her neck, trailing kisses there, and over her chin before he took her mouth again.

"I *don't* think you're incompetent. I *know* you know how to handle yourself. I trust you to be as safe as you can.... and I *still* don't want you to do this, even though I know you're going to anyway. I'm concerned about your safety, and I don't really give a shit if you like it or not, I'm still gonna care."

Sighing, Naomi pressed her head into the wall behind her, meeting Marcus's gaze with a wry smile. "Marcus... what are we doing?"

He shrugged, then stood up, offering Naomi a hand up, which she accepted. "I was just trying to pass some good dick your way, you're the one who made it all complex."

"Oh God." Naomi sucked her teeth. "What if I said something like that to you? I was just trying to give you some good pus – never mind," she said, rolling her eyes at the smile that spread across Marcus's face.

The feeling that washed over her – pleasant, soothing warmth – when Marcus wrapped her in his arms was familiar now, but still strange. Quentin had hugged her countless times over the many years they'd known each other, but his embrace never felt as safe and secure as *this*.

Settled in his arms, Naomi's mind wandered to the information she was holding on to about Marcus's father. It was nagging at her that she should tell him, but after his little speech about objectivity... should she? Kendall and Renata were just helping, but at this point Marcus was considered part of their team. Wolfe had taken something from both of them, but Marcus didn't know. Because of that, he was able to balance her lust for revenge.

Naomi closed her eyes. She never, *ever* wanted Marcus to feel the kind of powerlessness or pain that had led her to his door that night.

"What did you think was gonna happen?" Marcus asked, with his face buried in her hair. "You thought you would share your body, your memories, and your deepest fears with me, and I was gonna what... not be affected by it? I let you cry in my arms, when I could have left you standing outside my door."

Naomi pulled back, turning her head up so that she could see into Marcus's eyes. She hoped to see a lie, some type of betrayal, *anything* but the transparent honesty she found, something that would stop her heart cold from flip-flopping in her chest. "Why didn't you?"

"Because," he said, placing a kiss on her forehead, "Like I said... you're not at all, what I thought you were."

ELEVEN
UNKNOWN

[COMMAND: open private chat]

painted_pixel: are you there?

…..............

CrawDaddy: yeah. wasn't expecting to hear from you anymore.

…........

painted_pixel: i freaked out a little, about you wanting to meet. you could have been a crazy person, or one of them, trying to test my loyalty.

CrawDaddy: i could still be.

painted_pixel: yeah right, quentin. we both know that's not true.

…........

painted_pixel: quentin, are you there? i still need help. they want me to do something that could get me put away for the rest of my life.

CrawDaddy: so what do you need from me?

painted_pixel: i need you to help me figure out how to make it LOOK like I did it, without doing it. and it has to be done in a way that she stays safe.

CrawDaddy: okay... hey, remember when we agreed to never try to find out who the other REALLY was?

painted_pixel: yeah...

CrawDaddy: when did you break that?

painted_pixel: what do you mean?

CrawDaddy: you called me quentin.

[USER: painted_pixel no longer exists. Aborting chat.]

MARCUS

MARCUS ALMOST FELT LIKE A CREEP, reclining in a chair by the window while he watched Naomi sleep. A few moments before, she'd shifted positions, and the sheet pulled away from her nude body, leaving her exposed from the navel up. It was kind of voyeuristic, just sitting there staring, but she was so *beautiful*, with the light from the window pouring in over her rich, deep brown skin, and even darker nipples that he was honestly mesmerized, and stuck in the moment.

This was his first time at her townhouse, further away from the busy, energetic vibe of the city. It was peaceful out here, quiet, but Marcus understood that the solitude was the very reason Naomi had revealed she never stayed a night here alone. If someone decided to take her, who would know? Marcus hated that she lived with that kind of private anxiety, while she had to outwardly appear so fearless.

206

But... none of that had a place in this moment. Right now, she was at peace, her face and body completely relaxed, opposed to the bunched eyebrows and clenched fists she sported in the midst of her grievously frequent nightmares. Beside him, his phone began to ring, buzzing and vibrating against his leg. A glance at the screen told him it was Meagan.

"What's up sis?" he asked quietly, standing up. He padded over to the bed, where he gently pulled the sheet up to cover his sleeping lover. Naomi stirred, and her eyes fluttered open in obvious alarm, darting around until they landed on Marcus. She relaxed, then smiled, her face returning to a neutral expression as she drifted back to sleep.

"Marcus, are you there?" Meagan's voice was mildly annoyed, but mostly amused as she sought Marcus's attention. "I've been talking for like, a whole minute and you haven't responded."

"Sorry, sis." Marcus gently closed the door behind him as he stepped into the hall, heading for the spacious living room. "Naomi is asleep, I was trying not to wake her up."

"Mmhmm. Listen to you sounding all... boyfriend-ish. I like it, Marcus. I like it a lot."

He took a seat on the couch, propping his bare feet up on the ottoman. "Shut up, Meg. What's going on?"

"Well... you know our birthday is coming up, right? We haven't decided what we're gonna do. Like... you haven't even mentioned it at all."

Marcus sighed. Every year, he and Meagan made a big deal of their birthday, doing some big, crazy, mildly-dangerous thing. It was a tradition their father started, predicated on guilt from working so much. He may not have been around as much as they liked throughout the year, but he *never* failed to show up – and *out* – for the twins' birthday. One of Marcus's worst memories was, just a few days after Kenneth Calloway's death, opening the newly-arrived plane tickets and reservations for a shark dive in the Caribbean sea. He and Meagan had taken the trip anyway, and gotten permission to spread their father's ashes in the ocean. Ever since, they'd kept the promise to each other to spend their birthday together, with the exception of times when it just wasn't possible, due to a case, or Meagan traveling to be with her husband.

It *still* haunted Marcus that the news of his father's death had come with very little information. Even now, as an FBI agent, the circumstances surrounding the shooting were kept sealed in a classified file, above Marcus's clearance level. The assurances that his father was a good man – which Marcus already knew – did little to soothe the sting of not even understanding *why* he was gone. But, Marcus knew well that death in the line of duty was an occupational hazard, one made increasingly more likely to happen to *him* thanks to his recently acquired duties, and forced team-up with Agent Barnes and Naomi.

"Skiing," Marcus said, forcing himself to focus on the conversation with his sister. "Sophie can stay with Aunt Kelly, it'll just be me and you, like old times."

Meagan sucked her teeth. "Ain't nobody trying to be cold on vacation. Are you crazy? I wanna go somewhere *sunny*. Maybe scuba-diving? Or snorkeling? You feeling up to another trip to Barbados? Trevor will be on leave, and you can bring Naomi. It can be a couple's trip."

Marcus smiled, thinking about that very first euphoric moment of being inside Naomi. "I *did* have a good time in Barbados," he agreed. But would Naomi even *consider* taking a real vacation, as his *real* girlfriend, with his very real family? Did he *want* to take that kind of trip with her? "Let me talk to her, and I'll let you know."

"*Soon*, Marcus, 'cause we have to plan. Sophie wants to talk to you."

Before Marcus could say anything else, his six-year-old niece was on the phone. "Uncle Marcus, are you and Madame Mimi gonna have a baby?"

"*Sophie, what kind of question is that? What the heck have you been watching on Disney channel?*" He heard Meagan asking in the background as she laughed.

"Um... We haven't discussed that, lil bit, but we definitely don't have any plans for that right now," Marcus said, chuckling. "What makes you ask?"

"Cause Kenzie's mommy is having a baby, and she said that's what people do when they like each other, and kiss and stuff. They have a baby."

Marcus lifted an eyebrow. "And stuff?"

"Yeah, like sitting on the same couch, and I don't wanna have a baby, so I don't think I should sit on a couch with a boy."

"Uncle Marcus doesn't either, baby girl," he said, trying to stifle his laughter as Meagan got back on the phone.

"*Ohhh-kay*, so I'm gonna be having a little *talk* with Kenzie's mommy, and no more sleepovers over there, I see."

Marcus chuckled. "Yeah, maybe not."

"Hmph. *Maybe*?" Even over the phone, Marcus knew Meagan was rolling her eyes. "Anyway, I'll let you get back to your new boo. Thought I'd catch you early, since I know you'll probably be there all day."

Laying his head back on the cushions, Marcus stared up at the ceiling. He probably *would* be there all day, and something about that felt very... settled. He was surprised that he didn't mind. "Yeah. Love you sis. Kiss my niece for me."

"Duh. Love you too. Bye."

After he hung up, Marcus ambled back to Naomi's bedroom. The slight hint of mint in the air told him she'd been up, and brushed her teeth before climbing back into the bed. Now, she was turned onto her side, burrowed underneath the sheets. Marcus lifted an eyebrow at the subtle movement of her arm underneath the covers. Was she...?

"Why are you in here playing with yourself like I'm not here, huh?" he asked, speaking the words into her ear as he slipped under the sheets behind her.

Naomi laughed, shifting positions so she was facing him. "I'm not playing with myself, fool, I was scratching my leg."

"Mmhmm. You don't have to be ashamed, Naomi, everybody does it."

"Shut up," she said, playfully punching his shoulder. "If I *was* doing that, I wouldn't be ashamed of getting caught. It's *my* body, I can touch it if I want."

"Damned right." Marcus smiled, flashing his dimples as he ran a hand over her bare leg. "As a matter of fact, you should do it right now. That would *really* show me."

Sucking her teeth, Naomi propped her leg up over Marcus's thigh, drawing herself closer. "You think I'm really gonna fall for that? You just want a show."

"Guilty as charged," he said, smacking himself on the chest. He reached down to caress her thigh. "I would *love* to watch you like that. *Can I* watch you like that?"

Naomi shrugged, averting her gaze as she blushed. "I've... nobody has ever seen me do that. I've never done it front of anyone."

Marcus pulled his head back. "You serious? Nobody has ever asked you to...?"

Again, she shrugged, this time pulling her lip between her teeth before she answered. "I've been asked, and always declined. To me... it's just a very, *very* intimate thing, which probably sounds kind of odd, if you're sleeping with someone, but... I don't know, that's just *different* to me. Really personal."

Marcus nodded. "You don't have to justify that, not with me. No pressure. If you're not comfortable sharing something like that, you're just not."

"I didn't say that." She kept her eyes locked with his as she pulled back the sheets, then rolled onto her back, slipping her hand between her legs. She closed them briefly, biting her lip when she first made contact, then blushed again as she pulled her gaze away to watch herself. Marcus had his eyes on the same thing as he sat up to watch – her slim, soft fingers as they slipped and slid through the folds of her sex, then disappeared inside her body.

She seemed unsure at first, glancing up at him like she was wondering if this was what he expected. If she asked, he would tell her it wasn't. This was *better.*

Naomi closed her eyes, and after that, very quickly seemed to forget he was even there. Marcus moved so that he was in front of her, situated between her open legs. She stroked herself with two fingers, and strummed herself with her thumb as she used her other hand to roll her nipple between her fingers. The sensual aroma of her arousal was driving him crazy, but he looked on without touching as he grew hard. *Goddamnit*, he wanted to touch her so bad, but she seemed so lost in her self-pleasure that he didn't dare presume she would welcome his touch.

She serenaded him with quiet whimpers and moans of pleasure as she rolled her hips against her fingers, burrowing deeper, spreading her legs wider as her movements grew frantic. Her mouth dropped open as her thumb moved faster, and her chest began to heave as she pushed further, taking herself higher, and higher until her entire body tensed, but her hand kept moving until she let out a sound that was half moan, half gasp, half scream, half whimper, and *all* music to Marcus's ears.

This was *easily* the most beautiful, sexiest thing he'd ever witnessed. He was rock hard, *aching* to be inside of her, but he waited until her breathing evened before he leaned forward, kissing the inside of her knee. She shivered in response, which Marcus took as permission to keep going, trailing kisses along the inside of her thigh until he reached what was, in that moment, *heaven.*

Marcus took her hand, licking her sweetness from her fingers before he covered her with his mouth, imbibing the sweet remnants of her orgasm. She arched away from the bed, biting her lip to stifle a moan as he dipped his tongue inside, then kissed her sensitive peak before covering it with his mouth and sucking hard.

He kissed his way over her flat belly, up to her breasts, then licked a path to her neck. "I'm trying to figure out why you taste so good." he said, resting on his elbow as he cupped her chin in his hand. She smiled coyly, then lifted her mouth for a kiss. Marcus obliged, grinning against her mouth when she laved her tongue against his.

"I *do* taste good, don't I?"

Chuckling, Marcus positioned himself, then pushed inside of her. "You do," he murmured into her ear. "And you *feel* good too."

Naomi smiled, draping her arms over his shoulders as he began to stroke her in a slow, steady pace. Marcus closed his eyes, groaning in satisfaction as she lifted her hips to meet his, easily falling in step with his rhythm. He *loved* that she was always so into the act. There was no "laying there and taking it" for Naomi, she was present with him, fully engaged, as committed as he was to making sure they both enjoyed the moment.

"Marcus," she moaned, her voice sultry and low. "*You* feel good."

"Whaaat?" he grinned. "I *finally* get my props? About time I get some damned recognition around here."

She lifted her legs, crossing them around his waist as she cupped his head, pulling him down for another kiss. "Yes, Agent Calloway, I will give you your credit. You finally caught *Jolie Voleuse*.... but I don't think this is agency protocol."

"You're right," Marcus said, eliciting a squeal of pleasure from Naomi as he pushed deeper, increasing his pace. "You should be cuffed right now."

Naomi lifted an eyebrow. "Go get them."

Marcus paused, taking a moment to just look at her. *Damn* he loved when she was like this, happy and carefree. "We'll grab them for the next round."

MARCUS BOUNCED into the FBI field office feeling light on his feet. He and Naomi had spent the weekend together as he'd hoped, making love and eating in bed, then making love again.

Perfect day, he thought, taking a seat at his desk. That euphoria didn't last long, as he began digging into the mountain of neglected paperwork in front of him. Kendall and Renata were engaged in similar tasks, and it wasn't until late in the afternoon that they were able to step away to chat.

Kendall and Renata were *his* people. SSA Black may have been supervisor, but Marcus was the leader of their team. They were heading into their first job with Barnes's team, and he wanted to be sure they were in a good headspace.

"You know I'm good, bruh," Kendall said, shrugging as he leaned against the wall. They were tucked into a quiet corner near the window, overlooking the city. "They seem solid, and Naomi is bad-ass. I don't think they're even gonna need me, but I'll be ready with you in case we need to bust in. But... you know this is... kind of a complication, right? Have you mentioned…?"

Marcus shook his head. The "complication" only mattered if things went wrong, and he was praying they wouldn't. He and Kendall would be serving as security, even though Naomi would be going in alone. If anything popped off, he and Kendall would be the first ones through that gate. "I'll worry about that later. What about you, Renata?"

He turned to his pretty coworker, who pursed her lips with a shrug. "It's fine, I guess. I think we'll pull it off. It just … I guess I have to get used to working with that team."

"You mean working with the Cajun, *cher*?" Kendall teased, with a poor imitation of a Creole accent.

Renata blushed, then muttered, "Shut up, Kendall."

Shaking his head, Marcus smiled as he clapped his team members on the shoulders. "I just needed to know that I wasn't sending you guys to the wolves. If y'all are good... I'm good."

Kendall nodded, then headed back to his desk, but Renata held back, grabbing Marcus's arm. "Hey," she said, running her tongue over her lips as she fidgeted with the edge of the folder clutched in her other hand. "Um... I remember you telling me before that the file on your father's death was classified, right?"

Marcus lifted an eyebrow. "Uh... yeah. Why?"

Renata averted her gaze, taking a deep breath. "Well... I... um.... When I hacked Quentin the other day, I mimicked some of his files onto my hard drive. After that little... disagreement with you and Naomi, I was curious about the deaths of her mother and father, and... so, I looked into it, and Quentin had some information that may explain why your father's file was sealed."

Marcus cocked his eyebrow further, shaking his head in confusion. "Ren... I'm not following you here. What do the deaths of Naomi's parents have to do with the death of my father?"

The glossiness in Renata's eyes brought a lump to Marcus's throat, followed quickly by a sense of dread as she held the folder out to him. Reluctantly, he took it from her hands and flipped it open, his eyes skimming frantically over the information on the page. When his eyes fell on the report from the crime scene, his heart dropped into stomach as he read the names of the two other men that had died with his father.

He barely reacted to Renata's comforting hand covering his, and barely heard the soothing tone of her voice.

"Marcus... I am *so* sorry."

NAOMI.

JAB. Jab. Hook. Jab. Hook. Jab Jab.

"Naomi... I need to talk to you."

Naomi looked up, stopping mid-swing to see Marcus standing at the door to the office she shared with Quentin. Sympathy flooded her at the sight of his tense shoulders and clenched jaw.

Must not have been a good day at the field office, she thought as she stood, smiling brightly in an effort to improve his mood.

He didn't smile back.

As Naomi drew closer, she realized that he wasn't just scowling. He was scowling at *her*.

"Marcus... is everything … okay?"

He chuckled dryly, crossing his arms. "No. No, it's really not. I knew you would do anything to get to

Damien Wolfe, but I would *love* for you to explain why you didn't think I needed to know he killed *my* father too."

Coldness hit Naomi right in the pit of her stomach. She licked her suddenly dry lips, feeling lightheaded and dizzy as she tried to think of a way to respond. "Marcus... I... I didn't—"

"Don't you dare try to tell me you didn't know, when Renata took this file off *his* computer," Marcus spat, jabbing a finger in Quentin's direction.

Naomi held up her gloved hands in a calming gesture. She tried to touch them to his chest, but Marcus pulled away, turning his angry glare back to her. She lifted an eyebrow. Was he really this upset with her? "If you'll just let me explain –"

"Explain what? What bullshit reason do you have for keeping this from me?"

She shook her head, trying again – unsuccessfully – to gain a physical connection before he broke away. "It's not bullshit, Marcus. You said it yourself, *somebody* needs to be objective here. We're so close to finishing this, and I thought if I told you, you wouldn't be able to stay grounded."

Marcus scoffed. "And you thought that was *your* choice to make? Really?"

"I didn't think –"

"*Exactly!*" Marcus exclaimed, taking a step forward, nostrils flared as he bore down on Naomi. She backed away as he advanced, and tried to pull from her fearlessness reserves, but truthfully, she was terrified, and it had nothing to do with thinking Marcus was going to do her physical harm. "You didn't think about *me*, because all you think about is yourself. *Your* pain, *your* bad memories, *your* revenge. Did you think for one damned second that *hmm,* maybe Marcus has a right to know that Wolfe took his family as well? *Did you!?*"

Naomi's back hit the wall, but Marcus took another step, getting right in her face. "When I was comforting you, letting you cry on my shoulder, it *never* occurred to you that it wasn't okay to keep that from me?"

"Yes, it did," Naomi insisted as she clumsily removed her gloves in the small space between them. Swallowing past the hard lump in her throat, she fought hard to hold back a quickly building well of tears as she stared up at his face. "Marcus, I didn't want to tell you because I know how much it hurts. I don't want you to feel like I feel. To feel helpless."

She reached for his hands, but he roughly batted her away, shaking his head.

"Marcus, *please.*"

"Please? *Please*? Naomi, *please miss me with the bullshit*. You weren't concerned about me. You were concerned that if I knew, I would fuck up your grand plan for revenge, since *your* plan is the only damned thing that matters!" He took the last step toward her, his finger pointing dangerously close to her face before he was suddenly yanked backward.

"What the fuck is the problem, bruh?" Quentin asked, stepping between them and shoving Marcus away.

"Motherfucker, mind your business," Marcus growled, returning Quentin's push.

Quentin shoved Marcus back again. Fists clenched, shoulders squared, he said, "She *is* my business, and I wanna know what you planned to do, runnin' up in her face witcha voice raised. I already told you that's not a problem you want, Calloway."

Oh God, Naomi thought, scrubbing her hand over her face as she looked frantically back and forth between the two. This was *all* bad. "Guys, can you not –"

"I'm just trying to fucking talking to her," Marcus said through clenched teeth as he approached again.

Quentin shrugged, not backing down. "Looked like more than talkin' to me, when she's backed into a wall. If that's the kinda talkin' you wanna do, you talk to *me*. What's the problem?"

"The problem is that for *fifteen* fucking years I haven't been able to get any answers about my father. I come on this team to *help* you, to work with you, and I can't even have the fucking courtesy of full disclosure?

On *this*? Like I said, I guess *my* feelings about this are irrelevant. Your revenge is the only thing that matters."

"It's not," Naomi said, shaking her head frantically as tears finally broke free, spilling over her cheeks. "*You* matter. Marcus..."

"*Bullshit*," Marcus bellowed, charging in Naomi's direction. Quentin intervened again, catching Marcus by the collar as Kendall and Agent Barnes stepped in, both of their eyes widened in alarm.

Quentin shoved Marcus in Kendall's direction, and the other agent caught him by the arms, holding him back. "Bruh, you can *talk* from over *there*."

Marcus scoffed, snatching away from Kendall before swiping a hand over his face. Looking past Quentin, he aimed his words at Naomi. "You know... I would have expected this before... Before things changed between us. Would have expected you to be keeping shit from me, because you didn't owe me anything, but then you opened up, and.... this is what I get?" he stopped, looking toward the ceiling as he shook his head. "I'm *done*. Should have left your ass outside that night."

With that, he turned and walked out, slamming the door behind him. Naomi flinched, clutching her chest as a deep, intense ache swept through her, taking her breath away. Avoiding the eyes of the people in the room, Naomi picked up her boxing gloves, shoving them back over hands.

I should have left your ass outside that night.

Maybe he should have. If he had, perhaps her walls would have still been intact, and she wouldn't feel like she felt now, like her chest was being ripped in two.

Could you have been any more stupid, Naomi?

Probably not. Definitely not. This feeling now, this terrible, devastating mixture of hurt, and anger, and... *guilt* could have been avoided if she'd continued in the manner she *knew* got the results she was looking for. If she'd just kept everything to herself, Marcus wouldn't feel like she *owed* him anything. They were coworkers, not friends, not lovers, not.... anything else. Or at least... not anymore.

Diligence. Focus. Agility.

Naomi attacked the bag with fury, no holding back. Even if she broke or bruised something, it couldn't hurt any worse than how she felt now. How... *she* felt. Was Marcus right? Was it selfish of her to not give him information that would – *did* – devastate him? What was accomplished now that he knew? Was he any better off?

Diligence. Focus. Agility.

She put all of her strength into the next punch, imagining Wolfe's face there instead of the smooth black leather of the bag. Maybe it *was* selfish. Maybe Marcus *did* deserve to know, but what made that *her* problem? Naomi had been working on this since before they met. The first four years with the FBI, Barnes had held her back, clipped her wings. When he was finally letting her free, finally thought she was ready, Marcus had bumbled along, screwing things up, forcing them to include him in their plans, just to keep her cover from being blown. *He* messed things up, not her.

"Mimi," Quentin said, grabbing her by the shoulders. "You gonna hurt yourself, cher."

Naomi shook her head, squeezing her eyes tight as her heart raced. She choked back a sob as she pushed him away, then took a deep breath.

Diligence. Focus. Agility.

She repeated it over and over in her head, until she felt the words. She threw one blow, then another, mentally chanting those words in time with her punches until even through the gloves, her fists were sore.

Diligence. Focus. Agility.

Marcus was right. Nothing else mattered.

TWELVE
NAOMI

"NAOMI... ARE THOSE *BRUISES*?!"

Cursing under her breath, Naomi hurriedly yanked her slim, fitted pants over her legs as Inez entered the room. She was trying to hide the deep purple splotches that covered her ankles and lower legs from another morning going harder than she should in her classroom. She'd turned on the light that negated the effect of the two way mirror, making the room hidden from outside view, and locked the door. She turned her music up full blast, and danced with abandon until her recklessness had caused enough missteps and tumbles that she decided to stop before she *really* hurt herself.

Now, she was fresh from the private shower in she and Quentin's office, using the tiny changing room to dress in her outfit for the job — slim, comfortable black pants that gave her full range of motion, and had enough pockets to hold whatever little gadgets she might need, a black tank top, and the Kevlar-paneled black jacket that Quentin insisted she wear. She'd forgotten to lock *that* door, and now Inez had barged in, with a concerned expression that let Naomi know she'd been talking to Quentin, and was coming to check on her.

Why? Naomi had no idea.

The only people she was a danger to were Damien Wolfe and possibly Marcus, if the strangely persistent, debilitating ache in her chest didn't go away soon. No matter how hard she tried to clear him from her mind, his angry parting words echoed in her head.

"Naomi… what the hell is going on?" Inez took the last few steps into the room, taking Naomi by the hands. Naomi rolled her eyes, grudgingly allowing herself to be pulled into a seat on the padded bench.

"My God, Inez." Naomi shrugged into her jacket, and zipped it. "You're acting like I need an intervention or something. Yes, they're bruises. I just took a few spills in my classroom — it's not a big deal."

Inez lifted a groomed eyebrow. "You hurting yourself is not a big deal?"

"Don't be dramatic Nez." Naomi stood up, reaching for the door before Inez caught her by the hand.

"Hey… I want you to think about this, okay? *Carefully*. Are you sure you want to do this today?"

Naomi scoffed. *Of course* she didn't want to do this today. She didn't want to do this *ever*. None of it. If she could run off to some remote place, where she could dance and have hot sex and live in peace for the rest of her life, she would. But she could barely even see the sky with the dark cloud of Damien Wolfe hanging heavy over her.

It would be so much simpler to put a bullet in his head from a distance, but not nearly as satisfying. Naomi hadn't *always* wanted Wolfe's blood. For a long time, her memory of that night had been fuzzy, like she was seeing it through a frosty window. She wasn't clear on who pulled the trigger, couldn't hear the garbled words in her head, but three years ago, she'd come very close to taking a bullet herself, courtesy of an over-zealous security guard at a museum. That night was the first time she had the nightmare, triggered by the ear-splitting sound of a gunshot piercing the wall just inches from where she was hidden.

Before, she was content. Somewhat lonely, but settled well into her double-life, not even thinking about Damien Wolfe on a daily basis. But once the picture became clear, she couldn't un-know what she'd learned, and it took her back to the place of a 16 year old girl, watching the slaughter of her father by the same hand that had violated her mother, and something just... *snapped.*

So she was patient. She would play the role of a good little special agent, helping take down an organized crime boss, and when she'd successfully gotten close to Wolfe... she would just kill him instead.

"It's not about if I *want* to do it, Inez. I don't really have a choice."

Inez sucked her teeth. "Of course you have a choice. You don't have to do anything you don't want to do."

Shaking her head, Naomi leaned against the door. "You don't understand what it's like, knowing that there's someone out there who means you harm, and has the ability to do it with basically no repercussions."

"You wanna run that by me again, amiga?" Inez asked, propping her hand on her hip. "Because last I checked, I spent a couple of years getting my ass kick—"

"I know, Inez." Naomi held up her hands in a soothing, conciliatory gesture. "I'm sorry. I'm just—"

"Being a bitch because you're nervous about the job, and your head is messed up about Marcus? I'll allow it. *This time.*"

Naomi rolled her eyes. "I'm not even thinking about Marcus. He's... irrelevant."

"Hmphm. Since when?"

"Since he said he was done." Naomi shrugged. "I mean... how was I supposed to know that he was messed up about his dad? He never talked, he never opened up to *me*. He let me do all the spilling, and then he used my pain as a weapon against me."

"Because he's hurting himself, Mimi. You should try to talk to him."

"And say *what*?"

Inez placed her finger against her chin, sending her thick hair swinging to the side as she tilted her head. "Umm... I don't know, maybe start with an apology, and go from there?"

"An apology for *what*?" Naomi asked, crossing her arms. "I don't owe Marcus anything. It's not like we... it's not as if..."

"Not like... what? Not as if... what? Not like you've talked my ear off about him *many* times in the last few months. Not like he sexed you so good it made you wanna cry and fix the man a Sunday dinner – your words, remember? Not as if I didn't *see* how concerned he was about your safety last week at this table. Not as if I've *ever* heard such happiness in your voice like when you told me about him taking care of you that night you showed up at his place."

Naomi laughed dryly. "But it doesn't matter, does it? Because as I'm sure Quentin probably told you, Marcus wishes he had left me out there that night. He wishes we'd never connected, that I'd never darkened his door with my problems. I'll just... leave him alone... Which is what I should have done in the first place." Naomi looked away, swallowing hard in an attempt to wet her suddenly dry throat.

"Maybe if you explained where you were coming from –"

"I tried. He called it bullshit."

Inez sighed. "Really? You *tried*? I've always known you to make your point get across. You don't *try* Naomi, you *do*."

"I *couldn't.*" Naomi shook her head, trying to clear away the vivid of image of the hurt and anger in Marcus's eyes. "I felt the passion when we were intimate, felt the emotion in his eyes when he looked at me, but yesterday when he was screaming in my face, I felt *none* of that. It was just... *gone*, and it was like... that just paralyzed me, you know? I... I let him turn a little crack in my armor into a canyon, and I poured out. I told him everything, showed him *all* of me, and it meant nothing."

She stopped to swipe the tears from her cheeks with her thumbs, then shrugged. "Initially, yeah... I just didn't want him messing anything up. It was selfish, I can admit that, but at the same time... I'm doing a job here. *Everything* about this mission is need-to-know, and I couldn't see how he needed to know. Quentin and I were already emotionally involved, and Marcus balanced that. If he was going to be part of the team, he needed to be objective."

"So you were being professional?"

"At first," Naomi nodded. "But then... once he and I got closer, I *wanted* to tell him, but... Living with that kind of baggage... it changes you. It *haunts* you, and I didn't want to do that to him. I didn't want to impose that kind of anger, and trauma, and powerlessness on him, not just for the sake of telling him. I don't see how he can be *so* angry without even hearing me out. I didn't even know it was bothering him!"

"But *he* knows, Naomi. You have to try to see this from his point of view... he's been hurting for information about his father for all of these years, wanting to know what happened and why... and then he finds out that someone he cares for *has* the information he's been lacking. Can't you see how that would be like a punch to the gut... and a knife to the back?"

At first, Naomi shook her head, but then a sick feeling hit the pit of her stomach as she realized that... yes, she *did* see how Marcus could feel betrayed.

"Naomi... despite how *you* feel about it, Marcus deserves to know the truth — that his father died trying to take down a really bad guy – the same thing we're doing here now. I know you say he won't listen, but you have to call, leave a voice mail, text him, email... he needs to hear the whole story. He needs to hear that you just were trying to do your job, even if it was self-serving. He needs to hear that at some point, your feelings changed. He needs to hear that you cared enough to not want to hurt him. I mean... wouldn't you want the same thing?"

Slowly, Naomi nodded. "Yeah... I guess I would."

Both women flinched, startled by a sudden knock against the door. Naomi stepped back, and Inez swung the door open to be met with a smile from Kendall. "I don't mean to interrupt, ladies, but... we need to start this briefing. Job's in less than two hours."

"Of course," Inez said, straightening her posture as she flipped her hair over her shoulder and propped her hands on her hips. Her stance called attention to her fit-but-curvy frame – courtesy of her Afro-Latina heritage – and Naomi grinned through the last of her tears at the appreciative sweep Kendall gave her.

This wasn't the first time Naomi had noticed little hints that they were "feeling" each other. In their team meetings, Inez would pick at her nails, pretending to be unaffected by the raw masculinity and power oozing off Kendall. But, having known her longer than anyone at the table, Naomi knew the deal. Full, glossed lip pulled between her teeth, constantly shifting in her seat, playing with and tugging at her thick ponytail... Inez was *very* interested in Kendall Williams, as far as Naomi could tell. Every time he spoke, in a deep, sonorous tenor, Inez's hand went to her throat, as if she were quite literally "clutching her pearls".

Naomi cleared her throat. "We'll be right out," she said, lifting an eyebrow at Inez and Kendall's reluctance to give her their attention.

"Okay." Kendall finally tore his gaze away from Inez long enough to acknowledge Naomi. "But... seriously, we need to get on it. We're one man short."

"What?" Inez's expression returned to a serious frown. "Who isn't showing up?"

Avoiding Naomi's eyes, Kendall delivered his answer with what seemed to be carefully measured words. "Marcus. Nobody can get in touch with him."

TYPICALLY, Naomi felt a wide range of emotions going into a job. Her feelings ranged from complete confidence to near-anxiety, but she was always controlled, always prepared, always... diligent, focused, and agile-minded.... but not this time. This time, Naomi felt... *off*.

Thanks to a keen observation from Quentin, she knew that in exactly two minutes from.... *now*, the security cameras would move, sweeping the area once before they settled into a new position. Each time they switched, it created a *tiny* blind spot, and she had to make sure she was there at the right times.

She took a deep breath.

She wondered what Marcus was doing.

It had been all eyes on her when, just an hour ago, they'd all sat at the roundtable, doing their best to reconfigure the plan. Marcus was MIA, and even though no one was saying it, Naomi knew they were thinking it. This was *her* fault.

Inez asked again if Naomi were sure she wanted to do the job tonight, but if they didn't, it would ruin everything. The party for Wolfe's daughter was coming up in less than a week, and after that, all hell would probably break loose. It would absolutely *not* be in their favor for Rochas to still not be in possession of those diamonds. A manufactured double-cross wouldn't work without *proof*, and Lucas had the proof they needed. This job was happening, with or without Marcus in tow.

It wasn't just her, either. After he'd been practically worshiping at her feet since he met her, Quentin was suddenly being very standoffish with Renata. Not to the point that he was rude – that wasn't Quentin's style anyway – but he was definitely keeping his distance. When asked, he brushed Naomi off, told her everything was fine, and assured her that he was ready to do his job. His raised eyebrow asked whether she could say the same.

Of course she *could*, and she *did*, but saying so didn't make it true. Maybe if he'd picked up, instead of sending her straight to voicemail when she'd snuck away to call him right after the meeting, Naomi wouldn't feel quite so unsettled. Coldness, or another verbal battle, *anything* would have been better than the radio silence he was giving her, and apparently everyone else attached to the case.

"Can't dwell on it, Mimi," she muttered under her breath. Her timer bracelet, the gadget she hated and loved most, was telling her that she only had fifteen seconds

before she needed to move, and it would take her thirty to get to the next blind spot.

Diligence. Focus. Agility.

Naomi took off at a run, suddenly regretting the beating she'd given herself in the classroom that morning. Her legs were burning and aching, her body reacting sluggishly to her efforts to get to where she needed to be before her bracelet buzzed again.

She pushed, then pushed harder, willing her legs to *please* move faster. The silver band vibrated against her wrist, and then *one, two, three* seconds later, she was in position, clinging against the wall as her chest heaved, not with exertion, but with anxiety and adrenaline.

She was caught.

Naomi closed her eyes, taking a deep inhale as the bracelet vibrated again. Should she keep going, hoping that her slip-up had been missed by a guard, praying that even though Quentin and Renata had been unable to hack the security feed, maybe they could scrub her presence from it later?

The bracelet vibrated once more.

Maybe it was better to turn back, get the hell out of there before she ran right into a trap. The security was no joke – their intel had made that abundantly clear. She probably *had* been seen. Her phone vibrated against her thigh, and she silently cursed herself for not turning it off. Without pulling it out to look at it, she felt for the power button through her jeans and held it to shut the phone down.

Again, the buzzing at her wrist only amplified Naomi's racing heart. If she *had* been seen, she probably wasn't getting back off the property as easily as she'd entered. And if that were the case...

Naomi shot away from the wall as the bracelet signaled the passing of another two minutes. She was nearly at her checkpoint when the first fifteen-second notification went off. *Yes,* she thought to herself. *No more mistakes.*

And then she hit the ground. One moment, her feet were underneath her, and then she was crashing to her hands and knees, slipping in a wet patch on the grass. Naomi caught herself quickly and shot to her feet, colliding with the wall just as her bracelet told her time was up.

She fought the urge to cry as she steeled herself for the last sprint. Her pants were intact, but from the throbbing pain radiating up and down her legs, she was sure she'd busted at least one of her knees, and her wrist didn't feel much better.

Shit. Shit shit shit shit shit. Shit!

Naomi took another deep breath. She had exactly one minute to pull it together. She closed her eyes.

Diligence. Focus. Agility. Diligence. Focus. Agility. Diligence. Focus. Agility.

She opened her eyes. "Okay. No Pain. No Fear."

Naomi sprinted away from the wall, her eyes focused on that final checkpoint – a little walled alcove just across from the kitchen entrance. She thought about nothing except making it there, reminded herself that her life depended on doing so. She touched the brick lined wall with seven seconds to spare.

While her breathing settled, Naomi pulled a thin, stainless steel contraption from one of her pockets. To her, the thing looked no more sophisticated than one of those crappy portfolio calculators they gave away at the bank, but Quentin had been so proud to put the thing in her hands that she clamped her mouth shut and stayed quiet.

"This is your house key, cher," he'd said with a grin. He'd also given her instructions on how to use it, but Naomi still put in her earbud and pressed the small button on the outside that would connect her directly to Quentin.

She bit back her sigh of relief at the sound of his low drawl. It was comforting to her ears in a way it hadn't been in a while.

"Mimi, what the hell is going on? Are you okay?"

Naomi sighed. So they'd seen the security feeds. "Yeah... I'll be fine. You were able to get into the cameras?"

"Yeah, and good thing we were, because you would have been –"

"I *know.*"

"You've gotta pull it together, cher."

"I *know.*" Naomi took a deep breath then pushed it out, reminding herself that now wasn't the time to get testy, especially when he was just concerned about her. "Quentin... tell me how to use this thing so I can get inside."

Even over the phone, Naomi could feel his hesitation. "Are you sure, Mimi? We don't have to take this further. We've got control of the cameras, we can get you out of there, regroup when you're not..."

"No." Naomi squared her shoulders, allowing her gaze to dart around the hidden alcove. "If you've got the cameras, that's even *more* reason to do this. I'm going to the door."

Without waiting for Quentin to respond, she darted over to the plain, unassuming metal door that would lead her inside. Following Quentin's reluctant instructions, Naomi slid the back from the device, freeing the cords that she needed to connect to the side of the alarm box. She watched as the screen came to life, running through a random combination of numbers before one by one, they flashed from bright, *stop-right-here* red to *you're-all-clear* green.

Naomi didn't realize she was holding her breath until locks inside the door slid apart with a quiet snap. The silence in her ear told her Quentin was gone. From here on, it was up to her to get where she needed to be, while Quentin and Renata overrode the motion detectors to keep her from setting off alarms in the empty house. Naomi didn't need to be reminded that she was running on a tight schedule, or that it was gravely important that she stay properly timed. No more fuck-ups.

She stayed close to the walls, moving carefully as she hurried through the house. She relied on the signals from her wrist band, and the schedule in her memory to guide her up the stairs, down a hall, and into the office where Victor Lucas kept his private computer.

Naomi tapped her earbud again, connecting herself to Quentin as she pulled a flash drive from her pocket. "You ready?" she asked, positioning it above the glowing USB port.

"We're ready."

Naomi pushed the drive in.

From the long nights they'd spent at that table, going over these plans, Naomi knew that as soon as she connected that drive to the computer, she and her entire team were targets. While Quentin suppressed the network security that would alert the system of unauthorized access, Renata would be battling the decryption worm that was already working to break into the team's network.

There was nothing for Naomi to do except wait, while the drive did its job of transporting the files into the cloud. She was only waiting so that she could take the drive with her, leaving no traces that anything was amiss. When the light on the drive switched from red to blue, signifying that it was done, Naomi snatched it from the computer, powered the computer down, and shoved the drive into one of her zippered pockets.

She wouldn't experience the full pleasure of relief until she was out of the house, off Victor Lucas's property, but she felt much lighter as she headed for the door of the office. Carefully, Naomi pulled it open, peeking out before she stepped into the hall. Almost immediately, she felt a sense of deja-vu, her mind traveling back to the night of the job in Barbados. *That* thought brought about a graphic flash of what had happened later that night, and the vivid memory of Marcus pushing his way inside of her for the first time.

Naomi shivered.

Not the time. So, so, not the time.

Shaking her head, she headed stealthily down the hall, freezing in alarm when she heard the distinct sound of voices coming from around the corner.

Shit.

The house was supposed to be empty, for Lucas's weekly jaunt to a high-end gentleman's club in the city. Apparently, he'd decided to turn things into a private party, because as Naomi sank into an alcove to hide, she caught a glimpse of Lucas, two friends that she recognized from surveillance photos, plus one whose face she couldn't see. The sight of the men made Naomi's blood run cold, and the two heavyset security guards behind then turned it to ice. They were flanked by scantily-clad, giggling women carrying bottles of expensive alcohol.

Diligence. Focus. Agility.

Think, Naomi.

They had a plan for this, and she knew it, if only the synapses in her brain would start firing. The men were heading into Lucas's "fun" room, which according to the surveillance pictures was an eclectic mix of pool tables, flat screen TVs and stripper poles. Once they were in there, they would be occupied with their drinking and playing and fucking and whatever other debauchery they planned to get into.

Problem was, the security guards didn't go inside. They stood on either side of the door, watching the hallway, which gave Naomi extremely limited choices on getting past. Limited, meaning one.

She dropped to her sore, tender knees, cringing as she placed her weight down on them. Changing her mind, she balanced herself on her hands and toes, using that awkward stance to make it down the hall, hidden by the half-wall that served as a barrier between the second floor and the open alcove below it.

Naomi made it back to the office, positive that she hadn't been seen and immediately tapped the button on her earbud.

"*Quentin,*" she hissed, pacing with her hands propped on her hips. "*There are people in the house now. I need you to guide me out.*"

"Quentin can't hear you, *cher.* Signal blocker... keeps the strippers from putting compromising pictures on social media."

Naomi spun on her heels to find Tomiko sitting in the darkness on the other side of the office. While Naomi watched, the other woman stood, sliding her arms out of the silky white kimono-style robe she wore to reveal a sports bra and boy shorts underneath.

A vein twitched at Naomi's temple, and her nostrils flared as she clenched her fists. "Tomiko... how awful to see you."

"Does Quentin still say that all the time? *Cher.* That always annoyed me, not just from him though. All of those Cajun's, with that *terrible* accent, *cher* this, and *cher* that, like they were punctuating their damned sentences with it. Drove me nuts." Tomiko smiled, reaching up to tighten the messy bun in her hair.

Naomi didn't take her eyes off her. She knew how Tomiko operated, lulling you into a false sense of security before she attacked. She was well-versed in that particular brand of betrayal. Tomiko stretched her arms high over her head, showing off well-defined abs and a slight hint of the tattoo that she'd gotten with Naomi holding her hand for support – ballet slippers, with the ribbons tied at the top. Underneath, the nickname "Ballet Royale" was spelled out in inky-black script, branding Tomiko with the name she'd given herself all those years ago, back when she, Quentin, and Naomi were a team.

Now, Naomi watched her with caution. Their friendship was long expired, and Naomi knew from experience that Tomiko was a dangerous enemy to underestimate.

"You used to like it," Naomi said, lowering her voice to a bored register that contradicted the adrenaline pumping in her veins. "As *I* remember it... you used to practically melt over that little creole twang of his. You wanted Quentin pretty damned bad. What changed?"

Tomiko gave a dry laugh, her expression dropping into a sneer as she responded. "*I* changed. I met a *real* man, and I got over my silly crush on a *boy* who would rather chat with geeks than have a little fun with a *real, live, woman.* Too damned bad, too. What a *waste* of sexiness." She shrugged. "Who knows... maybe I can convince my big daddy to let him stay alive after this. I could use a new boy toy."

"I bet you could. What are you doing here, Royale?"

"I don't use that name anymore," Tomiko said, taking a step closer to Naomi, who remained where she was, visually calm, but ready to swing. "Too reminiscent of that dark period in my life where I aligned myself with the serfs – that's you and Quentin. Tomiko works just fine."

Naomi rolled her eyes. "Girl... whatever. Answer the question. You working for these people now? Is that why you were in Barbados?"

Laughing, Tomiko took another step forward, and Naomi still didn't back down. "Ah, Naomi... you're not in a position to ask questions, are you? I belong here... you don't. So what are *you* doing here?"

"You know I'm not answering that."

Tomiko smiled. "Oh... well... okay then. I guess I'll just have to *beat* it out of you."

She was *much* faster than Naomi remembered. Before she could blink, Tomiko was on her, aiming lightning-fast kicks and punches directly at Naomi's head. Naomi was expecting it, and easily dodged the blows, one after another until Tomiko slipped up, leaving herself open for Naomi to send a jab flying into her jaw.

The blow made Tomiko stagger backwards, and Naomi took full advantage of the chance to hammer Tomiko with punches. The two women fought toe to toe, each landing lucky, inconsistent blows until finally, Naomi shoved Tomiko to the floor. Straddling her chest, Naomi wrapped her hands around her neck, pressing her thumbs into the delicate flesh at her throat.

Tomiko caught her with a punch, her ringed fingers splitting Naomi's cheek. Rage flushed her chest, but Naomi kept herself controlled, briefly releasing her hold to pin Tomiko's arms under her legs before she took her by the throat again. A sick sense of satisfaction swept over Naomi as she watched Tomiko struggle for breath.

"I've imagined doing this for a *long* time," Naomi whispered, leaning forward to look Tomiko right in her terrified eyes as she kicked her legs and gasped for air. "I'm really just toying with you now... your ass could be dead already, and it would be *exactly* what you deserved for what you did to me, bitch. We were *friends*. I've never been anything but good to you, and you stabbed me in the back. *I. Want. You. To. Die.*"

With each word, Naomi pressed harder, and Tomiko's breath came less and less easily, until she closed her eyes, and didn't open them again. Naomi forced herself to release the pressure on Tomiko's windpipe. Chest heaving, she sat back, then swiped at the blood dripping from the open cuts on her cheek. She climbed off Tomiko, resisting the urge to kick her unconscious frame as she reached for the discarded robe.

Naomi pressed layers of the fabric against her face, trying to stem the bleeding as she searched her mind for an out. Her earbud had been dislodged in the struggle, and there was no way she could devote time to searching the room for the tiny device. She would have to get out on her own.

She turned to the door, stopping to look down at the wired pads that were suddenly attached to her thigh. "What the fu –"

A sense of helplessness washed over her. Her nerves were on fire, and even though she didn't exactly feel pain, she couldn't move. She was paralyzed, and shaking, she... couldn't do anything. A "pins and needles" feeling crept over her skin as she dropped to her knees, then fell to her side. The last thing she saw was one of the security guards from before, pulling back his fist before her face exploded   in   pain.

THIRTEEN
NAOMI

FOR THE FIRST few moments after Naomi opened her eyes, she had no idea where she was, or what the hell had happened, but she recognized that she no longer had her jacket, and someone was *dragging* her along the sleek, polished hardwood floor.

She wanted to throw up.

For a few awful seconds, she thought she'd been blinded until she realized that a small sliver of the floor, and her legs, were visible where the blindfold had risen up. She had no idea how long she'd been unconscious, but her cheek itched with dry, crusted blood, and her mouth was so dry it hurt.

There was a brief pause while a door swung open, then Naomi's ears were met with the muffled beat of music and the distinctly sweet smell of burning marijuana. She inhaled deep. Drugs of any kind weren't Naomi's thing, but maybe a contact high could soothe the pain radiating from what seemed to be *everywhere* on her body.

Her arms were over her head, handcuffs biting into her wrists. One of the beefy security guards was using the short chain to pull her along, stopping in what she perceived to the middle of the room to drop her in an unceremonious heap onto a chair. The disconcerting sense of lethargy that consumed her kept her from doing anything to facilitate an escape as she was uncuffed, then cuffed again, this time with her hands behind her back as she clenched her fists.

A few minutes later, she heard the door open again, and someone pressed a bottle of cold water to her mouth, tipping her head back to force her to drink. She swallowed greedily, savoring the cool refreshment in her dehydrated, burning throat before the bottle was taken away. The blindfold was snatched from her eyes, and finally, she could see.

Directly in front of her was Victor Lucas. He was handsome, but devilishly so, with sharply defined features, bright hazel eyes, and a chiseled jaw. Victor was far from what one would expect a "crime boss" to look like. With his dark framed glasses and crisp white button up, he looked more like he'd just come from an accounting job than partying with strippers. He wasn't frowning, but his arms were crossed over his chest as he gazed down at Naomi.

"The notorious *Jolie Voleuse*. Or… is it Arabesque? What are you calling yourself these days?"

Instead of answering, Naomi looked away, lowering her head. Almost immediately, pain ripped through her as one of the guards snatched her by the hair, lifting her head to face Lucas, who smiled.

"Oh, you're a feisty one, huh?" Naomi narrowed her eyes as Lucas began pacing in front of her, lowering his arms to shove his hands into his pockets. He stopped, studied her for a moment, and then said over his shoulder to one of the guards, "Bring him in, please."

Bring who in?

"See... Naomi, right?" Lucas said, sitting down across from her, but too far away for a well-aimed kick. "I've heard a *lot* about you. Beautiful renowned thief, with an FBI agent for a boyfriend, and the damned devil himself for an uncle. An eclectic mix, but I can't say I'm surprised. Tomiko won't shut the fuck up about you, so I knew you had to be interesting, but what I am *dying* to know is what the hell you're doing in my house."

Naomi swallowed hard, but still didn't answer. Her tongue was still heavy, brain still moving sluggishly, and she didn't trust herself to speak wisely. The events of the night were still a blur, and the last thing she clearly remembered was her hands around Tomiko's throat. And Victor Lucas had just thrown out Tomiko's name like she was a good friend.

Fucking perfect.

"Cat got your tongue, Naomi? I'm trying to be patient here, but your little... *tussle* with my lady interrupted a good time, and I'd like to get back to it... but I've gotta figure out what to do with you first."

"Let me have her."

Naomi tensed as Tomiko stepped into the room, stone-faced. She fought the urge to smirk about the thick layer of makeup she wore to hide the deep purple bruises marring her face. On Tomiko's light brown skin, they would look worse — much worse — before they looked better, and Naomi took great pleasure in that.

Tomiko accepted Lucas's embrace, then turned to Naomi with fire in her eyes. "Please, baby?" she asked, directing her words over her shoulder as she stepped closer to Naomi's chair. Naomi flinched, jerking her head away as Tomiko cupped her chin, caressing her face before trailing her hand under the strap of Naomi's tank top.

"Get your hands off me, bitch," Naomi muttered through gritted teeth.

Tomiko withdrew her hands, but remained in front of Naomi to get right in her face. "Baby," she said, still talking to Victor. "Just say the word... just tell me yes, and she and I can have *so... much... fun...* after I break her for messing up my face."

"I should have killed you when I had the chance."

"Ah, but you didn't. You've always been too much of a softy to *really* go hard, so now, my big daddy is gonna let me keep you as my new toy, and..." Tomiko smiled, biting down on her still swollen lip. She put her hands on Naomi's thighs, sliding them up towards her waist. "I'm gonna *train*—"

Naomi reared her foot back then let go, aiming a swift kick of her boot at Tomiko's shin. When she dropped, howling in pain, Naomi kicked again, catching her under the chin and sending her reeling back. "I *told* you to get your hands off me."

Lucas ignored Tomiko's wail, stalking to Naomi with his hand raised. She looked him right in the eyes, bracing herself for the blow, but before it came, someone grabbed Lucas's wrist, shoving him backward.

"Vick, what the fuck is going on here?!"

Wha— ...Marcus?

Naomi's heart dropped into her stomach. What the hell was he doing here, calling Victor Lucas by a nickname, like he was... a lump built in her throat as understanding washed over her. Nostrils flared, she looked away, focusing instead on Tomiko as she rolled onto her side. She could feel Marcus staring at her, his gaze burning against the side of her face as she fought hard not to spill a single tear. She couldn't believe that she'd been worried about him, concerned over his mental state while he was working for the enemy.

"What's going on is that we found your little girlfriend in my damned house, trying to *kill* Tomiko. You care to explain this shit, Mr. FBI?"

Naomi squeezed her eyes shut.

"What the hell am *I* supposed to explain, I don't know why she's here!"

Lucas laughed. "Calloway… you really want me to believe it's a coincidence that she's a known goddamned thief, and you and she just *happened* to be in Barbados when those diamonds got planted? Yeah, *planted.* Rochas can't lie worth shit, and his dumbass let the French police get involved when they got picked off from the apartment, so I know he didn't keep those diamonds for himself. And I find it *really fucking convenient* that once your FBI ass overheard that I had them, I suddenly have this chick in my house."

A few seconds later, the distinctive *click* of a gun being cocked echoed through the room, and finally, Naomi opened her eyes. Victor Lucas was pointing a gun at Marcus, and the two security guards had theirs ready.

Instead of fear, Marcus exuded steely resolve. He didn't flinch, barely blinked, and definitely didn't give Naomi the benefit of eye contact. "So what are you trying to say?"

"I'm saying that your loyalty looks a little funny in the light, Calloway."

Marcus scoffed. "Motherfucker… I'm not loyal to *you*. So yeah, you're probably right. I'm interested in money, and her breaking in here screws that up, so nah… I don't have shit to do with this, and didn't know shit about her supposedly being a criminal until your girl Tomiko ran her mouth. So unless you plan to do something with that gun, you can get that shit out of my face."

For what seemed like a long time, Lucas stared at Marcus, his face pulled into a scowl. Marcus remained cool, looking positively bored about what was going on around him.

"So you didn't know she was Wolfe's niece?"

Cocking his head to the side, Marcus let out a dry laugh. "Hell no, not before Tomiko said something. Why would I willingly get involved with anybody related to his ass? I'm not trying to get into *any* of the type of shit he does. That lying, manipulating, obsessive bullshit he's on probably runs in the family, but..." he glanced over at Naomi and smiled. "The pussy is A-1, so I was sticking around."

Naomi swallowed hard.

Don't you dare cry. Don't you dare cry. Screw him.

Nostrils flared, Naomi rolled her eyes and looked away, again settling her gaze on Tomiko, who'd finally been picked up from the floor and sat on a couch a few feet away by one of the guards.

"I feel you on that, man. May have to sample that myself, you know?" Lucas laughed, and vomit rose to Naomi's throat. Would Marcus *really*—

"*Ha-ha, hell*. I don't share, bruh. Just like you're stingy with your old lady."

Naomi held her breath as silence reigned between the two men, until Lucas spoke again. "You know, Calloway… the more I think about this, the more I'm wondering about you. I pay your ass to stay off the FBI radar, keep the feds out of my business."

"And I've done that — have I not? Even last year, when you and Tomiko got popped at the airport with those sapphires, who got you out of that?"

"Yeah, but I'm thinking maybe it's *you* I should have been watching."

"Vick…" Marcus's voice changed, taking on a lower, more dangerous edge, but Naomi refused to look up. "Get that motherfucking gun out of my face. You know goddamned well I didn't have shit to do with this. Why the fuck would I come out with you, come back to your house if I knew this bullshit was going down?"

"You were politicking pretty hard to stay at the club."

"Because the damned vibe is different. I'm not into this stripper-screwing private party shit like you, hell yeah, I wanted to stay at the club, watch some ass, conduct our business, and then go home. If I knew she was here, I would have pretended to take my ass home and gotten outta dodge."

"I'm not buying your bullshit. I think this is a setup. Who the hell are you *really* working for? Wolfe? What, he's suspicious of me? You're fucking his niece, so I bet that's who has you keeping tabs on me."

"I'm about to put that damned gun down your throat, Vick. You pulled it, you better be ready to use it."

She wasn't watching, but the tension covering the room was so thick that it felt heavy on her skin. It would be so easy to speak up now, tell Lucas that she was FBI, tell Lucas that Marcus *did* know about this, that he'd planned the shit, all while he was double-crossing… hell, *everybody*. And he had the nerve to be upset with *her* for keeping things to herself? How in the world did he rationalize this? Or… did he even bother?

All of this time, working for the other side, not saying *anything*. Not for the first time, Naomi was completely exhausted. She couldn't have gotten this more wrong, couldn't have fucked this all up any harder. The *one* time she'd let her guard down… it had to be *him*.

But no matter.

Giving up, getting herself killed wouldn't benefit herself or anyone else, and she had a hunch about something that just might save her life.

"I didn't know he was working for you."

Everybody went quiet, turning toward Naomi as she spoke. She caught the surprise in Marcus's eyes, and hoped like hell he didn't think she was speaking up for his benefit. "Silly me… I *actually* thought he was clean. He has nothing to do with why I'm here tonight."

Lucas didn't take his eyes — or his aim — away from Marcus, who was standing with his hands slung casually in his pockets like there wasn't a gun in his face. "Why the fuck should I believe you?"

"Because we have a common enemy."

That made Lucas lift an eyebrow, and he flicked his gaze toward Naomi. "Keep talking."

"Damien Wolfe."

Lucas scoffed, tightening his grip on the gun. "Bullshit. That's your uncle."

"Have you seen me in any family photos? Look... I don't really give a shit what happens to the suit over there, I'm trying to save my *own* ass. Fact is, I got in here to get access to your computer, to figure out where you were keeping those diamonds, and why you wanted them. I worked too damned hard getting those diamonds for you to mess it up."

"*You* took the diamonds?"

"*And* planted them with Rochas. You were never even a target — you made yourself one by taking the diamonds. The plan was to put Wolfe's suspicion on Rochas, and while he was dealing with that, quietly infect his organization and take him down. You weren't in our sights."

"*Our?*"

"Me and my partner. My *real* man. Our shit with Wolfe is personal."

"And why are you telling me? I could turn you over to him right now."

"Because you *want* him taken down. The first place your mind went was that Wolfe was suspicious of you. Sounds like a guilty conscience to me. You didn't take those diamonds to help Rochas, you took them to help yourself, 'cause you knew if Rochas got caught it would increase the scrutiny on *everybody.* Give me those diamonds back, so we can flip this on Rochas and be done."

Lucas narrowed his eyes, his gaze darting between Marcus and Naomi for several moments before he turned the gun onto her. "Or I could just kill you."

"Vick, will you chill? Why would you screw up a *golden* opportunity? If you really are trying to take Wolfe's place, be smart about this shit, man. Killing the man's niece is dumb as hell."

Naomi swallowed a wave of fear, struggling to keep her face devoid of emotion as Lucas's finger skirted the trigger.

"So what do you suggest, FBI?"

"I suggest you put the damned gun down first of all, before you accidentally kill her, cause I'm not helping you clean *that* shit up. Then me and my girl are gonna walk outta here pretending like everything is lovey-dovey, I'm gonna drive her home, stay a while, and we'll continue like shit is normal, until we figure out how to turn this back on Rochas, like her original plan. I *really* wish you had told me about this, cause now you've got me mixed up in some shit I didn't want."

Lucas shrugged, finally lowering the gun. "No... your girl got you mixed up in some shit."

"And I plan to handle that." Marcus shot Naomi a look of complete disdain, and Naomi gave him one right back before rolling her eyes and looking away. She was completely conscious that Lucas was watching, scrutinizing her every move, and it wasn't until he nodded, signaling to the guards that he was allowing them to go that she breathed freely.

Well, *more* freely.

The next events were a blur of activity. More arguing between Marcus and Victor Lucas, like they were part of the same team, had been together a long while, and understood each other. Plans for how to spin this with Wolfe, plans on keeping Tomiko quiet, plans on keeping *Naomi* quiet, which included another joke from Marcus about "filling her mouth". By that point, Naomi was too numb to be disgusted, too frozen from the depth of betrayal to feel the blazing inferno of anger lurking just beneath the surface, and much too hurt and confused to intelligently process much of anything.

The men finished talking, and one of the guards picked her up, slinging her over his shoulders like she was a stack of potatoes, and carrying her downstairs to the waiting car. Naomi recognized it as Marcus's.

They handcuffed her to the door handle and then tossed the key to Marcus, who caught it, climbed in himself, then sped toward the open gate while Naomi contemplated exactly *how* she was going to commit his murder.

FOURTEEN
MARCUS

THE SILENCE WAS THE WORST.

Marcus could have handled tears, curses, explosive anger, and attempts to take his life— anything except the cold, unrelenting silence suffocating him from Naomi's side of the car. With his hands still on the steering wheel, Marcus flexed his fingers, chancing a glance in her direction.

What is she thinking right now?

She didn't flinch, scowl, roll her eyes... nothing to suggest she was even conscious of his gaze. Marcus forced his attention back to the road with a barely audible sigh.

Not even three hours ago, he'd been alone in his apartment, ready to drown out his hurt and anger with Sports Center and a bottle of whiskey. He'd called in sick, not interested in seeing pitying faces or hearing sympathetic words from his team. Sophie was gone to visit her grandmother, and his sister was headed out with her friends. Before she left, Meagan pulled him aside, prodding him for information about his sudden shift in mood.

"It's nothing, Megs. I'm good."

Meagan rolled her eyes. "Oh, *please*, Marcus. I've known you for thirty-four years, remember? Plus the whole twin thing… it's not *nothing*. Tell me what's going on."

"It's… work stuff. I can't talk about it."

"Work stuff has you drinking now? Try again."

"What?"

"You're *lying*. I've only seen you pull out the damned *bottle* over women."

Marcus shrugged.

Shaking her head, Meagan plopped down on the couch beside him. "Explain."

"I *can't*."

"Can't, or won't? Come on, maybe I can give you some advice… I *am* a woman, you know."

"You're not about to leave me alone, are you?"

Meagan smiled, clapping her brother on the knee. "*Nope.*"

"Shit. Fine. I found out that Naomi… kept something from me."

"Something big?"

"Huge."

"Was she cheating on you?"

"No."

"Putting your health at risk, or putting you in danger?"

"No."

"Was she trying to hurt you?"

"No."

"Do you feel better about it now that you know?"

"No."

Meagan lifted an eyebrow, then raised her hands in front of her, palms in the air. "So… maybe it's *not* that big."

"Maybe it's not that simple."

"Or maybe it is." Meagan stood, then turned to face Marcus on the couch. "Did you give her a chance to explain why she kept it from you? Did she have a good explanation?"

Marcus scoffed, then reached for the bottle. "*No* explanation is good enough."

He was placing the whiskey to his lips when his phone rang in his pocket. As glad as he was for the interruption in a conversation he *really* didn't want to have with Meagan, he considered not answering, but this was a ringtone he couldn't ignore, unlike the calls he'd blocked from Naomi's entire team, plus his own.

That call had been a summons to come and kick it with Victor Lucas and his boys, an invitation that Marcus wanted to decline, but duty called. He'd been working with Lucas for two years now, gathering the evidence that would put the man behind bars for a much longer time than the smaller crimes Marcus was sanctioned to cover up for him. So, Marcus went along, and he was glad he did, because as hard as he tried to talk him out of it without looking suspicious, Vick was hell-bent on taking the party back to his house.

Marcus knew the team's plan front to back, and a quick glance at his watch told him that by the time they arrived, Naomi would still be in the house. As pissed as he was, he didn't want her caught. Victor insisted that he ride in the limo with him and the strippers, so Marcus knew he would be limited in his attempt to give some sort of warning.

He attempted calling Agent Barnes first, but the lack of answer told him that the team was knee-deep in making the job go off without a hitch. Next, he tried Naomi, not expecting her to answer, but hoping that if she *did* have her phone on, the fact that he was calling in the middle of a mission would tell her something was wrong.

But that didn't happen.

When they arrived at the house, no alarms blaring, no sign of an intruder, Marcus relaxed a little, hoping that as long as Vick remained occupied with woman and liquor, Naomi would be able to get out without a problem. Unfortunately, he'd forgotten about Tomiko, who wasn't even supposed to be in the country right now.

Marcus knew something was wrong as soon as Vick was summoned outside by one of the guards. Long minutes passed, and then an hour. His own cover was at risk, so he kept his cool, until one of the guards came to get him, taking him into another room.

Naomi was handcuffed to a chair in the middle, and Vick was running up on her with his hand raised like he was about to slap her. Marcus's heart leapt into his throat at the sight of a captured Naomi, the left side of her face a mess of cuts and bruises.

But why the fuck did he care? This was Naomi's mess. Little Miss Bad Ass Thief had gotten herself caught, and she was dragging *his* fate down with her. He kept his cool. His own life depended on getting *both* of them out of there.

But… did Naomi know that? Or was she sitting over there stewing over the ugly things he'd said, his harsh words and even harsher persona?

Marcus shook his head. Wasn't like it mattered. Maybe now she understood how that knife in the back felt, could understand what it was like to have something kept from you.

He would have let her sit over there and pout forever, wondering where his loyalties lay, but he thought about his concerned team members and pulled his phone from his pocket.

"Tell Barnes I've got her," he said when Kendall answered.

The other man let out a long rush of air. "Okay. Glad you called, we were getting ready to raid the place."

"That's what I figured. But... we're out, and managed to do it without blowing my cover."

"What about hers?"

Who gives a shit?

"Hers is wide open. She got caught, had to tell some things to get out of it."

"Damnit."

Marcus lifted an eyebrow, resisting the urge to let out a snort of laughter. "Yeah, it's too bad. Ask Barnes where he wants me to take her."

There was a brief conversation in the background, then Kendall returned to the phone. "He says bring her here, to the gym."

"Will do."

Marcus hung up, then glanced over at Naomi again. Still, she stared out the window, emotionless, unblinking. He turned his attention to the road, pushing aside the annoying heaviness in his chest. He didn't know why her silence bothered him so much. It wasn't like he was interested in hearing anything she had to say, unless it was a "thank you" for saving her life, which he certainly didn't expect to ever happen. It would require thinking of somebody other than herself, which he wasn't sure Naomi even had the capacity to do.

Once he was confident they weren't being followed, he guided them to the gym without incident. He got out, went around to Naomi's side to open her door, then used the key to unlock her handcuffed wrist and free her from the door handle.

He stepped back in surprise when instead of cooperating when he reached to unlock her other wrist, she snatched away, a snarl masking her face as she lunged at him.

Marcus dodged, expecting a punch, but a few seconds later, he realized that wasn't her goal. With unexpected speed, Naomi was on his back, using her own wrist as leverage as she pulled the chain of the handcuffs against his neck.

He struggled against her, torn between not wanting to hurt her and tossing her ass across the parking lot. He quickly grasped that he didn't have time to contemplate options — she was pulling those cuffs as tight as she could, despite the injury she had to be causing herself. Naomi was *really* trying to kill him.

With a grunt, he grabbed her arms and flipped her off his back, cursing when she caught herself on her hands and knees. Marcus barely drew a full breath before she was at him again, clawing and kicking and punching like her life depended on it.

"*Naomi!*" he bellowed, shoving her away from him. "I'm not your fucking enemy!"

"Could have fooled me, motherfucker." Naomi's tone and expression were both cold as she stood up straight, aiming Marcus's gun at his chest.

Oh Shit.

He had no idea when she'd disarmed him, but if the look on her face was any indication, she was serious about using his own weapon against him.

"I was doing what I had to do in order to get us out of there. I saved your goddamned life."

Naomi let out a peal of laughter, taking one hand away from the gun to brush tears from her eyes. "You didn't save me. *I* saved *your* sorry ass so I could save myself."

"I could say the same thing."

"But who has the gun, Marcus? I can't think of a single good reason why I shouldn't kill your hypocritical ass. I already let one backstabber live today, I don't really think I should let a second opportunity pass me by."

Marcus shook his head. "Nobody stabbed you in the back. I was doing my job!"

"*So was I*! So was I, Marcus. What I kept from you put you in *no* danger, but *this* shit tonight? How much differently could it have gone if you had told us you were working with Lucas?! Huh?!"

Looking around in the dark parking lot, Marcus raised his hand. "Could you lower your voice? Or you wanna tell the whole worl—"

"I don't *give a shit* anymore, I'm *tired.* I *trusted* you. I *cared* about you. I *gave myself to you!*"

"You think you're the only one who cared?!"

"I *know* I'm the only who cared. All that mattered to you was that "the pussy was A-1", remember?"

Brushing a hand over his face, Marcus pushed out a heavy breath. "Naomi... I said that shit because I was playing a role."

"No, you opened your door that night because you were playing a role. You should *have* left my ass outside."

"I was upset!" Marcus took a step forward, stopping in his tracks when Naomi cocked the gun, lifting an eyebrow. "I've been wanting answers about my father all of this time, and you *sat* on the information for your own selfish-assed reasons. I can't be upset about that shit?"

"*Not* selfish reasons, Marcus, not entirely. Just like you, I was doing my job. I didn't want to hurt you. If that's selfish, so be it, but you're the same damned thing."

"So I guess we're both hypocrites then."

"I guess so."

With one last disdainful glare, Naomi shook her head, lowered the gun, placed it on the ground, and then turned to go inside. Marcus stood in place. He watched as she disappeared into the gym, and he remained there long after the door closed behind her.

What the fuck just happened?

And why did his throat feel so dry, why did he feel so... numb? Marcus rubbed the back of his neck, then his temples, trying to ease the headache building between his eyes. When he was unsuccessful, he shook his head, then walked over to retrieve his gun. With it back in the holster, he closed his car door and then headed inside, following the anxious voices to the office.

When he entered, Naomi was nowhere to be seen.

"Inez took her in back to get cleaned up," Quentin said. The relief was evident in his face as he extended his hand in appreciation to Marcus. "Thank you for getting her out of that shit."

Marcus shrugged, ignoring the gesture. "I was just trying to keep my own ass from taking a bullet."

Immediately, Quentin's expression changed from grateful, to annoyed, then to angry. "Ya know, you got a lotta fuckin' nerve, bruh. Kendall and Renata already spilled the beans, told us the *real* deal to make sure you didn't catch a few shots yourself when we sent agents in for that raid. You been holding your own cards from the beginning — we've only known about your dad for a few weeks. You wanna talk down to Mimi like she betrayed you or somethin', when you did the shit first. I was gone let it slide til you walked in here with a fuckin' attitude. Your suit's still freshly pressed while *her* face is split open."

Marcus sucked his teeth. "And what the fuck is your gator-hunting ass gonna do, huh?"

"Man, will y'all cut this bullshit out?" Kendall stepped between them, pressing a hand into either man's chest.

"Hell no, if this motherfucker wanna get down, we can do it, but he's run outta chances to act like Mimi don't mean shit. Actin' like a fuckin' baby cause she kept a secret."

"We're talking about my *father*!" Marcus snapped.

"We're talkin' about her *life*. You think this shit is easy for her?! She was a goddamned kid when it happened! If she'd told you, the first thing you were gonna want her to do is tell every shitty detail of a traumatic event. That shit happened in front of her, while she hid behind a rotten couch in an abandoned house. She's been livin' with that shit for fifteen years! I think she's earned the right to be a lil selfish about her own memories, but you're too full of yourself to get that, right? Can't believe I thought your ass might actually be *good* for her."

Quentin shoved Kendall's arm away from his chest, then stalked away, disappearing into the room where Inez had taken Naomi.

Marcus's mind was running at a frantic pace, trying desperately to come up with a rebuttal that Quentin would never hear, but would justify his actions nonetheless. When he came up blank, he took a step back as if he'd taken a blow to the chest.

270

Was he being just as selfish as he'd accused Naomi of being? He was so wrapped up in being angry that she hadn't told him about his dad that he hadn't really taken stock of what he'd gained. He had closure, sure... but nothing had changed. Having or not having the information hadn't affected anything in his life, except that he now felt a deep, dark anger against Damien Wolfe for taking his father.

Exactly what Naomi claimed she didn't want to happen to him.

Even *she* hadn't denied the selfishness of her original reasoning, but the other explanations she gave, the ones he called bullshit... maybe they were just as valid as her simply being selfish. She was human, after all. Naomi was capable of complexities... *full* of them, actually.

Marcus sighed, thinking back to how he'd accused her of tunnel vision. Could the same be said for him? So desperate to close *something* big that he'd kept back information that could have cost her life... *shit*. At least she'd had more noble reasons than just "doing her job" for holding *her* information back.

He glanced toward the private room, wondering how Naomi was feeling, and what she was thinking. He swallowed the lump in his throat. He had no clue what would happen moving forward, no ideas of the next steps, but he *did* know one thing.

He couldn't have fucked this up more if he'd tried.

FIFTEEN
NAOMI

"MADAME MIMI!"

Plastering a smile on her face, Naomi turned to greet one of her students' parents. It was after class, and although she *loved* her baby ballerinas, all she wanted to do was shower, get home, and curl up on her couch with a big glass of wine. Scratch that — the bottle.

But, it wasn't just *any* parent that greeted her. It was Meagan, Sophie's mom. Marcus's sister. Naomi's heart turned a backflip in her chest. Sophie was occupied checking out one of her classmate's new baby brother, and most of the other kids and their parents were already gone. No escape.

Weeks had gone by since the disaster at Victor Lucas's house, and she'd seen Marcus only rarely since. Lucas had returned the diamonds to them, but Barnes didn't want to move forward until they'd had time to regroup, and re-evaluate the plan.

Naomi suspected he was really just giving her a break, and she wasn't going to complain about that. For a whole two weeks, she'd been able to devote her time to dancing and boxing and being in places she actually had a right to be. And *not* thinking about Marcus.

But now, Meagan was in front of her. They weren't identical twins, but Meagan was undeniably a pretty, softer version of her brother, and that made it hard for her thoughts not to immediately shift to him.

"Mrs. Terry, how can I help you?"

Meagan smiled, and the authenticity in her expression made Naomi feel a little guilty for her own plastic smile.

"Well... I know I'm stepping over a line, but...," *Here we go* "It's about Marcus."

Naomi squared her shoulders, standing up a little straighter as she faced Meagan. Clearing her throat, she asked "What about him? I'm sure you know that he and I are no longer... involved."

"I do," Meagan said, with a little nod. She shifted on her feet, letting out a puff of nervous breath. "Um... that's actually what I wanted to talk to you about."

"Mrs. Terry, I—"

"Call me Meagan, please." She reached forward, taking Naomi's hands in hers. "I don't know what exactly happened between you and Marcus. I just... I know that he's not himself, and he hasn't *been* himself for a few weeks. I've never seen him so subdued, so... quiet, like he's been, and I know it's because you two are no longer on good terms."

Naomi pulled her hands away, tucking them against her body. "I'm... sorry to hear that you're having troubles with your brother, but I don't understand what it has to do with me?"

"Well… he *misses* you. He hasn't said anything, but I *know* he does. The whole twin thing, you know?"

"That still doesn't explain what you're expecting from me…"

Meagan sighed as she lowered her head. "Nothing, I guess. I guess I just… I don't know, wanted to ask you to take him back so he can stop moping."

"Take him back?" Naomi let out a dry laugh. "Marcus would have to actually care for that to happen. He got what he wanted from me."

Naomi regretted those words as soon as they left her mouth, wished she could take them back and swallow them. Being loose-lipped was *not* her style, but… as usual, anything involving Marcus took her out of character.

"Do you really think that? That he didn't care about you?"

"Mrs. Terry —"

"*Meagan.* And my brother *absolutely* cares for you. It takes a lot for Marcus to *really* get upset, but when he does, he does a really great job of pretending not to give a shit. Trust me, I grew up with the man. The more awful he was, the more he cared, the more… wounded he was. He didn't really give me any detail, but he told me you'd kept something from him, and whatever it was… you kinda… gutted him." Meagan lifted her hands in front of her. "But, I'm not here to pass judgment, not at all, I'm just… before this… *whatever* happened, Marcus was really, really happy, and from what I could tell, it seems like you were too."

Naomi wet her lips with her tongue, then pressed them together as she glanced toward the door. Her shoulders felt tight, and she was overwhelmed with the inexplicable desire to *run.*

"I'm sorry, Naomi," Meagan said, her expression pained. "I can see I'm making you uncomfortable, and I *swear* I didn't mean to. This was… this was stupid, to even bring this up to you."

Shaking her head, Naomi managed to pull her mouth into a smile. "No… you're just looking out for your brother. I get it."

With a small nod, Meagan turned away to retrieve Sophie and left. Instead of leaving as she'd planned once her students were all gone, Naomi locked the door to her classroom, deactivated the mirror, and cranked up her music.

She had no idea how long she stayed in there, dancing to whatever played, trying her best to clear her mind. It was easy not to think about Rochas or Lucas. It was difficult not to think about Wolfe. It was *impossible* not to think about Marcus.

Wounding him had never been her intention. Even in her continued — but much-subdued — anger, knowing that she'd *wounded* him was like a blow to the chest. But *why*? It wasn't like Marcus was so innocent. She'd found out later that he *was* acting on official orders, and had been specifically told that his semi-undercover mission with Wolfe took priority over everything. Still, it didn't change the fact that he'd gone nuts on her over keeping something from him, when he was doing the same thing.

Or maybe it *wasn't* the same thing. At least not to Marcus.

A knock at the door pulled her out of her musings, and a quick glance at the clock told her it was nearly eight at night. Panting from her workout, Naomi went to the door, opening it to find Quentin on the other side, eyebrows drawn together as he scrutinized her face.

"You've been back here for a while, Mimi. You alright?"

Naomi nodded, managing to pull forth a smile. "Yeah… I'm okay. Just… lost track of time."

Quentin lifted an eyebrow, but didn't push. "Okay… well, we should probably head out. It's late, and I haven't seen you eat anything since lunch… come grab a bite with me."

"Your treat?"

Chuckling, Quentin grabbed Naomi by the hand to pull her out of the classroom. "When is it ever *not* my treat, cher?"

Naomi sucked her teeth. "You don't *always* pay for me when…oh yeah." She gave him a sheepish smile, realizing that she *couldn't* recall a time she'd ever paid for her own meal when they were out together.

Quentin flipped off the light in the classroom.

"Yeah, *exactly.*"

THE HALLWAY WAS TOO DARK. That was the first thing Naomi noticed as she stepped off the elevator onto her floor after dinner with Quentin. There were only three tenants total in the building, and her floor belonged only to her, so it wasn't surprising to have a maintenance issue, but still… something about one lonely light out of four made her skin crawl.

With her back against the wall, she surveyed the area. The tiny blue light on the security camera was blinking, which meant it was still functioning. It *also* meant Quentin was probably watching her right now — or would later, when he made it home from dropping her off — , wondering why she was acting so paranoid over a damned blown fuse.

Naomi let out a deep breath as she pushed away from the wall, but she also pulled out and unsheathed the utility knife she kept tucked in a case attached to her keys. Better safe than sorry.

In her apartment, the first thing she did was flip on the lights. Their warm, artificial glow did nothing to quell the unease gnawing at her stomach. Swallowing hard, she reached into her purse for her gun, then began moving systematically through the condo, checking to make sure she was alone. She'd only made it through one room when the loud ringing of her cell phone nearly made her crawl out of her skin.

Shaking her head, Naomi took a moment to compose herself before she pulled it from her pocket, glancing at the screen before she answered. "Yeah Q?"

"Mimi, I just stopped to get gas, and I see an alarm breach notification from your place on my phone. Everything okay?"

Immediately, she raised the gun, keeping her knife tucked in her hand as well, and balancing the phone against her ear as she turned around the room. "When?"

"Five minutes ago. Did you turn it off and reset it when you came in?"

Naomi's shoulders sagged in relief. "No," she said, chuckling as she lowered her weapon. "I didn't. The hallway lights were out, so I was freaked out. I completely forgot."

"Don't tell me you're over there being Little Miss Law & Order, clearing rooms?"

"Quentin, you *know* I am." Naomi laughed, shaking her head as she turned the safety back on her gun, and sat it down on the desk. She headed back to the front of her apartment, where the light on the alarm panel was flashing, but not making a sound.

"Why don't I hear the alarm going off?"

Naomi shrugged, forgetting that Quentin couldn't actually see her from his car. "No idea. I must have turned the volume down the *last* time I accidentally tripped it and couldn't get the damned thing to stop droning. I'm fine though."

"Okay." Quentin laughed. "You know what I'm doing as soon as I get home right?"

"You're gonna watch me make an ass of myself?"

"Would *not* miss it."

Sucking her teeth, Naomi shut off the alarm, then turned back to her empty apartment. "Whatever Q. I'll talk to you later."

"Later."

Naomi hung the phone up with a sigh, then went immediately to her kitchen, suddenly feeling silly about her paranoia. She pulled a bottle of wine from her cooler and uncorked it, pouring herself a generous glass before she sat down at the counter and flipped on the TV in her kitchen.

Ten minutes and an empty wine glass later, Naomi turned off the TV. A shower, comfortable pajamas, and her freshly laundered sheets beat out reality TV any day. She was down to her underwear, and just about ready to step into the shower when her phone rang again. Rolling her eyes at the screen, she picked it up, answering as she turned on the hot water.

"Quentin, I do *not* want to hear you teasing—"

"Mimi, shut up and listen. Get the *fuck* outta there, *now*. Somebody cut your cameras."

"What? I do—" The lights in the bathroom went out, and Naomi's heart began to race. She'd left the bathroom door open, but *everything* was black. The only light was from her cellphone screen.

Don't panic. Don't you dare panic. Diligence. Focus. Agility.

"Naomi, I'm on my way, but I need you to get out of there, okay? Please just *listen*."

"I'm listening," she whispered, pulling the phone away from her long enough to tap the buttons to turn on her flashlight app. It gave her better visibility to pull on a robe and slip her hand inside the "emergency" drawer she kept in every room for a knife that packed a little more punch than her portable one.

"Okay. Watch yourself. If you can get out of there, do it, if you can't, hide. *Stay alive*, Mimi. I'm getting in my car, and calling the rest of the team. *Stay alive*."

He ended the call, and Naomi lowered the phone, using it like a proper flashlight to scan her bedroom before she stepped out of the bathroom. Clothes were optional. What she really needed was to get to the door of her bedroom, make it across the living room, and out the door.

Or would the window be better?

She had the penthouse apartment, three floors up, but the fire escape would keep it from being an ugly drop. That was closer. That was *faster.* She swept the room with the light one last time, and once she was confident that it was clear enough for her to get out of that window, she shot out, wasting no time getting to it.

Her hands were calm, steady as she flipped open the first lock, but when she reached for the second, it wouldn't budge. Naomi only gave herself a few moments to struggle with it before she cursed, then decided she would just have to break it.

Her vision had already adjusted to the low visibility of the area. In the dark, she scanned her bedroom for something light enough to wield, but heavy enough to break the glass. Her eyes fell on the cute little three-legged bedside table she'd purchased not even two months ago. She hated to ruin the glossy, pristine wood grain finish, but didn't hesitate to drop her knife into the pocket of her robe and head for the bed to grab it.

She swept the contents from the top and grabbed it by one of its intricately carved legs. Before she could make the two steps back to the window, something took hold of her ankle and yanked hard, sending her crashing to the ground. Her first instinct was to kick, and kick she did, making contact with the soft flesh of her attacker's face as he came from under the bed. She slammed her foot down again, causing another yelp of pain from her assailant before the grip on her leg loosened.

Naomi didn't have time to think, she just acted, pulling herself up from the floor and retrieving her knife from her pocket. It wasn't leaving her hand again. How many people were in her apartment? Just this one? A dozen? Not taking her eyes off the one who'd grabbed her, and was still on the floor, Naomi picked up the lightweight table with one hand, using a single swing too smash the window.

She didn't have a chance to look at the damage before her bedroom door swung open, and two more people were in the room, both wielding knives that in the shadowy light looked much bigger than hers.

Okay, Naomi.

She squared her shoulders, nostrils flared. "Come on," she said, forcing her voice into a derisive tone. "Do whatever the fuck it is you came to do."

There was a short pause, as if the intruders were deciding what to do, then they both lunged at once. Naomi easily dodged one, delivering an elbow to the temple that dropped him to the floor, but a blistering flash of pain went through her arm as the other brought his knife down with a slash that could have disconnected her wrist from her body if she hadn't moved in time.

As it was, her wrist was still attached, and despite the agony in her arm, she intended to follow Quentin's instruction to stay alive. The trespasser lunged at her, and she used every bit of strength she could find to dodge the slash of his knife, and put her own through the space under his ribs, pushing hard to puncture his lung.

He collapsed to the floor, struggling for breath, and Naomi took a moment to gather her own.

Get out of here Mimi.

She was *trying*. Naomi stepped over her wheezing assailant to try again to get to that window, but a sudden restraint around her neck pulled her backwards. She clawed at the hands, and when that didn't work, reached behind herself to claw for the eyes, but her ability to breathe was going fast, taking every ounce of strength she had with it. She stopped fighting, because she couldn't do anything else. Closed her eyes, because she couldn't do anything else. Started slipping away... because she couldn't do anything else.

Bang. Bang.

Her heart stopped. She was falling, and her head hit the floor, *hard*. The cord around her neck was loose, dropping away from her body as she clapped both hands over her ringing ears. She squeezed her eyes shut, shaking her head.

No, no, no. n—

"*Naomi. Naomi, hey.*"

She shook her head harder. "No."

"Naomi. *Naomi.* You're okay. You're okay."

That voice was familiar. She opened her eyes to finding Marcus kneeling over her, his eyes wide with concern. There was a gun in his hand. And blood at his feet. But everything was blurry, and fuzzy, and her eyes wouldn't focus.

"Naomi, listen to me, Beautiful, keep your eyes open, okay? You can't go to sleep."

"I can't," she mumbled, but her mouth felt like it was full of cotton.

"You have to, you hit your head. *Please.*"

"I *can't.*"

Her eyelids were too heavy. There was too much pain, from her head, her neck, her arm, it was too much. Sleep was better. Sleep was much, *much* better.

"Naomi."

"Mimi! Is she okay? What the fuck happened?"

"Where is she?"

Why are all of these people talking while I'm trying to sleep?

MARCUS.

284

MARCUS RUBBED HIS TEMPLES, lowering his head to the table as he listened to Barnes and Black go back and forth, droning on and on and *on* as they argued over who had been responsible for the attempt on Naomi's life.

His head was still spinning, heart still racing as the memory of Naomi being held by the neck in mid-air flashed to the forefront of his mind. He hadn't thought twice about putting two bullets through the attacker's side, and probably would have put slugs through all three intruders' heads if Quentin, Kendall, and Barnes hadn't arrived at virtually the same time, breaking his rage before he could even begin the violent rampage he *wanted* to go on.

The scar on her face from the night at Lucas's house wasn't even fully healed yet, and now she had a list of new wounds. Barnes had forced him to ride with Kendall to take Naomi back to the gym, while he and Quentin smoothed things over and handled the police. A private doctor had been called, and even the report of no concussion had done little to quell the anger burning in Marcus's chest. She still had a knot on her head, bruises around her neck, and seven stitches on her arm to close a deep knife gash that was dangerously close to leaving her permanently handicapped.

Somebody, Marcus really didn't care who, was going to pay for that shit. Truthfully, he was still steaming about the stuff at Lucas's house. Once he'd gotten confirmation on Tomiko's sealed history with Naomi and Quentin, he felt even worse about not telling his new team.

But… nothing he could do about it now. All of that was done, the fallout had already happened. The attempt on Naomi's life last night was another story. Saying nothing, he pushed his chair back from the conference table and left.

THIRTY MINUTES LATER, he was pulling into the underground parking garage of Inez's house, just outside the city. The neighborhood was gated, quiet, secure, and most importantly, barely anyone knew about it. It was a perfect place for Naomi to stay while she recovered.

Recovered.

He hated the sound of that. Hated the knowledge that she was upstairs hurting, and he'd very nearly been too late to do anything about it. Marcus had been shocked when Quentin called *him*, asking if he were anywhere near Naomi's apartment. Marcus let out a dry laugh as he reclined in his seat. He *had* been close by, taking the long way home from a trip to the shooting range with Renata and Kendall just so that he could drive by her place and tell himself the lie that he didn't want to knock on her door and try to talk to her. That corny, emotional-assed detour had saved Naomi's life.

Marcus wanted to see her. Wanted to talk to her, touch her, provide *some* measure of comfort, but he wasn't sure he was capable of that anymore. Would she even accept that from him, after everything that had happened? He considered pulling out, taking himself back home, but Inez already knew he was there, as he'd had to get her approval to get into the neighborhood.

Won't know unless you try.

He climbed out of his car, entering through the garage door, per Inez's instructions over the phone. He found her in her kitchen, speaking in a flirtatious voice that made it obvious the conversation was *very* personal. She pointed up the kitchen stairs, giving him some type of convoluted hand sign that he took to mean Naomi's room was two doors on the left.

Marcus followed those directives, then took a deep breath before he knocked on the door.

"Come in."

Shit.

The defeat in her voice almost made his chest cave in. He opened the door, and found her sitting at the window, staring outside. Seeing her there, barefaced and bandaged, reminded him of that day in the Parisian hospital, which now seemed *so* long ago.

She glanced up when he entered, and a litany of emotions ran across her face, but a contradictory mix of anxiety and relief came through strongest.

"Hey… what are you doing here?"

Did she really need to ask? Why *wouldn't* he be there, after what'd happened, unless she still thought he didn't… *shit.* Of *course* she did.

"I… was in the neighborhood. Wanted to swing by."

Naomi lifted an eyebrow. "Thirty minutes outside of the city is within radius to be "in the neighborhood, swinging by" now?"

"It is when the undertaking is important."

She went still, and Marcus watched her throat bob as she swallowed. "What does that mean?"

Marcus shrugged, stepping fully into the room so he could close the door. "It means I wanted to check on you… see how you were holding up."

Sighing, Naomi shook her head. "Well, let's see… my nemesis has information that could get me killed because I broke into her criminal boyfriend's house, and he works for the demon I'm trying to terminate, and I had to divulge a good part of my plan to him to keep from getting killed, and now, I have yet another evil ass man over my shoulder. Oh, and three men broke into my apartment last night to try to kill me. So… I'm *great.*"
She got choked up over the last few words, and looked

back toward the world outside as Marcus sat on the window seat beside her.

There was silence between them for a long moment before Naomi cleared her throat. "I'm sorry. I'm just…"

"Scared?"

Still staring out the window, Naomi pulled her lip between her teeth, gnawing at it for a moment before she turned to him and nodded. "Nothing like this has ever happened. They came into my *home*, where I'm supposed to be safe. I don't even know who to be afraid of anymore."

Marcus closed his eyes, taking a chance on pulling her against him as she broke down in tears. She sobbed against his chest, soaking his tee shirt, but he didn't care. He pulled her closer, and to his surprise, she climbed awkwardly into his lap, burying her face against his neck.

"We're gonna figure it out, okay?" he said, once she'd calmed. "You're gonna be fine."

"You don't know that."

He pulled back, adjusting their position so that he could see her face, and wipe away the last of her tears. "Work with me, would you? Stop being so contrary."

"I'm just saying," Naomi said, shrugging as a hint of a smile took over her mouth.

Marcus took her face in his hands, turning it from side to side as he examined her. "Wait… what is that? Is that… a *smile*? Goddamn, it's been a *long* time since I've gotten one of those."

"It hasn't been *that* long."

"Yes it has. Can I talk to you about something else?" he asked, running a hand over her bare leg. She was dressed in a tee shirt and cotton shorts that stopped high on her thighs, and her skin felt deliciously warm under his touch.

"You saved my life, Marcus. The least I can give you is a conversation." She turned a little, laying her head on his shoulder. "I'm guessing this is the follow-up to your sister's attempt to soften me up?"

Marcus wrinkled his brow, narrowing his eyes in confusion. "What? Meagan talked to you about me?"

Shit. I'm gonna kill her.

"Never mind."

"None of that *never mind* stuff," Marcus said, tipping up her chin. "What did Meagan say to you?"

Naomi looked down, those thick, lush lashes of hers lending a sensual quality to the sadness in her eyes. "Nothing, Marcus." She turned away again, looking to the window. "Just tell me what you want."

"I *want* to do this…" Marcus heard the hitch in her breath, felt her body melt into him when he leaned forward, wrapping his arms around her to pull her body against his. Her hair was pulled up into a messy bun, freeing him to press a kiss onto the exposed bruise wrapping her neck. When she didn't resist, he made a path up to her ear. "I'm sorry."

Her body tensed. She obviously wasn't expecting *that.*

"I've been thinking about this shit for a whole month, trying to come up with every justification for saying the things I said, acting the way I did, and… I just can't. I stand by my feeling that *you should have told me*, but… it doesn't excuse me. And you were right… I was being a hypocrite." He stopped, planting another kiss before he continued. "I *don't* regret opening my door to you. You're *not* the only one who cares. You're not out here by yourself."

Naomi's shoulders sagged as he repeated "*I'm sorry*", over and over while he kissed her neck, slid his hand under her tank top to caress her skin, then slipped under the waistband of her shorts. She opened her legs, allowing him better access as he pushed a first, then second finger inside of her. Marcus watched her face, basking in her change in expressions as he stroked her. She was *so* beautiful, rocking against his hand as her breathing grew more and more ragged the closer he brought her to climax.

He *needed* to touch her this way, but it had little to do with sexual gratification. From the beginning, a physical connection had been their *best* connection. Maybe his attention to her body could offer something words couldn't. Marcus kept going, pushed deeper, harder, and faster until she was trembling from her release.

After that, there was a long moment of silence while Naomi caught her breath. She looked up at him and cupped his face in her hands, pulling his mouth down to meet hers. "*I'm* sorry," she whispered against his lips, draping her arms over his shoulders. "I should have told you."

Marcus nodded. "It all happened the way it happened. Nothing we can do about it now. I don't even wanna talk about this. Do we *have* to talk about this shit?"

Naomi shook her head. "No. Like you said… it's done. But we're still here."

"We *are*. So… what do you wanna do about that?"

He felt a strange sort of lightness in his chest as she gazed up, locking onto him with her warm, expressive eyes. "I want you to make love to me."

"Naomi," Marcus sighed, closing his eyes briefly to get himself from under her spell. "You're not in any condition for us to do that. You're probably not even supposed to be out of bed, are you?"

"So be gentle."

He groaned as she shifted to straddling his lap, pressing the heat between her thighs against his growing erection.

"Marcus… I think I need you."

She whispered those words against his mouth before she drew him into a kiss, and how the *hell* was he supposed to resist?

"Are you two lovebirds decent? I'm coming in either way, just thought I'd ask!"

Marcus and Naomi both froze at the sound of Inez's voice, coming from the other side of the door. Sure enough, a moment later, the door creaked open, and Inez poked her head in, looking at them through her fingers as she covered her face with her hand.

"What is it, Nez?"

Marcus lifted an eyebrow at the tinge of irritability in Naomi's voice, and Inez apparently picked it up as well, because she giggled as she stepped into the room. "*Sorry* for interrupting your little sick and shut-in booty call, but there's something you need to see."

She switched on the TV, turned it to a news station, then stepped back for them to see.

"*Notorious, ruthless businessman Victor Lucas was found very early this morning outside a popular gentleman's club, dead from an apparent overdose. Police are being vague with details about the death, probably because Lucas was said to have connections to organized crime. He is a known associate of tobacco tycoon Damien Wolfe, owner and CEO of Lone Wolfe Tobacco Products. Wolfe is rumored to have ties to organized crime as well. We'll give you updates on this story as it develops."*

"A drug overdose?" Naomi asked, turning to Marcus. "It didn't seem like Lucas had a drug problem."

Marcus shrugged. "Didn't to me either, but… shit happens."

"Shit happens?" Naomi lifted an eyebrow as she surveyed Marcus's face. "You don't think it was an accident, do you?"

"I think it's… interesting timing. You get attacked last night, Lucas turns up dead this morning…"

Naomi sighed, then glanced at Inez. "What do you think?"

"I think the attempt on you last night was Lucas… and I think Wolfe found out and handled it."

Shaking her head, Naomi turned back to Marcus, her expression skeptical. "No. Why would he retaliate on my behalf?"

Marcus and Inez exchanged a glance, but neither said anything, both opting to look down.

"Oh," Naomi said, clearing her throat. "Right. Blood, and all of that jazz."

"Mimi…"

"No, it's fine. It's the truth, right? Marcus, you said it yourself, the lying and manipulating, the evil, it probably runs in the family. He killed everybody else, and now he's protecting his legacy. I probably have at least until his daughter becomes of age, right? She just turned sixteen, so I guess I'm good for the next… two years?"

Marcus grabbed Naomi's hands and pulled them up to his mouth to kiss her fingers. "Naomi… stop. Don't do that to yourself. We're gonna figure out what happened, rethink the plan now that Lucas is dead, and keep moving forward. Okay?"

Naomi rolled her eyes, attempting to turn away, but Marcus caught her chin, turning her back towards him. He kissed her, massaging her tongue with his until she *relaxed*. "Okay?" he repeated, when he finally pulled away. "Don't tap out on us. We're all on your side, Beautiful."

"Okay." She sniffled as she looked down at her hands, avoiding Marcus's eyes, but he'd already seen the fresh round of tears. Across the room, the door closed, and Marcus knew without looking up that Inez had stepped out, giving them privacy.

He kissed her again, and this time she kissed back, pressing herself against him as she draped her arms around his neck.

"Marcus… do you remember when you told me anytime I wanted to escape, I just had to let you know?"

Meeting her eyes, Marcus nodded. "Yeah. Why?"

"Consider yourself informed."

MAYBE HE'D COME ON TOO strong.

That was the only explanation for Renata's sudden withdrawal from communication with him. At first, she'd seemed pleased by his flirtation. On more than one occasion, he was *sure* he'd played a role in bolstering her mood, which usually bordered on melancholy. She was all smiles with those adorable dimples, twirling her braids around her fingers as she studied her computer screen, or figuring out shit he'd been working on for weeks.

There was nothing about Renata that *wasn't* appealing to Quentin. Except, of course, the fact that she'd been avoiding him since the job at Lucas's house.

To be fair, there hadn't been much for her to do, but still. Quentin knew that if things were the other way around, he'd *find* reasons to show up at her job. As it was... Quentin wasn't *exactly* welcome in a federal building of any kind. But that had nothing to with his problem now.

Quentin sat back in his chair, and his mind drifted to Naomi. He was worried about her, with everything that was happening, but now that Calloway had stopped being a dumbass, he seemed solid. Inez had reported that they were together now, treating her guest bedroom like their own private playhouse. *That* was more information than Quentin needed, but if Mimi was happy, he was happy for her. He was much more interested in *Renata's* bedroom activity.

Maybe… there was a boyfriend.

Although Quentin tried not to make a habit of looking into people just for the sake of looking, he woke his computer from its sleeping state and pulled up Renata's unofficial personnel file. He paused on a picture of her smiling with Marcus and Kendall. The caption said that it was from two years ago, and her eyes held a light that Quentin had yet to see. Her face usually held a hint of a smile, but those eyes… they told another story.

He kept scrolling until he ran across another picture from the same event — an FBI family day thing. This one was Renata and a young girl. According to the caption — Taylor, her daughter. She looked to be on the early end of her teenage years, and Quentin mused that her appearance must be an even mix of mother and father. She had Renata's cinnamon-brown skin and dimples, similar braids, and a slightly rounder version of Renata's nose, but the similarities ended there.

Still… something about the little girl seemed eerily familiar. Quentin stared at that picture for a full ten minutes before something in his mind finally clicked. He brought up his internet browser and searched "Kennedy Wolfe Sweet Sixteen".

In seconds, images from the teenager's birthday party filled his screen. She was something of a celebrity socialite because of her father, without the drugs, alcohol, and general mischief. Quentin scanned the pictures until his eyes fell on one that was particularly interesting to him. Kennedy Wolfe, hugging and trading air kisses with another girl.

Taylor Parker.

Quentin leaned back in his chair again, allowing his mind to wander as he processed what he was seeing. He looked up ,Taylor's birthdate, then sat back again. He checked to confirm the date of his own father's death, which he knew without looking, but just needed to *see* it, then sat back again.

He shook his head, scrolling through Renata's file a little more. The next picture he saw took his breath away. It was Renata, standing in the civilian waiting room of their FBI field office. Next to her was a piece she'd custom-painted for the room.

Quentin closed his laptop and packed it up.

He needed to pay Renata a visit.

―――

SHE WAS on her third glass of wine.

When she'd received that anonymous call, asking how she would — hypothetically — bypass a sophisticated, off-site security system, complete with cameras, she had no idea that the information would be used against Naomi. Not that she could have refused to answer the questions anyway.

Renata was under the impression that the person on the other end of the line would be robbing a bank, a jewelry store, a rival's mansion, *anything* except attempting a hit. Or kidnapping. Or whatever the hell they were planning to do.

She poured her fourth glass.

It didn't last much longer than the other three as she mused over whether her life would have been easier if fifteen years ago she'd just… no. Because then, there would be no sweet, beautiful Taylor.

Her hands weren't steady enough to continue her painting, so she dropped her brush, but kept her glass and emptied the bottle. She'd already finished off the last of the tequila — hadn't even bothered with the margarita. She drank it straight from the bottle, hoping that it, or maybe the wine, or whatever else she had left in the cabinet would dull the aching sense of loss that permeated her senses.

It didn't. Nothing did.

Every time she thought she was closer to being free, getting back to normal, there was another phone call. Renata never knew who it was anymore, but knew she couldn't rebel.

Her life depended on it.

So… for now, Renata would allow herself to be used as on-call, hi-tech hell-raiser, for whoever *the devil* kept on his payroll, until he was ready for her to move forward with *his* job. Then… maybe… if he saw fit to keep his word… she would be free. And Taylor would be free.

Maybe she could try to disappear again.

A knock at the door roused her from her near-unconscious state. She stumbled to the door, not even bothering to look out the peephole before she flung it open to find Quentin on the other side. Even — or perhaps, *especially*— in her drunken state, she felt especially affected by the nerdy-rugged-athletic-*sexy* vibe he put off. He was unshaven, his tee shirt was missing its sleeves, and he looked *pissed*. And *sexy*.

Renata giggled.

"Mr. LaForte," she slurred, leaning seductively against the door frame as she smiled. "How can I help you?"

"Painted. Pixels."

That dropped the smile from her face, and brought soberness rushing back to her mind.

"Wh… Quentin, what are you talking about?"

Still wearing a scowl, he pulled a picture from the side of his laptop bag. A picture of Taylor, at a birthday party. She looked happy.

Thank God for small favors.

"You care to explain what your daughter is doing in a picture with Wolfe's daughter?"

Renata swallowed a wave of nausea, then stepped back, intending to close the door in Quentin's face but he caught it, closing it himself as he stepped inside.

"Renata…. You've got a *lot* of shit to explain to me right now, but start with this. *Explain this!*"

"There's nothing to explain!" Renata yelled, her eyes darting around the room. She checked every day for bugs, but what if she'd missed one? What if they were listening to her now?

"Renata… I'm two seconds away from calling the entire team, and I can tell you now… Naomi might kill your ass. *Start. Talking.*"

"Okay! Okay…" Renata took a deep breath, shaking her head as tears welled in her eyes. "She's in the picture because… Damien Wolfe…. He's Taylor's father."

— the end… for now —

NEED THE NEXT BOOK?

No worries! It's already out!
You can purchase *Release Me If You Can* now.

ABOUT THE AUTHOR

Christina C. Jones is a best-selling romance novelist and digital media creator.
A timeless storyteller, she is lauded by readers for her ability to seamlessly weave the complexities of modern life into captivating tales of black romance.

As an author, Christina's work has been featured in various media outlets such as Oprah Magazine Online, The Griot, and Shondaland.

In addition to her full-time writing career, she cofounded Girl, Have You Read - a popular digital platform that amplifies black romance authors and their stories.

A former graphic designer, Christina has a passion for making things beautiful and can usually be found crafting and cooking in her spare time.
She currently lives in Arkansas with her husband and their two children.

To learn more, visit www.beingmrsjones.com or follow her across most social media @beingmrsjones

Made in the USA
Las Vegas, NV
26 April 2024

89151527R00174